More Than a Memory

Marie James

Copyright

More Than a Memory
Copyright © 2016 Marie James
Editing by Ms. K Edits

EXTRAS

Acknowledgments

Here we are once again. More than a Memory is my 12th book!!! 12 times I've written this part and still I cry each time! I'm surrounded by some of the most perfect people. People who are supportive, caring, and not afraid to speak their mind when I jack things up!!

In no particular order!!!

Monica Black... you my new friend are absolutely amazing!! MTAM wouldn't have even come close to where it is now without your keen eye and suggestions! I will recommend you as editor to any and ALL authors who are looking!!

Brittney Crabtree you are my rock and foundation! I can honestly say I've found a best friend in you and wouldn't change that for anything. We could obvs live closer, but even the states between us don't keep us apart!!

Laura Watson! You chick rock your ass off!! You have helped me so much over the last couple of months, I would be completely lost without you! Thanks for taking time out of your day to pimp, analyze, and help any way I needed. Without that support, I never would've finished this book on time!!

My BETAS... you women are amazing!! Brit, Sadie, Laura, Tammy, Shannon, Diane, and Brenda have been my support for a very long time now!! I appreciate each and every suggestion, edit, and foul word you send my way! I hope to have you ladies for many more books to come!!

Give Me Books: You gals rock it each and every time!! Thank you for letting me reschedule my cover reveal when I got wrapped up in The Tudors and completely forgot about it!! Can't wait to work with you on the next one!!

JA: what can I even say? You're my rock, my soul mate, and the man I'm grateful I get to wake up to each and every day! My heart is yours for eternity! You are my Bryson Daniels, Kadin Cole, and any and all other fabulous men I'll write about in the future. I couldn't write such a wonderful hero if I didn't have one at home.

Readers! You lady devils are amazing! Thank you so much for picking up my books and spending time with my characters! Because of you, I can keep writing and get my visions out!

If you enjoyed this book... leave a review, loan it to a friend, or tell people about it on social media!! Thanks everyone!! Hope to see you around for the next one!!

~Marie James

Synopsis:

"I'm your new roommate."

Four simple words turned my life upside-down.

I can't let a man—a baseball-playing stranger no less—move into my apartment. Even if he doesn't have anywhere else to go.

Bryson Daniels is too familiar—too much like *him*.

He'll discover my secrets - my obsession.

I was already questioning my insanity, but one unlucky collision in the hallway may be enough to send me over the edge.

How can I bear having one man on my mind when another still lives in my heart?

Chapter 1

Olivia

"You look better." I smile at my computer screen.

What were once vibrant blue eyes peer back at me, red-rimmed and dull.

"I still feel like shit."

Prominent shadows under his eyes, lines of exhaustion across his forehead, and the downturn of his once always smiling lips are evidence of his tiredness, but it's to be expected.

"You're gorgeous. Even better looking than the day I fell in love with you."

"And what day was that, sweet cheeks?" His eyes brighten marginally. We've had this conversation more than once.

I love the nickname he gave me so long ago. He was trying to act mature and look important in front of his friends. In high school, many guys thought acting like a douche was the best way to get the girl. It was never "beautiful", "pretty girl", or hell, even my first name. Years later, the intentionally derogative name stuck. I used to hate it, but now I wouldn't want to be called anything else.

"First day of freshman year," I say with a knowing smirk. Even when he was propped up against the wall with a small group of buddies our first day of high school, spouting offensive comments my way, I knew he was mine.

"I was covered in acne and had braces."

"Like I said, even better looking than the day I fell in love with you." He chuckles at my wink. I love the sound of his laugh. I haven't heard it as much lately, and today, it's a balm to my saddened heart.

His face grows serious and his Adam's apple bobs with a rough swallow. "I miss you so much."

"Can't be more than I miss you." My face falls and my eyes tear up, unable to keep the pain contained at hearing the devotion in his voice.

"I'll be home soon. I promise."

I reach out and stroke his face on the computer screen. I miss him more with each passing day. "I love you."

"I love you, sweet cheeks. Chat with you later?"

I nod just before the screen goes dark. Chat with you later… never goodbye.

***

I'm knee deep in *YouTube* videos when my phone rings. I ignore it like I always do the first time and continue to watch the panda bear as it swings upside down on a rope ladder. The phone rings again and I sigh, scooping it up off the table.

"Yes, Mother?" I don't even have to look at the screen. She's the only one who calls me anymore, and for that, I'm grateful. I lost my tolerance for fake, nosy people months ago.

"How are you?" The lighthearted tinkle of her voice drives me nuts. At least, it seems to these days.

"Fine." *Miserable.*

"You know why I'm calling, Olivia. Are you ready to discuss it?" She's been hounding me for weeks. It's either talk about it now or wait and try to put her off again tomorrow. The longer I take to discuss the issue, the greater the chance of her showing up on my doorstep—and that's the last thing I need.

Closing my computer, I sit up straighter on the couch, strengthening my resolve for what's coming.

"Now is fine," I say, the words coming out in a huff. I pick at the stickers covering my laptop, my lips purse as I wait for my mother to preach the same sermon she's been shoving down my throat for months.

"Are you planning to go back to school this semester?"

"No," I say, blinking into the empty room, my voice portraying every bit of the shitty attitude I have toward the topic. She already knew the answer. It's the same every time she asks.

"You need to come home then." Her voice grows deeper, which means she's losing her patience—another thing that seems to be happening more readily these last few weeks.

"I'm not coming home."

Her sigh is so loud, I have to pull my phone away from my ear. "I knew you were going to say that."

Then why did you ask?

"I'm going to rent the other room," she says, a coolness in her voice, as if she didn't drop a damn bomb in the middle of my living room.

I chuckle with a flippant defiance. "Don't be ridiculous."

"I need help with the rent."

Annoyed, I almost hang up on her. She's clearly lost her mind. My mother hasn't worked a day in her adult life. My father has been beyond successful in numerous business endeavors. We're what people would consider upper-upper class. She spends half of my apartment's rent on her hair each month. She's far from desperate in needing assistance to pay for the empty room.

"Think of something else. The rent excuse isn't going to fly." Frustrated with the broken record, I grab my laptop and head to my bedroom. A long nap after this conversation is a must.

"I'm tired of you being alone." Her voice holds more emotion than I'm used to. It's genuine. She's dedicated her entire life to me, and I know it breaks her heart to see me making decisions she can't control. I feel like a failure, but that's what happens when life fails you.

"I'm fine. I promise," I say with growing frustration. Lying back on my bed, I focus on the rotation of the fan blades—constant, never-ending, reliable when so many things in life aren't.

"Are you taking your medicine?"

I clench my teeth until I swear, they're about to crack. "I don't need the medicine."

"The doctor said—"

"I know my body. I don't care what the doctor said."

"Have you been eating?"

I sigh, not caring if the sound rings loud in her ear. "I eat."

"Have you left the apartment this week?"

I scrub my hand over my face. "What's with the twenty questions? I'm not coming home. I like it here. I'm not leaving."

"Well," she says with more indignation in her voice than before.

I sit up on the bed and listen with sharpened focus for the first time since she called. Not one good thing ever comes from my mother using *that* word.

Well, pads are better than tampons. Insert embarrassing middle school volleyball game here.

Well, trucks are better than cars. They don't have a back seat. Almost lost my virginity in the bed of a truck.

Well, I sold that desk because you don't use it anymore. All of my money from working the previous summer was stashed in a hidden compartment in one of the drawers.

"A young lady is coming in an hour to look at the apartment. I suggest you make it presentable."

I roll my eyes so far back, I can almost see my own ass. Like this damn place isn't spotless already.

"Damn it, Mom! I don't want a roommate."

"It's time. She'll be there shortly." With that, she hangs up the phone.

I fall back onto the bed with a huff and toss my phone to the side. My last roommate was my best friend from high school. We started college together last fall, full of hopes and dreams, then I dropped out shortly after spring semester began and she continued her journey. She's now in a sorority on campus, and I haven't seen her in months. I could say I miss her, but we've changed so much over the last year, I guess I miss who we used to be.

Refusing to sit idle any longer, I get up with a renewed determination and a devious plan. Fifteen minutes later, the apartment is a wreck. Dirty clothes thrown everywhere, the mini-blind cords pulled so they hang askew, food wrappers from the trash on the floor and counter, and dishes piled up in and around the sink—clean dishes, but enough for a good visual alarm. I'm not crazy enough to dirty a bunch of dishes.

I sit on the couch and can't help the calculating smirk settling on my lips when the doorbell rings. My antisocial mask in place, I pull the door open.

"Olivia?" The pretty brunette standing in the doorway takes in my appearance and has the class not to wrinkle her nose. My hair is all over the place and my clothes are practically torn to shreds. "I'm Emerson Daniels. I spoke with your mother about the room available."

"Ollie," I offer, ignoring her outstretched hand.

I almost feel bad for what I've done to the apartment—almost. Looking at her bright smile brings more sadness. In a different lifetime, I could've been friends with this girl. She has an air about her— sophisticated yet down to earth.

Stepping away from the door, I sweep out my arm, indicating for her to come inside, and point down the hall. "Last door on the left."

I ignore her as she tours the apartment on her own. My fingers itch to open my laptop, but I space out, watching a penguin documentary on Netflix instead.

"Is there a laundry room?" she asks, walking back into the room. I pop up on the couch, startled by her reappearance, and search for the time. The apartment is only so big. How long had she been checking it out? *What* had she been checking out for so long?

She picks a towel up between her forefinger and thumb and places it on the end of the couch near my feet before settling into the armchair.

I put that towel there to deter anyone from sitting and getting comfortable. I almost smirk at her—almost.

A soft smile tilts her lips up and I overanalyze the response, wondering just what in the hell my mother told this girl. "Laundry room?" she asks again.

"Stacked washer and dryer just off the kitchen."

She acknowledges me with a quick nod but doesn't get up to verify. I turn my attention back to the television, praying she takes a hint.

"This is a great apartment," she says, talking more to herself than me as she gazes around the living room.

I know it is. I also know trying to trash it up was a futile attempt at giving it less appeal. There's only so much damage that can be done on short notice.

"Only two blocks from campus," she murmurs, and I wish she'd take her contemplation out to her car. "How far is it to the baseball complex?"

I cut my eyes to her but refuse to give the appearance of her owning my undivided attention. The last thing I need is a cleat-chasing roommate.

"All the way on the opposite side of campus," I say, even though it won't make a difference. She doesn't seem deterred.

"Okay then," she says with a quick slap to her knees before standing. "We'll make it work. Can't beat furnished with a laundry room."

"Great," I mutter without getting off the couch.

"I'll contact your mother and make sure the contract is signed and emailed back, then move in next week," she says, clapping her hands. "I'm so thankful we found this place. I think he'll be pleased."

The door closes behind her with a thud and my eyes narrow in annoyance. All the work I put into destroying my apartment was futile.

If she shows up with her boyfriend and the expectation is he's either moving in or spending all his time here, she's got another thing coming. A roommate is bad enough. One who has a man glued to her isn't even an option, unless she stays mostly at his place. That would totally be acceptable.

I spend the next hour de-trashing the apartment. I wish I could leave it nasty as a way to try to deter her one last time when she arrives next week, but I couldn't live in the filth for a couple hours, much less several days. My mother calls it OCD, but it's just due diligence.

An email alert draws my attention as I settle on the couch with a dry box of cereal. Opening my laptop, I check for the unread mail. Just as I suspected, it's a copy of the signed contract from a Bryson Daniels. Well, at least rent will be on time if her father is taking care of the lease.

Chapter 2

Bryson

Just my damn luck. I lean forward and tilt my head, angling it closer to the windshield, trying to find a break in the pelting rain. The sky opened up five minutes ago and hasn't relented since. This is what I get for complaining about the heat when I had to pull over an hour ago to change my flat tire, which I'm sure was karma for driving past the crazy-eyed hitchhiker ten miles outside of my hometown. I was finally leaving La Grande and Eastern Oregon University behind me. The last thing I needed was to get shanked in my truck by a man with more desire to get away than I had.

Taking a fortifying breath, I push my way out of the truck and manage to grab my duffle bag, but everything else will have to wait. The apartment I'm moving into is furnished, so everything I brought with me is in the backseat, at my mother's insistence. Apparently, she actually bothered to look at the forecast before I left.

Making a mad dash to the covered awning over the apartment door, I manage to step in a puddle large enough to soak both of my damn shoes. I'm frustrated as hell by the time I knock on the door. As if traveling over five hours from home isn't stressful enough, let's add sopping shoes and planning to live with a dude before meeting them to the tension of the day.

I knock again when the first rap goes unanswered.

Finally, the door pulls open and the most adorable blonde looks up at me. Petite and almost fairy-like, she only comes up to my shoulder. My frustration washes away as my award-winning smile floats across my face. That's not false advertising either—I was named "best smile" in high school, and it's caught more women than I care to mention.

Her eyes narrow at the sight of me and my face falls. She must be Ollie's girlfriend. The last thing I need is to get kicked out of the only apartment we were able to find on such short notice. Plus, poaching really isn't my thing.

"Hey, I'm Bryson." I drop my duffle bag to the ground and stretch my arm out for a shake, but she ignores it. *Tough crowd.* "Are you Ollie's girlfriend?" Her eyes narrow further. "Sister?" I ask, hope filling my tone.

"*I'm* Ollie," she says, venom in her voice. "Who the hell are you?"

"Bryson," I answer. "Daniels? I guess we're roommates."

"Like hell," she says, crossing her arms over her chest and taking a step back. "I thought Bryson was that girl's dad."

"It is. He just happens to be my dad as well. I'm a junior. Look," I say, trying not to let my renewed frustration rear its ugly head, "it's no big deal. You have a room. I need a room. Two plus two equals I'm your new roommate. I'm paid in full through the end of the school year."

I grab the strap of my duffle and walk further into the apartment. Brushing past her, I ignore the look of confused disgust on her face and take in the small, yet very tidy apartment. The snap of the door closing either means she's accepted my arrival, or she's planning to kill me and doesn't want any witnesses. I can't discern the look in her eyes, but since I see no weapons, I'm hoping it's the former.

"My room?" I hold up my arm, indicating my heavy-ass bag.

"Stay here," she demands as she swipes her phone off the living room table and stalks down the hallway.

I follow, unable to take my eyes off her. Even in sweats, this woman is deadly. She disappears behind a door, and I take it upon myself to wander down the hall, ducking my head inside rooms until I find mine—not a difficult task with only a couple options to choose from. The room is simple. Dresser, bed, night tables—more than I'll really need. A place to crash and not having to drag baskets full of dirty clothes across town were my only two requirements, and Emerson assured me there was a washing machine inside the apartment. Seems like the perfect setup.

"No," I hear Ollie hiss through the wall. "I'm not saying that, Mother."

Two things. One, what kind of name is Ollie? I need to find out, because I'll be damned if I call that woman Ollie. Two, why are the walls so damn thin? So much for getting any action. Here, at least.

"Well, he's not ugly, that's for sure." I can't help but smile. "No. I said no. He doesn't seem like a serial killer."

I find myself leaning closer to the wall to hear the rest of her conversation, ignoring the slim ounce of guilt trying to sneak its way up at invading her privacy.

"You're not one bit sneaky. I know exactly what you're doing, and it's not going to work."

Having heard enough, I drop my duffle bag on the bed and head out of the room in search of the washer and dryer. I have a meeting first thing tomorrow, and being the procrastinator I am, I didn't wash my clothes before packing everything up.

I find the small laundry room and look in awe at the pristine labels on the shelves beside the stacked washer and dryer. Turning around, I take in the rest of the kitchen. I only thought the apartment was tidy when I first walked in, but this place is beyond spotless. I was concerned before, but now I'm not sure this is even going to work.

I pull my phone from my pocket and call my sister.

"You told me I'd fit in here. You said my roommate is just as filthy as I am. You also failed to mention she's a fucking girl!" I say as soon as she picks up, before she can utter a "hello."

She's silent for a long moment, and I actually wonder if she's taking me seriously for the first time in our lives. A second later, raucous laughter comes through the line before a clatter echoes in my ear, bursting that dream. I can picture her dropping the phone on the floor and holding her hands to her chest in the same way she's done all her life.

I wait, my eyes fixed on the ceiling as I tilt my head back. It's the only thing I can do. Emerson does what she wants, at her speed, and won't be rushed.

"First," she begins with a snort, "that apartment was disgusting. Well, not as bad as your old one, but it was up there."

"This place is surgical room clean. Everything is fucking labeled." I turn in circles, scanning every inch of the kitchen, and tug open the refrigerator door. "Even her damn food is all neat with the product labels facing the front." I cringe at the obsessive order of this place.

My sister giggles again. "I knew she made that apartment dirty on purpose. The towels in the bathroom were perfect, and the tub was sparkling clean."

I look around the corner to make sure her bedroom door is closed before whispering, "You don't even know, Emerson. This place is so clean, I think she may murder me if I leave clothes on the floor."

"So, quit being such a slob and don't leave clothes on the floor."

I huff. *Like that will ever happen.*

"She's pretty, right?" she asks with the same misplaced hopefulness she always gets when she's talking to me about women. I groan in frustration. My sister is always in my business.

"Don't start that shit. This girl is about to throw me out. I'll be homeless. Once she gets off the phone with her mom, I'm out of here."

And it's not like I can just go home, I mentally add, since saying it out loud is pointless. I fought to get out of La Grande for two years and finally put my foot down this summer. My mother insisted I stay close to home the first couple years to "acclimate" to college life, and I did, since she and dad were footing the bill my scholarship didn't cover, but not anymore. There's no way I can get anywhere in baseball stuck at Eastern—hell, they haven't had a first-round draft pick since Ron Scott skated into the minors in 1970. This is my shot and running back isn't an option.

"You're so damn dramatic. How I ended up with such a sissy for a brother, I'll never know. Sharing a womb with such an awesome girl must have increased your estrogen or something."

I scrub my free hand over my face at my twin's broken record on the subject.

This isn't the first time Emerson has mentioned being the power twin.

"Besides," she continues, "her mother knows exactly who's moving into the room. I was very upfront with her. She knew you wouldn't be able to make it up there to check the place out. She told me that was fine as long as someone looked before signing the lease. Now, whether she relayed that information to Olivia is on her."

Olivia.

It's a perfect name for the tiny blonde hiding in her room—so much better than Ollie.

"She had no clue I was the one staying here. She didn't say as much, but I think she was under the impression you were going to be her roommate. You didn't mention it?" I leave the small kitchen and head into the living room, which is sparsely furnished and almost surgically sterile.

This situation doesn't surprise me. Emerson pulls wild shit like this all the time.

"I don't remember *not* mentioning you. I never said I was moving in, though. Nonetheless, you're there. Her mom knows who you are, and she's fine with you living there. Her mother made it very clear Olivia wasn't going to be happy about anyone moving in, but she did say she wouldn't be openly rude about it. So don't worry. Get unpacked and make sure you make it to the field house for the meeting tomorrow." She's always mothering me. Four minutes older and running my life.

"How do you know about my meeting tomorrow? You're worse than Mom."

"I linked up your email calendar with mine. I don't want you missing any important stuff while you're on your own for the first time." Meddling ass.

Before I can berate her for sticking her nose in my business once again, I hear the door down the hall open. "Hey, Sis, gotta go. She's coming out of the room and I don't want to seem rude."

"Since when? You're always ru—"

I hang up before she finishes her sentence, prop myself against the counter, and wait for the gorgeous blonde to make her entrance.

Chapter 3

Olivia

After my mother laid down the law on "her apartment", I had no choice but to let it happen. My only other options were to move home or figure out a way to pay rent without my trust fund—neither was viable as far as I was concerned. It seems Bryson Jr. would be staying here. I can handle this; no big deal. Other than the fact that I value my solitude and want to spend every single second alone, it'll be just like it was yesterday.

My arms heavy and shoulders low, I trudge back into the kitchen after I get off the phone with my mother. Arguments with her always make me want comfort food, and for me, that's Hershey's Kisses, tiny little mouthfuls of chocolate. As I round the corner, I nearly jump and my hand flies to my chest, as if that will calm the thudding of my heart. Bryson is leaning against the counter, looking even more handsome than I allowed myself to remember... and trying to scare the ever-loving shit out of me.

My face turns up, meeting warm brown eyes and an overly cocky grin. I shake my head as he sweeps his eyes down my body, unabashed. *Nope. Not dealing with this right now.* Without a word, I turn and walk back to my room, where I'll hide until he goes to bed. It's not like I keep normal hours anyway.

I peruse various internet sites on my laptop, clicking without care or direction, and wait for him to go to bed. I draw my gaze away from my computer screen when I hear him walk past my door several times. I could've offered to help him move his things in, but with the extensive arm muscles even his t-shirt can't hide, I was certain he could handle it.

After an hour of silence, I decide to try my luck and finally leave my room, heading back into the kitchen. I crinkle my nose at the dirty cup in the sink. I have a feeling it's only the beginning—a small annoyance I'm certain is going to get worse.

I wash the cup, then place it in the dishwasher. Reaching into the cabinet above the stove, I grab the bag of Kisses, pull three out, and replace it in its proper bin on the shelf. My hands are still stretched over my head when I feel his eyes on me. Although he enters the room with ridiculous stealth, the air around me changes, becoming charged.

I ignore him, hoping he'll take note of my mood and walk away. Most men tend to willingly avoid unhappy women.

The doorbell rings and I flinch with a start, dropping one of the chocolates to the floor. He grunts when I bend over to retrieve it, and I snap my head up, my spine stiffening. To say I'm appalled is an understatement. That's a lie, but I should be upset, all things considered.

When I turn to face him, the only thing I find is his retreating back. The person at the door has to be for him, so I don't even bother walking in that direction. After grabbing a bottle of water from the fridge, I make my way out of the kitchen, only to be blocked in the doorway by Bryson with a large pizza box in one hand and a two-liter of soda in the other.

The smell hits me and my stomach reacts immediately, growling, begging for a slice. Embarrassed, I place a hand over my abdomen and try to skirt past him.

"Don't run away, Olivia." He places the box on the tiny table in the kitchenette. "Join me."

"No thank you." My stomach rebels against my decision, making its displeasure known.

"Look," he says with a sigh, "I know you don't want me here, but I'll try my best to make this work. We looked everywhere. This was literally the last room available for forty miles."

I turn back and pull out a chair opposite of him with a sigh. "My mother blindsided me with you. I thought the girl who came to look was moving in."

"Emerson," he confirms as he opens the box and spins it in my direction. "She's my sister. Twin, actually. I couldn't make it, so she came to check things out."

"My mother informed me earlier she knew you were the one moving in, but she left that little detail out when we discussed everything." *More like when she insisted.*

"If it's any consolation, I showed up today thinking 'Ollie' was a dude." He takes a huge bite of pizza but does his best to chew without opening his mouth. I force myself to look away. Handsome, personable, and clearly a caveman.

"I get that a lot." I open my bottle of water and pick at the toppings on my pizza.

"Every other Olivia I've met goes by Liv," he says around another bite.

I shrug. "My dad wanted a boy."

He nods in understanding.

"Your sister asked about the baseball complex. Do you play?"

He has the grace to swallow his food before responding. "Yeah. I played at La Grande. Their program is subpar. Figured I'd get a better shot at making a career out of playing if I was in a better program."

"You must be pretty good to have the potential to go pro."

The husk of his laugh comforts me for some reason. He shakes his head and wipes his mouth with the back of his hand. "I'm not *that* good, but a decent shot at the minors would be great."

The baseball team at Oregon State is incredible. One of the best group of guys I've ever known. "My boyfriend used to play baseball." I look down at my hand, fingering the diamond encrusted band. *Fiancé, actually.*

"He played here?"

"No. In high school. He stopped playing before graduation." I stuff my mouth with pepperoni, hoping he leaves it alone and doesn't ask any more questions.

"You dated in high school?"

Damn it. I nod.

"Wow, that's a long damn time. He doesn't live here?"

I shake my head, my eyes skirting to the sink. "I have some ground rules we really need to discuss," I say, moving my gaze back to him. I may be using the change in topic to deflect his questions, but after remembering the cup in the sink, I know it's a must—for my sanity and his safety.

"Ground rules?" he asks, raising a brow.

"Yes," I say after taking a sip of water. "They're important to me. I'll be upfront with you, Bryson. I didn't even want a roommate. I was fine on my own. This is my mother's doing."

"Okay. Ground rules, then. Lay it out."

I point over his shoulder. "If you dirty a dish, you need to wash it immediately and put it in the dishwasher."

He grins. "Simple enough. Clean dishes in the dishwasher."

I cringe. "No. Gross. When the dishwasher is full, you have to run it."

"But I already washed the dish. So, you mean rinse the dish, then put it in the dishwasher?"

I almost question his GPA, but I can accept what I'm asking isn't the norm. "No. I need you to wash the dish, then put it in the dishwasher where it will be washed," I say, enunciating every word to spell it out for him.

"Again?" His tone forces me to realize he's toying with me. Either he's amused by my need for things to be super clean, or he's trying to force me to realize how silly my rule is.

I nod, narrowing my gaze. "Moving on. Towels have to be washed after each use." He quirks an eyebrow at me. "Don't give me some complaint about conserving energy or wasting water, I don't want to hear it. My nerves wouldn't be able to handle wet towels hanging in the bathroom."

"What if I take them to my room?"

"Are you being obtuse? I'm not going to go into your room—that's your private space—but it will drive me crazy if I know there's a damp, mildewing towel in there. I think it's best if you just wash it."

"Okay," he says with a sigh, leaning back in his chair, his hands clasped against his stomach. I force my eyes away from his trim waist. "We'll wash a load of towels each day. I can throw my workout clothes in there as well. They do better on a sanitize cycle anyway."

"*We'll*? There's no *we* here. I'm not washing your clothes, Bryson."

He grins at me. "Okaaay. I'll wash *your* towel then. Really, I don't mind."

My stomach turns as my face contorts in disgust. I try to hide my reaction, but I fail miserably. "Gross. My clothes aren't coming in contact with yours. As a matter of fact, that brings me to rule number three. I need you to pour bleach in the machine and run it on a quick cycle after you've washed your clothes. I'll do the same."

"Once the load of laundry is done, the clothes are clean, Olivia. I don't see a point in running an empty load. I'll agree to not reusing towels—I'm not some 'save mother earth' tree hugger—but that is beyond wasteful."

I sigh and lean back in my own chair, mirroring his posture. "It's nonnegotiable. I need things to be clean."

He looks around my kitchen. "I noticed. Is this one of those germaphobe fetishes?"

I chuckle. "Fetish? No, definitely not a fetish. That word implies something of a sexual nature."

He humphs with a deviant glint in his eyes. "Isn't it, though? Sounds like you're getting off on your rules over there." I glare at him. "Fine. I'll waste a load of water and some bleach. Listen, it's clear you could spend the next hour telling me the ground rules, and I'll do my best to follow each of them."

I narrow my eyes.

"Seriously. I'll do my best, but there's no way I'm going to remember all this. You need to email it to me."

"I can do that," I state, nodding. I may even make up some labels for each rule and post them around the apartment. If the extensive rules happen to run him off, so be it.

My cell phone alarm goes off and I silence it but stand from the table.

"It's video chat time with Duncan," I say as Bryson gives me a questioning glance.

Not wasting any time, I wash my hands and head out of the kitchen.

"If he knew I had a male roommate, he'd shit a brick," I mutter to myself.

"Wait," Bryson's booming voice stops me in my tracks, "you're not going to tell him I'm living here?"

I shake my head and walk out of the room.

If only it were that simple.

Chapter 4

Bryson

Olivia walks away and my gaze drifts down to the subtle sway of her hips before dropping to her ass. I almost laugh at myself. She's in sweats and an over-sized hoodie, not even the slightest hint of her curves, or possible lack thereof, and I can't keep my eyes off her. There isn't a drop of makeup on her face and her hair is a tangled mess on top of her head, stray strands hanging out everywhere. She's obviously not trying to impress me in the slightest, yet here I am, checking out an ass I can't see.

I push away from the island and gather our plates, berating myself for finding Olivia to be so gorgeous. She's not single. She's going to talk to her boyfriend. I'm just grateful my jeans are restrictive, since I couldn't stop the grunt that escaped my lips unchecked when she bent over, exposing a sliver of silky skin.

I wash the dishes and put them in the dishwasher to be washed again, shaking my head at how freaking ridiculous her rules are. After clearing the trash and cleaning up the rest of the kitchen, I head back to my room to change. Since I drove here straight from my parents' house, I haven't had a chance to check out the town, or campus.

Mumbling from Olivia's room catches my attention as I walk past her door. I should be a good roommate and just keep walking, but the baritone voice on the other side of the door makes me curious.

"Duncan," Olivia grouses. Even her whiny voice is hot. I can imagine her whining for me to... I shake my head to clear those thoughts. *Wasn't I just acknowledging her boyfriend and how she's off-limits?*

"I'm sorry, sweet cheeks." *Sweet cheeks? Seriously, dude?* "I'd be there if I could. I'll be home soon."

"I'm just bored," she sighs in exasperation.

I lean in closer, leaving less than an inch between my ear and the surface of the door, recognizing how creepy this is. Too bad that's not going to stop me from listening—and now questioning Emerson's claims of the high amounts of estrogen in our mother's womb.

"I know you are. Call one of the girls, go to a movie or something. When was the last time you left the apartment?" I don't hear her respond. "That look tells me you've been cooped up so long, you can't even remember. You need to get out and live a little."

"I don't have any interest," is her response. "Why don't I just fly there?"

"Can't happen, sweet cheeks. You know what my parents said."

"They're just trying to keep us apart. You even told me that yourself. I'm going nuts being away from you," she says, emotion evident in her pleading voice.

"They're paying for this, Olivia. If you want me home at all, I have to go by their rules. You know that. We talk about it almost every day." The growing frustration in his tone fills her room as his voice gets louder.

I leave the hallway to change for a run, their conversation becoming muffled through our shared wall. Although it makes me feel less creepy, the thin walls are going to be a problem.

"Bringing a girl over is going to suck," I mumble as I tie my sneakers, then wonder if she has a "no members of the opposite sex in the apartment" rule. I huff at the thought. She may insist that I pre-wash dishes, but I'll be damned if I can't fuck in my own room.

Grabbing my phone and earbuds, I head out of the apartment toward campus.

***

"Damn it," I mutter to myself when I pull open the heavy door, interrupting the baseball meeting already in full swing.

Coach looks up and frowns in my direction but continues to talk to the team. If I didn't waste five minutes this morning pre-washing my to-be-washed dishes, I would've made it on time.

If Olivia had been around this morning, she would've gotten a little piece of my mind.

I grab a seat, but only seem to focus on Coach when he says something important. At least I have that going for me. I can't seem to let go of the frustration I feel over my current living situation and the effect my tardiness will have on my time here. Her rules may have just fucked my college baseball career.

"Rough start?" the guy sitting behind me says after Coach dismisses the meeting. I turn to face my new teammate, who sticks his hand out. "Liam Ashford, third base."

"Bryson Daniels, short stop," I say, shaking his proffered hand.

"Don't worry about Coach," he says, nodding toward the empty lectern. "He'll forget you were late before he sees you again. Just don't be late for practice and never miss a game."

Sound advice.

"Thanks, man," I say, rising from my seat, my mood lifting a fraction. As I make my way toward the exit, Liam follows.

"You coming to the party Sunday night?" He pushes the door leading out of the complex hard enough for both of us to clear it before it closes.

"Sunday night? As in the day before school starts?" The extracurricular festivities at La Grande never started until after the month-long honeymoon ended at the beginning of each semester. "Don't the parties start after the first week, at least?"

He laughs. "Any excuse to party here, man."

We descend the steps and begin walking down the sidewalk.

"Dorms?" he asks, pointing across campus.

"Nope. I'm in an apartment over on twenty-first."

"Alone?"

"No, I have a roommate. Female, hot as fuck. Has a boyfriend, though."

"Don't get mixed up in that shit, bro. Shitting where you eat is never a good thing."

"You're telling me." I run my hand over the top of my head. "We just met yesterday, but I get the feeling she's going to pretty much keep to herself."

"Lucky bastard. My dorm mate is an asshole. Well, if you don't want to hit the party Sunday, there's another one next weekend," he offers. "And the weekend after that. Pretty much always a party happening somewhere."

"Oh, I'm interested in parties," I confirm with a wide smile. Hell, I wish I was going to the one on Sunday, but responsibility forces my hand. "I'm only sitting the first one out because I still have to get unpacked."

We exchange phone numbers before he takes off toward the dorms. I turn back around to sit on the steps leading into the sports complex. The last thing I want to do is head back to the apartment.

I pull up my phone and check emails, finding the one from Olivia I've been dreading. I wait for Olivia's emailed list of rules to load, which she was generous enough to send in an easily printable PDF. Letting my eyes wander, I notice a small memorial garden off to the side of the steps. Bright flowers and a small plaque catch my eye.

My phone buzzes in my hand, alerting me to another email. *Corrected List of Ground Rules.* I groan, my mood plummeting straight back to pissed off at the few dozen rules she probably forgot. Before I pull that one up to load, I consider making my own list of ridiculous rules. I wonder how she would feel about "No Wine Wednesday" or "No Shirt Saturday". I can easily claim religious requirements.

Taking a deep, cleansing breath, I pull up the list and brace myself for what's coming.

I laugh out loud at the structure of it. There's a header, return address, and the damn thing is color coded by order of importance.

Reading through the list, I realize most of her requirements are about cleanliness. I'm now certain she's a germaphobe. The list begins to branch away from her desperate need to keep things clean, making it easy to tell where her added items begin. When I see *No porn/sex in the living room*, I can't help but laugh. Does she actually think I'd whip my junk out on the couch and rub one out?

Girls coming over are okay, I just can't bang them on the couch. I'm not really interested in having an audience, so that rule doesn't bother me in the slightest.

The final rule on the list, *No parties of any kind or groups larger than three people*, makes my brow furrow. The apartment is so small, three damn people would be about all it could hold. I can't seem to withhold a sigh as I walk back to the apartment. Living with Olivia Dawson may be easy on my eyes, but she's going to drive me crazy.

Chapter 5

Olivia

It's been several days since Bryson showed up, and I'm beginning to think this roommate thing will actually work out. He's pretty much kept to himself, and although he hasn't gotten all of the rules down a hundred percent, he's trying. The only issue is how thin the walls are. Though it's unintentional on his part, Bryson wakes me up every morning when he's getting ready. I can tell he's trying to be quiet, but I'm a light sleeper and some sounds can't be muffled. So, I lie in bed awake from the second his alarm goes off until I hear the front door close and the lock click into place.

After he left this morning, I couldn't go back to sleep. I ended up on the couch watching television and drinking coffee, which lasted about an hour before I fell back asleep. My sleep cycle has been disrupted for months. I don't go to bed and sleep for hours at a time like most people. I tend to live from one three-hour nap to the next. I have no schedule, no obligations, and nowhere to be, so I just sleep when I get tired.

I open my laptop and a second later, the door opens and Bryson walks in. The man is gorgeous. I've tried to ignore it, rationalize it, and even deny it, but it can't be done.

His tousled dark hair is messy perfection, shorter on the sides and much longer on top. A clean-shaven, strong jaw and plush lips are appealing even in profile as he closes the door behind him. He drops his keys and change into a small bowl he's placed on the entry table near the front door. Thick fingers reach into his back pocket to pull out his wallet and he casually drops that into the bowl as well.

Surprise meets his gold-speckled eyes when he sees me sitting on the couch. We haven't seen each other much since he moved in, so finding me on the couch must shock him. A big, strong hand grips the strap of his backpack as he lowers it to the floor. I watch the movement in awe, unable to resist the sight of his muscled forearm. I've always thought the best features on a man are his hands and arms, and Bryson has them in spades. My eyes continue to wander, taking in his thigh-gripping jeans and tight t-shirt until meeting his amused gaze. I look away, embarrassed at getting caught checking him out.

"Hey," he says as a grin spreads across his face. He sighs and drops into the armchair. "First day of class. Boring as usual."

I blow out a small breath, relieved he didn't call me out on my blatant perusal, and pull my legs up, tucking them closer to my body. My eyes follow the Sony emblem traveling across the black screen of the television, unable to look at him. I have no idea why he makes me uncomfortable, but I know it's my issue and not something he's done. I fight the urge to get up and go to my room. As much as I want to, I don't want to seem rude. I tuck the blanket covering me tighter around my body, shielding myself from the discomfort I feel whenever we're in the same room.

"When do your classes start? This evening?" He props his sneakered feet up on the edge of the coffee table and pulls them back to the floor at my chastising look.

"I don't go to school," I mumble, eyeing the entry to the hallway leading to my room. I should've left when he first walked in.

"How old are you?" he asks, his eyes studying my face harder. "You don't look old enough to have graduated already." It's a common misconception. I'm a young woman living two blocks from a college.

I frown in his direction. The last thing I need is to get all cozy with the hot roommate. Just the idea of it makes me uneasy. He waits patiently and the slight lift of his eyebrow lets me know he'll wait all day if he has to.

"Nineteen," I say, giving in. "Twenty in March."

"I turn twenty-one in October," he shares, unprompted. "I'm majoring in business, just in case the whole pro-baseball player thing doesn't happen for me. What are your life plans?"

I can't help the humorless laugh that bubbles up from my throat. "We haven't known each other a week and already you want a deep conversation?"

This is the last thing I want to talk about. I refuse to have this conversation with my own mother, so there's no chance of getting into it with a man who's practically a stranger. I look around the room, my mind scrambling to think of some way to divert his attention off of me, but I come up empty-handed.

"What you're saying is you're undecided? On sabbatical? I thought most girls have their entire lives planned out by this point."

I close my eyes against his words. I could argue that my whole life *is* planned out already, but plans change, whether you object to the new direction or not.

I say the only thing I can think of to shut down the conversation. "My parents are rich, so I don't have to work."

Although this would normally turn most guys off, he seems unfazed by my admission, but I'm unwilling to stick around for more questions. I don't feel like he's grilling me for information. It's more just friendly conversation, ice breakers of a sort to get to know each other better, but share time is over.

I gather my laptop and bottle of water. As I stand from the couch, the blanket once covering my legs falls away and I immediately regret coming to the living room this morning in my pajamas as Bryson's eyes linger on my legs. I didn't take into consideration the inappropriate length of my shorts or the possibility that he would be home before I had the chance to change. I blame the impromptu nap earlier for losing track of time.

"Jesus," he mutters, refusing to pull his eyes from my exposed skin.

Unwanted arousal heats my blood at his attention before shame flushes my cheeks. He smirks up at me, reading the situation wrong. I have to look away when I notice his fingers flex and the tendons in his forearms tighten.

Without a word, I go to my room, shutting the door once I'm safely inside. Frustrated by my oversight and Bryson's reaction, I pull on sweats and my hoodie, even though I have no intention of leaving this room. Bryson knowing how much he actually affects me gives him too much power.

Pacing the length of my carpet, I glance at the clock on my dresser, biting my fingernail. It's too early, but I have to see Duncan. Annoyance flares inside me as I debate breaking my own rules. Consistency and structure are the only ways I feel like I have control over my life these days, and being unable to stick to regimented times throws both into the wind, but...

Giving in to the urge, I sit on my bed, open my laptop, and log in.

I smile when the video opens.

"Hey, sweet cheeks." The sound of his sleepy voice makes me smile. "It's early. What's bothering you?"

"I miss you."

"You say that every time we talk." Sadness looms in his eyes, tainting his voice.

"I miss you more every day. I wish I was there with you." Right on cue, my eyes well with tears. I wipe them away as they begin to roll down my cheeks.

"Sweet cheeks," he says, his features softening. "Please don't cry. I wish you were here too. I'll be home soon."

"Not soon enough." My words echo through the speakers.

"I have to go. Chat soon?" He smiles, and my heart breaks a little more.

"I love you."

Chapter 6

Bryson

"What do you mean you haven't seen her?"

I take a deep, cleansing breath as Emerson grills me about Olivia. After our conversation on Monday, it became apparent she's avoiding me.

"She keeps to herself. I can't force the chick to hang out."

"Maybe she doesn't want to hang out because you say idiotic shit like *chick* when she does see you. You're never going to find a good woman if you don't stop being so damned misogynistic. You realize that, right?"

I want to reach through the phone and shake her, especially since she's beginning to sound exactly like our mother.

"I thought you said she was pretty," she says, digging even deeper.

I can't deny my attraction to her and wouldn't even try. Hell, it wasn't until I saw the look in her eye when she noticed me watching her that I realized the chemistry I've been feeling wasn't one-sided. She freaked out and I haven't seen her since.

"She has a boyfriend. Poaching girls, no matter how hot they are, isn't my thing. You know that."

Her indignant huff is beyond annoying.

"Drop the attitude," I demand. "You know getting involved with her is the last thing I should consider. I'm grateful she has a boyfriend and is off-limits."

"I bet," she mutters, and I roll my head back, my gaze reaching skyward.

I don't know if it's Olivia's proximity, but I've questioned my rules about hooking up with girls who aren't available more than once—and that doesn't sit well with me. I've honored our unspoken agreement to stay away from each other, and it's not like I wouldn't be able to control myself around her, it's the knowledge that I really don't want to.

Emerson starts asking me about the other girls on campus and I force her off the phone. I can't handle her meddling this early in the morning. Just a few minutes ago, I heard Olivia head back into her room, so it's now my turn to grab something to eat from the kitchen and head to class.

I'm taking five classes this semester—two on Mondays and Wednesdays, two on Tuesdays and Thursdays, and one four-hour class on Fridays. I must have been drunk when I made my schedule because sitting and listening to a four-hour lecture every Friday is going to be pure torture; not to mention, its economics. Even a one-hour lecture would be bad.

I enter my class, ready for it to be over so I can get a jump on the weekend. Grabbing a seat in the back, I pull out my notebook and the textbook that costs several hundred more than it's worth—not very economical when a book costs almost as much as a new laptop.

With ten minutes before class starts, I spend my time watching people enter the classroom. Oregon State has tons of great looking women. I've been blessed so far with the female pool in my first four classes this week, and I'm hoping my luck holds up. I'm not looking to get involved with a chick, but I'm not averse to doing a little window shopping, given the opportunity.

Liam walks in, catching my attention with a quick nod and wave. He stops and talks to several people before settling into the seat next to mine.

"You're stuck in this fucking class too, huh?" He waves to a couple guys I recognize from the meeting last week as they walk in. Business is a common degree for ball players; it was the same way at Eastern.

"I was just questioning my sanity..." my voice trails off as my eyes linger on the smoking hot woman standing across the room. She doesn't look like the other girls in class. She seems older, more mature—definitely fuckable. "Damn."

Liam follows my gaze to the tall blonde, and my fists clench as she leans over to talk to another girl already seated. When she cuts her eyes in our direction, a devilish gleam in them, I realize she knows exactly what she's doing. She's well aware a mere inch of fabric is the only thing keeping her nipples from being visible for the entire class.

The sway of her hips as she straightens and makes her way over to us entrances me. My cock jumps in excitement, my eyes still glued to the deep V of her cleavage. Some women know how to flirt with a sly smile, and some know how to seduce without even batting an eye. This woman has seduction in spades.

"Simone," Liam says, nudging my arm. "She's a fucking tiger."

"Boyfriend?" I ask as she stops to say hi to another guy sitting a few chairs away.

"Cleat chaser," he mutters just before she saunters up to us. I shift in my seat and clear my throat when her eyes land square on mine before she diverts her attention to the seat next to me.

"Hey, Liam." Her voice is raspy, but I can't tell whether it's her natural tone or she's trying to sound seductive.

I'm already concerned with how much effort she put into her appearance for an eight o'clock class. Trying too hard makes me uneasy. High maintenance women aren't my thing, and I know her full face of makeup and the luscious curls hanging past her shoulders took over an hour to accomplish. Casual, laid back, and spontaneous are more my speed. If I show up at a girl's house to surprise her with an impromptu date, I want her to be able to throw on some jeans and head out, not wait around while she consults websites for the best shades to wear with certain clothes.

"What's up, Simone?" Liam asks without taking his eyes off the door. It's clear he's window shopping today as well. Either that, or he's waiting for someone specific.

"Just came to say hi. I'm Simone," she says, holding her hand out for me to shake. "Do you play ball?"

Cut right to the chase, why don't we?

Liam huffs beside me. Cleat chasers aren't uncommon around the diamond—hell, every sport has a group of females who follow the players' every move. We call them jersey chasers. Some are hoping to marry a star, some just want to brag about banging an athlete, and some are just attracted to the attention hanging around a team brings. None of them really have a clue what's actually going on during a game because they're too busy scoping out their hopeful for the after-party.

I get the feeling Simone belongs to the third group. She seems like the type who belongs to no one and everyone at the same time and loves every second of it—which is fine by me.

"Bryson, short stop."

"Mmmm," she purrs, taking the empty seat beside me. I ogle the bounce of her breasts in her thin top, praying her wardrobe malfunctions, but my unlucky streak that started with this class continues as her shirt holds up. Light shines off the teardrop diamond hanging around her neck and I place the blame for struggling to pull my eyes from the exposed skin of her chest on that.

Her hand lingers on mine, as if the way her eyes roam up my arm isn't enough for me to understand her intentions. One of the benefits of being a ball player is never having to hunt for interested women. Even third strings get their fair share of attention. Gorgeous, hot-as-fuck women flock to athletes, and no matter how far out of my league this woman seems to be, I know she's not. None of them are. I don't take advantage of the girls who follow the team, but I'm not ashamed to reap the benefits.

She's empty-handed, no books or backpack, which isn't uncommon for students the first week of school. "You haven't gotten your books yet?"

Liam chuckles again.

"I'm not in this class," she says with a sweet grin.

Liam's weight shifts beside me and he rolls his eyes as he looks in her direction over my shoulder. "Simone, you're not registered at this school."

Her eyes snap to him and she raises a brow, her glare glacial. I wonder if there's any bad blood between them, or even with her and the other guys. As much as I'd like to take this chick for a ride, cleat chasers aren't worth the turmoil they may cause for the team. I've met women who pride themselves on pitting team members against one another. Most are sent from rival teams as a distraction.

"I graduated over the summer," she says, bringing her eyes back to me. "Will I see you at the party tonight?"

"We'll be there," Liam answers for both of us.

"I can't wait to see you there." She trails her finger up my arm as the teacher enters the room and places his briefcase on the lectern.

She walks away, the sway of her hips riveting me once again. I know exactly where I'd put my hands when I slam inside her for the first time. Simone is seriously on my radar.

"I hope you're not intent on love," Liam whispers beside me, his eyes staying on the professor as he discusses the syllabus for the semester. "That girl runs through men like Sunday morning Taco Bell."

I laugh at his graphic description. "Nah, man. Love isn't even on my radar. Just looking for a little fun."

"Search no further. Simone is one hell of a good time."

I look over at him to gauge his response, and even though I find nothing menacing in his eyes, I decide full disclosure is still the best way to go. "Hooking up with her a problem?"

He chuckles and covers his laugh with his hand when the teacher stops talking and locks eyes with us. The professor moves his attention back to the rest of the class and continues speaking, but Liam waits a few minutes before angling his head closer to mine. "Simone is kind of like a rite of passage. She's the first one to jump on the new guys when the school year starts. I'm not even surprised to see her here, even though she graduated last year. You're going to be an extra nice treat, since you're not a freshman. Have at her, man, just make sure you wrap it up. I'm not saying she's got anything, but she's been around."

I nod. Most jersey chasers jump from guy to guy, so that tidbit of information isn't new.

"Surprisingly tight pussy, all things considered." His smile fades and my brows draw together, thinking he suddenly has an issue with the idea, until I follow his gaze.

His eyes bore into the back of a brunette's head as she leans in close to another guy, whispering in his ear. I turn my attention back to the teacher. Drama is something I try to avoid at all cost. Even though Liam is the closest thing to a friend I've found on campus, it's not enough to go wading through his shitstorm.

Chapter 7

Olivia

My full bladder reminds me I fell asleep before relieving it. I pull sweats on over my sleep shorts, but don't bother with the hoodie. A quick trip to the restroom and back doesn't call for the full body armor this morning. Since it's Saturday, I don't anticipate Bryson being up just as the sun is coming over the horizon.

The doorknob moves away from my hand the second I reach for it and I freeze, my eyes wide as Bryson stands before me wearing nothing but a towel and a smile. My gaze skirts across his sculpted chest and abdomen, and I tighten my fist. My fingers itch to trace his muscles and tickle the dark line of hair leading into the plush fabric below his belly button.

His throat clears and my eyes snap up to his. He's not even trying to avoid the awkward way I was staring at him. A knowing smirk marks his handsome face, forcing a frown to harden mine. His cocky attitude rubs me the wrong way. Combine that with the anger I feel for even being attracted to him in the first place, I'm nearly in a rage within seconds.

"I know I would normally dart off to my room after getting caught gawking at you, but I really need to pee." I look around his arm into the bathroom. Meeting his knowing gaze is no longer an option.

When he steps past me into the hallway, the heat rolling off his skin ignites the same reaction to mine. The tiny hairs on my arms stand up, as if reaching out to him as he slides a mere inch from my body. I can't blame him. We don't live in a luxury condo or anything. It's not what I wanted when I moved away from home and started college, so the hallway isn't wide enough for two people to walk past each other without touching. Considering Bryson's size, I'd literally have to turn sideways to get past him.

"I don't mind you looking," he whispers in my ear. He's too close for comfort, a few inches inside my personal space, but that doesn't keep my body from leaning toward him a fraction.

Straightening, I shuffle back and shut the door in his face. His chuckle pierces through the wood as I sit on the lid of the toilet, doing my best to catch my breath.

He has to go. There's no way I can continue to live in this apartment with him. For the first time since he arrived, the urge to pack up and move home hits me. The notion is unwelcome and only lasts as long as it takes to inhale a few fortifying breaths.

His scent is everywhere in the humid room, and as much as it should unnerve me, it's actually refreshing. The aroma of Bryson's bodywash or shampoo is thick and masculine—nothing like the way I'm used to the bathroom smelling. I take comfort knowing it's the opposite of Duncan's scent, which has always had more of a rich, expensive edge to it.

I take care of business but remain in the bathroom for several long moments. After getting my stupid hormones under control, I head to the kitchen for coffee, crossing my fingers Bryson already left. He doesn't stick around much. This last week, he seemed to only be home when it was time for him to crash.

The coffee begins its dark drip into the carafe when I feel Bryson approach from the hallway. When he doesn't say anything after a few moments, I turn around, questioning whether he walked up at all.

I wasn't wrong. He's leaning against the counter, a smirk on his face. I groan internally, knowing he's going to bring up the whole towel thing. A gentleman wouldn't mention it again, but I'm discovering Bryson Daniels is far from a gentleman.

I do my best to feign nonchalance at his presence but hate how the sight of him makes my breath catch and my nipples tighten in my tank top. His eyes move down as if they waved a flag in his direction.

"Coffee?" I ask, ignoring my body's reaction to him.

"Nah, I think I'll have a beer," he says, pushing off the counter and reaching for the handle of the refrigerator. The kitchen is almost as small as the hallway, but his hand grazing my hip as he bends down to grab his drink out of the fridge feels intentional.

I sidestep away from him. "It's a little early for that, don't you think?" I ask, glancing toward the clock on the microwave. It's just after seven.

The bottle hisses when he twists off the top. Thankfully, he moves back against the other counter, putting as much space between us as the small kitchen allows. He raises his eyebrows at my words. "It's evening, Olivia. If you didn't sleep all day, you'd know that."

There isn't a hint of chastisement in his voice, just plain fact. I pull my phone out of my pocket to verify and reach over to turn off the coffee pot. No sense in drinking it now. I don't set out to have hours opposite most people. Some days, it just happens that way.

"I'm heading to a party off campus," he says, holding the beer out to me. "Wanna go? You can drink. I'll drive."

My eyes glance over his distressed jeans and nice button-down shirt with the sleeves rolled up. I didn't think anything of his attire before, just assumed he was getting ready for the day. And now that I think deeper, it's still not surprising, given the time. A young, single guy dressed nice on a Friday evening, kind of par for the course, isn't it?

The thought of a college party makes my stomach turn, even if the idea of hanging out with Bryson, regardless of the fact that I've been dodging him all week, is enticing. But I've avoided any form of social situation for months, and a smiling ball player isn't enough to make me want to change that.

"No thank you."

"You sure? I don't mind. It's my first party here, so I have no intention of getting smashed or anything." He winks at me. "I'll make sure you get home safe."

"I have no doubt," I say, walking past him into the living room. "Parties really aren't my thing. I would normally be polite and say something like 'not this time', but the answer will always be no. Feel free to never ask again."

"You don't go to class, I've never seen you leave the apartment, and the only two people you speak to are your mom and boyfriend. I don't know if that's very healthy, Olivia." He sits down in the armchair as I curl up on the couch.

"I didn't realize you were a psychology major," I snipe, reaching for the remote with every intention of turning the volume up until he takes the hint and leaves.

He leans forward and snatches the device out of my hand before I can even hit the power button.

"What do you do for fun?" He places the remote out of my reach on the table.

"Sleep," I quip.

"Sleep is a necessity, not a means of entertainment." His lips twitch and I contemplate asking him to tone his sex appeal down a notch, but I'm not certain he even realizes how tempting he is.

"Naps are the highlight of my day," I tell him. "I look forward to every one I take. Sometimes, I'm thinking about my next nap when I'm dozing off for a current nap."

He shakes his head, but a beautiful smile lights his face. *Colgate commercial, anyone?*

"Are you afraid to be around people? Is that another part of your germaphobia?"

I gawk at him, my hackles rising further the longer this conversation continues. "Germaphobia? Just because I like things clean does not mean I'm a damn germaphobe. And for your information, I'm not anthrophobic either."

"I don't know what that word means, but your brain is incredibly sexy. Do you know lots of big words?" His smirk forces me to realize he's messing with me.

"Do you always flirt your way out of situations your mouth gets you into?"

"I usually use my mouth to get me out of those same situations." I watch, riveted, as he licks his lips.

"Not gonna work this time, buddy."

"Too bad," he whispers before rising to his feet and walking out.

Guilt isn't too far behind the closing of the front door. I know my decision to stay away from him is the right one, but it seems like I almost gravitate toward him. I fire up the television as a means to ignore the thoughts going through my head.

The guilt triples when my daily alarm goes off, reminding me it's time for Duncan. I feel lower than dirt when I silence the alarm and make no move to turn on my laptop.

Chapter 8

Bryson

"Where exactly is this party?"

Liam settles into the passenger seat of my truck as I pull away from his dorm room.

"It's a Sigma Chi party," he says.

"A frat party? That's where we're headed?" I don't have an issue with frat guys, but they tend to stick together and aren't very welcoming to guys they think are there to poach their girls.

"Sigma house has two sororities across the street. The Delta Phi Lambda is stuffed full of women. Those bitches are smoking hot and easier to fuck than hookers."

I cut my eyes over to him. "My sister is a Delta at Washington State," I inform him through gritted teeth.

"Is she hot and easy?" Liam asks with a lopsided grin.

"Do you have a death wish?" I snarl.

He holds his hands up in mock surrender. "Calm down, dude. It was a joke."

He wasn't joking when he said it, but by the tone of his voice, I can tell he now regrets the words. I narrow my eyes and turn my gaze back to the road, deciding to let it slide this time. One more mention of my sister, though, and I'll lay his ass out.

"Turn up here," he says, pointing to a row of taillights. "We might as well park down here and walk to the house. Probably won't be able to find anything closer."

Pulling into a grassy field, I park between two other cars, the owners unloading and grabbing things out of the trunks.

The walk to the Sigma house is quick. Music blares through the sound system and out the front door. Hips gyrate to the heavy bass on the porch and across the sloping lawn. My eyes skirt across the crowd, short skirts, high heels, and barely there shirts—if you can call them that—fill my line of sight. Women have to make up at least two-thirds of the party, from what I can see, all different levels of inebriation, their tits and ass on display for anyone who's not blind. I nod in approval as couples pair off and find dark corners to make out in. A ball player I recognize from practice hands me a beer, and I twist the top. As I take a long pull, my eyes dart back and forth, trying to decide where I should post up for a while.

A warm hand slides up my back, and I grin, turning toward the attention.

"Hey there, handsome." Her drawl is slow, betraying her attempt to sound sober.

Simone, the sexy-as-hell non-student.

"Hey, Simone." I nod toward the red cup in her hand. "You get an early start?"

She grins and lifts the cup to her lips. "Always."

"This party is pretty big," I say, looking around, trying to ignore her fingers as they skate down my stomach and hook inside the waist of my jeans.

"The first frat party of the semester is always big." She stumbles closer to me, and I have to catch her by the arms to keep her from knocking us both over.

"Easy," I whisper in her ear as she lays her head against my chest.

"Wanna get out of here?" Her face tilts up and her eyes meet mine. She blinks rapidly, and I lift a brow, trying to decide whether she has something in her eyes or she's attempting to look sexy and failing. I appraise her. She's still sexy, but nowhere near as put together as she was that first day in class.

"I just got here. Do you need a ride home?"

She nods and bites her lip. "I need a good, *hard* ride."

I grin down at her. Only nine o'clock and she's drunk and ready to fuck. I wonder if she was a Delta before she graduated. With that thought, I make a mental note to check on the Delta girls in Washington. If Emerson is slutting it up in college, I'll lose my damn mind.

Simone presses her tits harder against my chest, and as much as my dick needs the attention, drunk girls are not my thing. I've seen too many friends hook up with a chick who has buyer's remorse the next day and shouts rape.

Simone doesn't seem like the type to complain even if the entire team gangbanged her, but I'm not willing to take my chances. Besides, if a girl can't participate, there's really no point. Most guys are just looking for a girl to sink inside of, but I'm more interactive than that.

"Do you want to give me a ride?" she whispers against my jaw.

"You're drunk, beautiful." I push her hair off her forehead. She is gorgeous, in an overly done up sort of way.

She nips my bottom lip and the sweet scent of strawberry daiquiri, or something similar, wafts up. It's not entirely unpleasant, and I don't push her away when her tongue brushes my lips.

Just because I don't like drunken sex doesn't mean I'm not down for a little impromptu make-out session.

I suck her cold, fruit-flavored tongue into my mouth, and her breath hitches. Her hands move to rest near my zipper, and my cock thickens, angling toward her touch.

"You want me," she pants, her fingers finding my straining erection over my jeans.

"You're drunk," I remind her even as my cock thrums behind the denim.

"I can fuck drunk," she assures me, taking my lips again.

Her body swivels against mine, rubbing seductively, enticing me to break my own rules. I pull my mouth from hers, my cock straining against my zipper, and trail kisses down her neck, the chemical taste of her perfume stinging my tongue as I lick her skin. I drag my head away and take a long pull on my beer. You'd think it would be a turn off, but I can't recall ever hooking up with a girl who didn't leave makeup, perfume, or lotion of some sort on my tongue.

Her eyelids flutter open, her eyes glazed over and heated. She turns her attention to the zipper of my jeans as the beer washes her taste from my mouth and I stop her just before my dick pops out. We're still standing in the front yard of the frat house. I haven't even made it inside and she doesn't give one fuck that she's about to flash my junk to all the sober people walking up.

"Whoa," I tell her as I button my jeans.

She half-stumbles back a step and sticks out a pouty bottom lip. Honestly, she'd be adorable if it weren't for the disheveled hair and slightly ruined makeup.

"Let's get you out of here," I say, wrapping an arm around her.

"Finally," she says, her tone husky.

She steadies herself against my side as I pull out my phone to let Liam know I'm giving her a ride.

It takes three times as long to get her back to my truck than it took for Liam and me to get to the house. It's to be expected, I guess. I'd pick her up and carry her, but I'm not going to be the guy seen carrying some drunk chick away from a party.

It takes almost as long to get her into my truck. High heels and being overserved do not mix. Eventually, we're both secured inside the cab and heading toward her place.

"Is this it?" I ask as the GPS tells me I've arrived at the address she gave me.

I peer up at the two-story house and let out a low whistle.

"Yours?" I ask as Simone unbuckles her seatbelt.

"My parents," she says, sliding closer and straddling my lap. "They're not home. You could come up."

"Not tonight, beautiful." Reaching over, I grab her phone from beside us on the seat and enter in my number. "If you remember me tomorrow, give me a call."

Desperate lips crash against mine, and I let it happen. I know my limitations, and Simone is nowhere near them. She begins to rock on my dick and I grip her ass, allowing her tongue to sweep against mine. Her soft mewls turn into loud moans, and I wince in pain as she grinds too hard. Mistaking my wince for pleasure, she continues her assault, forcing me to pull her off my lap. The last thing I need is her breaking my cock before I get to fuck her with it.

Lying back on the seat of my truck, she attempts seduction by spreading her legs, forcing her tight dress to inch higher up her smooth thighs. My mind flashes back to Olivia's gorgeous legs as she stood from the couch the other day and I thicken even further in my jeans.

I kiss Simone with renewed fervor, forcing her to moan into my mouth. Knowing that sound is now going to get me in trouble, I pull my lips from hers.

"Fuck, you tempt me."

"That's the point."

"Not tonight." I pull her to a sitting position and climb out of the truck.

When I make it to her side to help her down, she's beyond excited. "Coming in?"

I shake my head. "Just making sure you make it in safe."

Ten minutes later, I'm driving back to the apartment, a deep ache in my nuts. I'm either chivalrous or an idiot. Simone had a lot to drink, but she seemed more buzzed than inebriated when I left her house. Normally, I wouldn't turn down a buzzed chick. Hell, you couldn't really go to a college party and find a girl who hadn't been drinking a little bit, but after the thought of Olivia crept into my mind, I wanted to be anywhere but there.

***

The ding of a text message forces me to push the blankets away from my head. I've been lying here awake for a while but refuse to get up. I grab my phone off the bedside table—several texts lighting up the screen—Liam, Emerson, and multiple ones from Simone.

Liam's texts are bragging about the chick he bagged last night and how I missed the best striptease ever. Apparently, some chicks climbed onto the dining room table and went wild, *Coyote Ugly* style. I frown, hating that I missed it.

Emerson texts about random stuff, including how much she despises the Ubers in Pullman, rude jocks, and an insanely itchy spot on the back of her calf, which she insists is necrotizing fasciitis. A trip to the emergency room the last time she thought she had it resulted in the doctor pretty much calling her an idiot and giving her an itch stick for her mosquito bite. I blame binge watching *Grey's Anatomy* and the news pertaining to what's going on in Texas as her reasoning behind the self-diagnosis.

Simone's texts are a combination of apologies and requests to meet up later. I don't think she has anything to apologize for, but the gesture is nice.

Ignoring Liam and my wacko sister, I text Simone back with plans to meet up later this evening.

After a quick shower, and no sign of Olivia, I head out to get breakfast.

Once back at the apartment, I linger in the kitchen, making as much noise as possible, but my elusive roommate never shows her gorgeous face. After fifteen minutes, I leave the food I got for her in the fridge with her name on it and head back to my room. I hardly ever see her eat and hope she enjoys the breakfast burrito.

Chapter 9

Olivia

After he left last night, I couldn't get him out of my head, and the shame I felt over that wouldn't ease. I needed to know how long I had to deal with this—how long before my life would go back to normal without Bryson screwing everything up. I thought I could adapt, had even convinced myself everything would be okay, but it wasn't working any longer. When my mother texted back, telling me he signed a two-year lease with the option to extend after he graduated, my chest tightened. I didn't know how I was going to survive this.

When the text about kissing him came through—as in, her asking me if he's kissed me yet—I stopped responding. She loves Duncan as much as I do, so how she can so readily shove me off onto another man is beyond me. Now I question whether she actually sought out a male roommate rather than just accepting Bryson because he was the first interested.

My heart wants me to avoid him at all costs. My body wants to spend every moment with him that I can. I'm honestly torn. I dream about how his lips would feel on mine, about him coming into my room and holding me at night. These dreams all end the same—he morphs into Duncan seconds after our connection is made.

Avoiding him isn't making things better—it doesn't keep the thoughts out of my head. Every Duncan chat makes me feel guilty for feelings and thoughts I can't control. My mother doesn't understand, and my friends are long gone. I almost gave in and asked for help in a live forum the other day, but writing it down gives the thoughts life and that's the last thing I want to do.

I wait half an hour after I hear him leave this afternoon, making sure he isn't just heading out to grab lunch or something, before I escape my room to shower and get ready for the day. After spending my normal hour washing and shaving—I may not leave the apartment, but I'm not disgusting—I pull on sweats and a tank top and head to the kitchen to make coffee.

Finding the bag on the top shelf with my name on it when I open the fridge to get the coffee creamer makes me smile. Bryson is sexy as sin, flirty, and buys breakfast for his roommate. This man is going to be the end of me, I just know it.

The bag contains one of the biggest breakfast burritos I have ever seen, and I don't waste a second getting it on a plate and heating it in the microwave.

I moan at the first bite as a zesty cheese sauce hits my tongue. Fast-food places don't deliver, so it's been a while since I've had one of these.

"Damn," Bryson says, startling me. I drop the burrito on the plate and clutch my chest, trying to tame the rapid increase of my heart. "Mine wasn't *that* good."

Spinning around, I face him with narrowed eyes. His smile is playful, but his eyes are hooded as he watches my mouth while I chew.

"I thought you were gone," I say, still flustered by his appearance.

"Clearly." His arm brushes mine as he reaches into the fridge to grab a water.

"Thank you for breakfast."

"Probably would have been better at eight this morning when I got it, rather than four in the afternoon." He cocks an eye at me, a little too close for comfort. "You've been avoiding me."

I size him up, the lie sitting on the tip of my tongue, but I decide against telling him anything other than what he already knows. This apartment is too small not to run into each other more than we have. "I have."

I want to tell him being around him makes my pulse race, even when he's not sneaking up on me, or that my palms grow sweaty around him, but I can't. Vocalizing the effect he has on me isn't an option, especially forbidden feelings that aren't fair to Duncan.

He leans against the cabinet opposite of me but doesn't speak. The expectant way he's looking at me makes my skin tingle and my nerve-endings come alive. The silence between us becomes thick, but he doesn't question my confession.

"How was the party?" I ask around another bite, needing to break this apparent showdown we have going on. Plus, small talk is safe, right?

"It seemed like it would've been a good time, but I didn't stay long." He continues to watch my mouth, which unnerves me.

I frown down at my food before wrapping the rest of the burrito up and putting it back in the fridge. I don't have a problem eating in front of people; however, him watching me like he wishes it was *him* I was eating makes me self-conscious. Turning away from the fridge and back toward him, my gaze lands right on his crotch and I avert my eyes, ignoring how he's adjusting himself.

"You have plans tonight?" I narrow my eyes at him. "Of course, you don't have plans."

"I do," I argue, crossing my arms over my chest. "A Netflix marathon of *Criminal Minds* is on my agenda."

His lips twitch as he tries to hide a grin. "So, you're into crime shows?"

I huff a laugh. "Not really, I've just watched pretty much everything else."

"I can change my plans. Want to go watch a movie you haven't seen?"

"Like Redbox?"

He shakes his head. "Not here. Like at the movie theater."

I shake my head in response.

"I know you have a boyfriend, Olivia. I'm not hitting on you."

Mild disappointment washes over me, his declaration putting a dent in my self-esteem. "I know you're not."

"But the answer is still no?"

I nod. "What are your plans?"

He looks away, almost as if he doesn't want to answer. Maybe he didn't really have plans after all.

"I'm meeting up with a chick from school."

My face falls, my reaction angering me, but I school it back to passive. I have no say over what he does or who he does it with, but I didn't realize how lonely I'd become until my heart panged at the knowledge that he's leaving. I'm on dangerous ground.

"That sounds like fun," I lie, pushing away the lingering twinge.

"I can stay here," he offers.

I stiffen at his words. The idea of spending even more time with him scares me more. The hopeful look on his face is unnerving. I don't want him to stay, but I'm struggling with the fact that he's meeting up with a female rather than some of his baseball buddies—things I have no right to be concerned over.

"That's ridiculous, Bryson. You should go out. Have fun with your friends. You don't need to hole yourself up in this apartment. You have no obligation to keep me company."

He watches my face, his eyes scrutinizing every emotion, reading into each nonverbal clue, and I pray he can't see through the indifference I barely manage. I hold my breath and let it out as he stands up from the counter, thankful he didn't find anything.

"I'm going to get ready then."

He watches me for another long moment before heading out of the kitchen to his room.

My shoulders drop and a sigh escapes as I head back to my room and close the door behind me. I lean against the wood, attempting to get myself under control. Regret, sadness, loneliness... hurt? I don't understand why, after so long, I would feel any of these emotions, especially when it comes to Bryson. Especially when it's not in a way that he's hurting me, but where I'm hurt because he's not staying.

I know I'm doing this to myself. For months, I've lived in self-pity, refusing to interact with anyone, and I've found solace in my reclusiveness, but now I'm questioning everything.

* * *

The front door unlocking startles me awake. It wasn't until I heard the door close and lock that I left my room again, and I only made it through a single episode with Dr. Reed before succumbing to the sleepiness I feel all the time.

I smile, but before I can lift my head from the couch to greet Bryson, I hear a feminine giggle.

"Shhh," he says. "You'll wake my roommate."

Lying on my left side, my back facing the open living room, all I find when I open my eyes is the fabric of the couch, preventing me from identifying the girl he's brought home. Is she pretty? Does she have long blonde hair like I do? I hate that I'm not facing outward because it's thwarting my ability to get a gauge on his preferences but wanting to know his predilections upsets me more than the cackling girl he's brought home.

There are a few hushed words and more giggling. "Think she'd want to join us?"

Not in a million years.

"I wish," Bryson mumbles before leading her down the hall to his room.

For a man who claims he's not flirting with me, he sure didn't have a problem throwing that little nugget of information out there.

I stay on the couch until I'm certain he's not going to come back out, then hightail it to my room, not even bothering to turn the television off and risk drawing attention to the sudden silence.

I turn the lock on my bedroom door, which is something I never do. I've never felt unsafe or uneasy with Bryson here, but I have no idea who this girl is, and I'm not taking a chance of her somehow ending up in here.

The loud giggling, throaty moaning, and occasional bump of the headboard against our shared wall draws my attention. I can practically picture what's going on in there, and the images on replay in my head are almost enough to drive me insane.

I glare at the wall, pissed at how inconsiderate he was by bringing her back here. And to think I was worried about Emerson living here and having a boyfriend. At least the annoyance with a female roommate having sex in the next room wouldn't be filled with emotional confusion over the parties involved.

Pulling up the most aggressive playlist on my phone, I put in my earbuds and pull a pillow over my head, but it does nothing to help the situation. I can still hear them. Well, I can hear *her*. He's not making a sound. I want to bang on the wall and tell her she's not auditioning for a damn porno, but I'm afraid the interruption would only make it last longer.

I haven't had trouble falling asleep in months. It's been the easiest thing for me to do since Duncan left, but tonight is different. Tonight, my brain won't pull itself away from the image it conjured up of Bryson's face and what it looks like when he's about to orgasm. Do his teeth scrape over his lips as he tries to hold back a moan, or does a soundless gasp escape his perfect mouth? Does he lean in, kissing her as they mutually fall over the edge?

The room goes silent, leaving only the music in my ears, and minutes later, the front door opens and closes. I can't help but feel sorry for the girl, but at the same time, I smile as my mind calms and weariness takes over. Contemplation of why I'm giddy about Bryson being a premature ejaculator is still bouncing around in my head as I succumb to sleep.

Chapter 10

Bryson

"Shhh," I tell Simone as I unlock the apartment door. "You'll wake my roommate."

Expecting Olivia to be in her room, I freeze at the outline of her back on the couch. The television is turned down low and an episode of what I assume is *Criminal Minds* flickers on the screen. The way her hair is fanned out on the throw pillow makes my finger itch to touch it.

Simone follows my eyes, noticing Olivia for the first time. Her eyes light up with a spark of excitement. "Think she'd want to join us?"

Generous offer, and normally I'd be all over a threesome, but the thought of it tonight doesn't appeal. It's not Olivia. In fact, it's Simone who would ruin that situation for me. If I ever had any type of chance with Olivia, I sure as hell wouldn't share her with anyone.

I shake my head and urge her down the hallway to my room. "I wish," I mutter as I give her one last look before following Simone.

I remind myself that Olivia is spoken for. She's not even an option for me, and that pisses me off. What kind of man thinks a long-distance relationship is a good idea when it's Olivia he's walking away from?

Can he not see her pain? Does he have no idea how she spends her days, holed up in this apartment, sleeping all the time. Her depression is blatant. There's nothing normal about a twenty-year-old woman being so socially withdrawn, she doesn't go to the grocery store to buy her own food.

"What are you thinking about, handsome?" The scrape of Simone's nails down my t-shirt covered chest brings my attention back to the moment.

"You, baby," I lie.

I allow her to pull off my shirt and refrain from rolling my eyes when she swirls it around her finger before throwing it to the floor.

Licking the tip of her finger, she drags it down her body until it disappears under her skirt.

"Want a taste?" she coos, and I try not to cringe as my stomach turns.

Normally, I'm a very generous lover, leaning more toward giving than receiving, but knowing she's fucked every guy at school who wears cleats makes the idea of putting my mouth on her pussy less than pleasant.

Before I can say *not gonna happen, sweetheart*, she's reaching for the buckle of my belt. I stop her hands before she can pull the leather through, suddenly not in the mood. I can turn the question I just asked about Olivia back on myself right now. What kind of almost twenty-one-year-old man has a flaccid cock when a sexy sure thing of a fuck is purring right in front of him? Me, apparently.

"You seem distant. Something bothering you?" I hear her words, but the look on her face forces me to realize she doesn't really care. I'm as nonessential to her as she is to me. Match made in heaven, right?

I sit on the bed and allow her to straddle my lap.

Hot, willing chick grinding on my lap and I'm thinking about the noises Olivia made when she was eating her burrito this afternoon. Her simple moan caused the erection that wouldn't go away until I jacked off in the shower. I picture Olivia, just as I did this morning, on her knees, greedily sucking my cock. I stir in my jeans, realizing she's gotten under my skin if all it takes is a conjuring of her image to get me hard.

I let the thoughts of Olivia drift away when Simone's lips meet mine. On instinct, my hands reach up and grasp her breasts. She moans into my mouth at the attention and begins to shift her center against my thickening cock.

The action of her hips makes the headboard hit the wall, and I cringe knowing Olivia can hear everything going on in this room right now. Most days, that wouldn't bother me, but Olivia is different.

"Slow down, baby." I grab her hips in an attempt to calm her thrusting and look over at my door.

I hear Olivia's door open and close with a soft click, as if she doesn't want to disturb us. If she sits on her bed, her head is literally less than a foot from mine. The thought douses my libido, but Simone doesn't seem to take notice as she continues to grind against me.

"Let me take care of you," I whisper against her lips, reaching under her skirt.

I find her wet and ready. With deft fingers and the palm of my hand, I bring her to orgasm quickly. Well, at least I think I did. Since we hit the bed, her actions have been so over-the-top, I can't really tell, and I question whether or not it's intentional since she knows Olivia is here.

I brush her hand away when she reaches for my belt again. "What's wrong, handsome?"

At this point, I'm wondering if she remembers my actual name. "Nothing. These walls are just super thin."

"I know," she says with a wink. "I used to fuck a guy on the third floor. Anyone in the apartment can hear what's going on. Are we trying to make her jealous?"

She tosses her head back and moans like a whore getting fucked for the first time in months. If I had any doubt about her intentions, they're clear now.

"No," I whisper-hiss. "I'm trying to be considerate."

She bites her lip and looks down at my crotch. "I can be quiet."

I laugh, an honest to God hard laugh, and grab her by her bare ass. "You couldn't be quiet if you tried."

My lips meet hers again, and she whimpers when I stand with her in my arms. I shift her weight so she knows I'm going to let go, forcing her to lower her legs to the ground.

"We can go back to your place," I offer. Stroking it in the shower is never as satisfying as it seems in your head. Olivia is spoken for, so fucking this girl isn't completely a turnoff for me, I just don't want to do it here and force her to listen to every single gasp and moan.

"Can't," she says, sticking that lip out again. "My parents are home. They won't let me fuck in the house. The last guy stole some jewelry. It was a big mess."

"A real winner," I mutter as I reach down for my t-shirt.

She shrugs, as if it's no big deal. "I try not to judge."

"Very generous of you."

"I'm a nice girl," she says with a smile as she pulls her dress down barely enough to cover her ass. "But I can suck you off in your truck."

Grabbing my hand, she all but drags me out of the apartment, seeming more eager about giving me head than I am—and that's saying something.

"Park there," Simone says, pointing to the driveway of an empty house. "They moved out last week, so we won't be bothered."

By the time the truck is in park, she has the top button of my jeans open and my zipper down. Even with her warm breath on my neck and her talented hands on my released cock, I'm having trouble keeping my head in the game.

"What's wrong, handsome?" Simone asks when my dick can't seem to get up more than half-mast.

I lean my head back and close my eyes, letting my mind wander to that untouchable blonde down the street. The image of Olivia in my head, along with Simone's hot mouth, gets me where I need to be—thick, hard, and ready to blow within minutes. My teeth grind as I resist the urge to say the wrong name when my orgasm strikes.

Say what you want about slutty girls who spread their legs for everyone, but Simone has the most expert mouth I've ever had the privilege of deep throating. No gag reflex on a college campus is a difficult thing to find. That girl has dick sucking skills for days.

"See you around," Simone whispers in my ear before climbing out of the truck and walking half a block to her house.

Picturing Olivia while another chick is sucking me off should be shameful. I should probably be disgusted with myself, but I can't seem to fathom an ounce of it. My only regret is that now the thoughts of Olivia have been joined with the sounds and pleasure of an amazing orgasm, which make me want her even more, as unobtainable as she is.

The second I get home from dropping Simone off, I shower and change my sheets. Even with as tired as I am, the last thing I want to smell all night is Simone's perfume.

I settle on the couch and begin an episode of *American Dad* while the sheets are in the washer. Laying my head on the pillow Olivia was using earlier, I let my eyes flutter closed. If Simone's scent is all bad girl and sex, Olivia's is everything soft and pure. I can easily admit the latter does more for me than the former.

Chapter 11

Olivia

"I love you," Duncan says from the computer as Bryson walks into the living room.

"Chat soon." Smiling, Duncan ends the call, and I look down at the time on my screen before closing my laptop. It's early afternoon, and the apartment has been empty since I got up this morning.

Looking up, my gaze meets gorgeous brown eyes and a chiseled, bare chest. Sweat glistens on Bryson's tan skin, reflecting the light from the window.

"Duncan?" he asks, plopping down beside me on the couch.

I nod and turn my focus back to the television, though it's only on for noise. I hadn't been paying attention to what's playing, and even now, my focus is distracted at best with Bryson sitting next to me.

From the corner of my eye, I watch him wipe sweat off his face and chest with his t-shirt. He smells divine, like hardworking man and clean sweat. I resist the urge to close my eyes and breathe him in.

"Hot out there?" I ask with a smile. He works out more than most guys, but I guess if he's looking at a pro or semi-pro baseball contract, it's required.

Why I'm engaging him in conversation, I have no idea. I can only chalk it up to the really good mood I've been in all day. Despite the way the evening ended, I woke up feeling rested and happier than I have in a long time. Even the pain I normally feel after my time with Duncan isn't hitting me as hard today. I'll take all the blessings I can get.

"Humid as hell," he answers. "What are you watching?"

I have to look back at the television before I can answer him. I had been staring at him, my gaze glued on the drops of perspiration clinging to his skin.

"Um, *Gilmore Girls*." When he makes a disgruntled sound in the back of his throat, I hand him the remote. "You can watch something else."

I start to stand, but he places a hand on my bare thigh, and I immediately regret not putting sweats on when I got up this morning. My skin tingles under his touch as my mind flashes back to the last time he caught me out here in shorts.

"Don't go." I look over at him but can't read the look in his eyes. "Stay. We can watch anything."

I swallow against the dryness in my throat and look down at his hand. Following my gaze, he snaps it back as if he hadn't realized he was still touching me.

"I've seen all the *Gilmore Girls* episodes," he confesses.

I can't help the laugh that slips from my lips. "Seriously?"

"Emerson," he mutters. "Chick shows were all she ever wanted to watch. Sitting and watching them with her was easier than listening to her bitch."

"Poor thing," I tease. "Watch what you want. I'll stay, so long as it's not *Field of Dreams* or *Moneyball*."

"Problem with baseball movies?" He cocks an eyebrow at me, probably thinking I have some issue with baseball players, but it's far from the truth.

"No," I grin over at him. "I've just seen them all a million times."

Tears start to build behind my eyes against my will, and I clear my throat, trying to push down the emotion clogging it. I frown, my mood beginning to sour, and I wonder if my mom knew he was a ball player when she rented him the room.

He notices the shift in atmosphere, but the doorbell rings before he can ask me anything. The questions were there on the tip of his tongue. This interruption has only postponed his curiosity for another time. He's not going to let it go.

Bryson peers at me a moment longer, his eyes skeptic, before shaking his head and standing. I watch him walk to the door, focusing on how the muscles in his back shift with his motion. Considering I haven't had anyone ringing the bell looking for me in a long time, whoever the visitor is has to be for him. I just pray it's not the girl from last night. As much as I want to avoid his inquiries, I let myself invest in the idea of spending time with him this afternoon.

My fears are washed away when he returns holding several bags from the Chinese food place down the street. The tangy smell of Asian seasoning hits my nose and my stomach growls.

"Come on," he says, angling his head toward the kitchen. "Grab some food before we start our Potter marathon."

"I never took you for a Potterhead," I tell him as I get off the couch and follow him into the kitchen.

"The Weasleys are my boys," he says, grabbing plates out of the cabinet.

I can't help but laugh. "Seriously? I would think you'd be more of a Harry follower, or even Draco."

"Obviously, but those twins are epic," he says, winking at me.

How does the small bat of an eye make my heart race, and why do I pray he does it more often?

"I would have given their pranks a run for their money. My life goal has always been to catch my sister off guard." Discontent fills his voice as he reminisces.

"I take it you weren't always successful?"

His laugh causes chills to race up my arms. It's almost as glorious as the wink. "It may be the twin mind-reading thing, but she always knew what I had planned. She was even able to turn a few things back on me."

"You sound a little bitter about it," I say as he hands me a plate.

"You would be too if you spent a week working on the perfect way to scare someone and they don't even blink when you carry your plan out."

I grin at the juvenile agitation he still has over failed pranks with his sister.

Standing in the kitchen loading up our plates with beef and broccoli seems almost natural. The way I watch his muscles bunch and flex as he scoops fried rice onto his plate is also natural... in a lion watching its prey kind of way.

He clears his throat and my eyes snap to his. I try to keep the embarrassment off my face at being caught salivating over him, but when I realize he's only been pretending to put food on his plate while I watched in awe of his working body, my cheeks heat.

I take the spoon from him, my eyes diverting to the food, and place a small pile of rice on my plate, mumbling, "Thanks."

"You may want a little more than that. You seem pretty hungry," he whispers in my ear as he walks out of the kitchen. The graze of his back against mine is intentional. The heat radiating off his skin is pure bliss.

I hang my head in shame, mortified, and contemplate heading to my room for the rest of the evening.

"You're going to miss Harry getting dropped off at his horrible aunt and uncle's house if you don't hurry, Liv!"

I smile at the nickname he's never used before. A few friends in school started calling me that, but it never overpowered the "Ollie" my dad has been using since I was born.

I join him on the couch and wait for the awkward conversation to pop up again. It's not the first time he's caught me appreciating his body, and if he keeps living here, it won't be the last. In my defense, he's practically half naked and cut like an Olympian. I'd like to meet a heterosexual woman who wouldn't do a double take at a shirtless Bryson Daniels. I imagine the list would lean toward the geriatric end of the spectrum, or the blind.

"What are you doing?" he chastises as I scoot a sliver of watercress away from my food. "That's the best part!"

I hold my plate up for him as he stabs the evil vegetable with his fork and pops it into his mouth.

Plush lips, strong jaw, and masculine slashed eyebrows—this man has everything going for him.

I give my head a slight shake and turn my attention back to the television. He seems relaxed and unfazed by sitting on the couch beside me. I, on the other hand, am full of turmoil. His thigh is touching mine, his shoulder bumps mine every now and then, and my body shakes slightly when he laughs, ever aware of his proximity.

"You seem like a Hermione," he says as Harry and Ron sit down beside her in the library.

I watch her with sad eyes as she struggles to remain proud and unaffected by the naysayers trying to pull her down. I'm nothing like her. She stands up to those who throw negativity her way. She faces adversity with her head held high. I cower and hide.

"I wish I were as strong as her," I say, my voice low. "I used to be like her."

"What changed?" I tilt my head in his direction, finding the softness in his voice matches the compassion in his eyes.

Looking away, I shake my head, trying my best not to let the tears stinging my eyes fall down my cheek.

"Hey," Bryson says, reaching over and hooking a finger under my chin, "forget I said anything."

His finger is gone just as fast, and I miss his touch immediately. My appetite gone, I lean forward and place my half-eaten plate of food on the coffee table, the idea of hiding away in my room sounding better by the second.

"Nope," Bryson says. Picking up my plate, he puts it back on my lap and points to the pile of broccoli. "None of that. Only those in the Slytherin house refuse to eat their vegetables. You're not Slytherin, are you?"

I grin at his silliness. "Hufflepuff all the way."

I pop a chunk of food in my mouth.

"That's what I thought."

My mood lightens immediately. Bryson has a way of making me smile, even when I don't want to, even when I want to wallow in self-pity and sleep all day. Maybe my mother was right. Maybe having him around isn't so bad after all.

"The books are so much better than the movies," I tell him.

"These movies are cinematic gold, Liv. There's nothing better than the movies."

"Have you read them?" I look over at him, wishing he would put his shirt back on. He kills my concentration.

"Reading's not really my thing," he admits with a shrug.

"Everyone has read the Potter series, Bryson. You're not human if you haven't."

"I guess I'm an alien then," he says with a grin.

"I guess that's why you're inhumanly fit." I cringe at my words, but all he does is wink at me before turning his attention back to the movie.

We spend the next four hours in front of the television, arguing over whether Harry should have ended up in Slytherin rather than Gryffindor. I side with his original house, but Bryson held his own, insisting anyone who can speak to snakes is evil, which I couldn't argue with.

Chinese food turns into popcorn, and my sad mood from earlier turns into smiles and belly laughs.

When my phone alarm goes off, Bryson stops the movie.

Just as I'm about to tell him to turn it back on, he stands from the couch.

"Duncan time," he declares before walking to his room.

I clean the living room quickly and head to my room as well.

With a smile on my face, I log on to my laptop.

The glint in Duncan's eyes makes my body tremble.

"Hey, sweet cheeks. I have an idea for tonight. You may want to grab your little toy for this."

Chapter 12

Bryson

I grab some clothes from my dresser and shove the drawer shut, growling out a frustrated breath—talk about ruining a great night. Her phone goes off at the same time every night, and I should've paid more attention to the clock, but time just slipped away. We were actually having a good time, joking, and then that boyfriend of hers, who has her on one hell of a strict schedule, had to rear his ugly head in the form of an alarm.

I head to the shower, wondering why I'm so irritated by this. Normally, I'd shower right after working out, but the sight of her sitting on the couch in those short-ass shorts kept me from my routine. I'm not complaining one bit, but the hit on my mood becomes too obvious.

By the time I make it back out into the hallway, I hear his voice coming from the other side of the door, but it's the buzzing sound and faint moan that stops me in my tracks. I lean in closer, certain she's not in there doing what my mind automatically assumes.

"That's right, sweet cheeks. I see how wet you get for me. Even on video, I see that tight pussy glistening."

She releases a breathy moan and my cock stiffens at the sound. I picture her laid out on the bed, legs spread wide, fingers working over her slick, needy flesh. I hate that he's seeing her when I'm only a few feet away, willing and able to give her everything she's wanting from him.

"Duncan," she pants.

"No talking, Ollie. Just feel me."

Her moans deepen, drowning out the sound of her buzzing toy. My cock responds to her throaty whimpers by flexing, throbbing, and begging for attention.

I grip my dick, stroking over the fabric of my basketball shorts, giving it the attention it demands.

"Damn," Duncan and I groan at the same time.

The sound that escapes my throat doesn't even faze me. She could open this door right now, and I don't think I could stop myself. I close my eyes and picture her laid out on her bed, her fingers and toy at her core.

"If I were there right now, I'd lick you clean. Taste yourself," he commands.

"Jesus," I mutter, taking a step back from the door. "What the fuck are you doing, Daniels?"

As much as I hate not sticking around to hear her climax, the sound of her boyfriend's voice makes me want to barge in and smash her computer to bits.

I lock myself in the bathroom and finish what I started in the hallway, gasping her name as I shoot my load down the drain.

***

"Morning," I grumble, my sights set on the coffee pot. I don't try to hide my crappy mood when I find her sitting at the small kitchen table bent over a cup of coffee.

I slept like shit last night. Knowing Olivia was just on the other side of the wall, knowing she's the sexiest fucking woman I've ever seen, and knowing she's off-limits, even if I think her boyfriend is a complete fucking idiot for leaving her here to do God knows what wherever he is, had me on edge.

She doesn't answer me, so I ignore the fact that she already introverted again. I don't have time to keep pulling her out of her shell every day. She has a boyfriend for that. I take in her slumped shoulders and the way both hands are wrapped around her cup. The depression is rolling off of her in waves, but she doesn't seem like the type to self-harm, so I just let it be and stand against the counter, drinking my coffee rather than joining her at the table.

"Thank you for last night," she says, her voice soft, but she doesn't look up from whatever has her mesmerized in her cup.

You should thank Duncan. He's the one who got you off.

"Welcome," I mutter, downing the last half of my coffee, not caring as it burns my throat all the way down.

I hate being this guy. I'm not the guy who gets jealous over another man's girl. I don't get attached to a woman who's out of bounds—hell, I don't get attached, period.

Out of spite, I wash the cup without soap and place it in the dishwasher. I don't have the patience for her rules today.

Without another word, I grab my backpack from the entryway table and head to class, realizing I spent the evening with her on the couch watching movies I've seen a million times instead of completing the assignments due today. Just another thing to be pissed about as I drive to school.

And it pisses me off even more that I'm pissed about it. I didn't have an ulterior motive when I ordered extra food yesterday. I didn't have some plan to get into her pants. I just had the urge to spend time with her. I hate how she spends every day locked in that apartment with no social life or human interaction aside from me. I don't really pity her. She seems quite content to watch television and sleep her life away, but there are moments when I catch the pain in her eyes, flashes of something I can't describe—a need for something more than she's able to give herself. That's what draws me in.

***

"What did those dumbbells ever do to you?" Liam asks, walking into the room as I let the fifty pounders tumble to the ground, my muscles screaming for mercy.

I ignore him and move over to the squat rack, in no mood to entertain anyone right now. My early classes sucked today, just like every day, but usually I'd head back to the apartment to do homework during my three-hour break in classes on Mondays and Wednesdays. Not today. Today, I'm in the weight room at the sports complex avoiding everything Olivia.

Liam watches while I tackle the weights without saying a word. I can't face another sleepless night, and muscle fatigue is a surefire way to ensure I sleep better tonight.

"You want to grab a beer? A couple of the guys are heading over to Cody's."

"I have class," I grunt, placing the bar back on the rack.

"Yeah. You look like you're in the mood for class."

He has a good point. I tried focusing on getting the assignment I flaked on while watching movies with Olivia done earlier, but I couldn't concentrate, so there's really no point in showing up empty-handed.

"I'll meet you there. I have to shower."

"I'll wait," he says, sitting on one of the weight benches. "My truck has a flat, and it's too fucking hot to try to change that fucker right now."

"Give me ten," I tell him, grabbing my bag and walking to the showers.

Twenty minutes later, we're walking through the door to Cody's. I haven't been here yet, but I've heard of the place from a few of the guys on the team. It's more crowded than I expected it to be on a Monday evening, but the noise and people milling around keeps me from focusing on my bad mood.

We start with a few shots, and I know I'll be walking home before the night is over. I'm nursing a beer when Simone shows up with an easy-to-read look in her eyes.

She wraps her arm around my shoulder. "Hey there, handsome. You look like you could use some company."

"I'm not sure he's in the mood, honey," Liam says from the other side of the small pub-style table.

I smirk at him. He's got it all wrong. The anticipation of easy pussy always puts me in a better mood.

"What can I do to lighten your mood?" she asks, leaning in closer to my ear. "I bet you wouldn't turn down my mouth, would you?"

I grin at her. "I still haven't had your pussy."

She bites the corner of her red lip. "We could easily remedy that, handsome."

"That so?"

Nodding, she runs her hand up my thigh, and my cock twitches at the invite.

"Jesus, Simone. At least wait until he's home before you whip his dick out," Liam says.

Ignoring him, she nips at my ear and grabs my cock.

"I can't drive," I tell her, angling my beer toward the row of empty shot glasses.

"Easy fix, baby. I rode with a friend and haven't touched a drop."

I stand with her still plastered to my side, reach into my back pocket, pull out some cash, and toss it on the table.

"Later," I say to Liam with a grin.

"Double bag that shit, man," are his parting words as we leave the bar.

For a woman in heels, Simone drives my truck like an expert, making it to the apartment in record time. It may be a little vindictive on my part, but I'm glad Olivia is sitting on the couch watching television when we show up. She doesn't seem surprised when we stroll in, arm in arm. Her eyes dull and the corners of her mouth turn down slightly at the sight of us, disappointment clear as day.

"Hey," I say with a nod as we walk past.

She doesn't look at me, but I can't help but notice the twitch in her jaw as she continues to stare at the television.

Too bad you have a boyfriend. I'd rather be fucking you.

Simone hits her knees and has my cock down her throat within thirty seconds of the door closing us into my room.

"Fuck," I groan, not holding back. I may have been considerate Saturday night, but it's open season now.

After I come down her throat, I'm ready to fuck five minutes later. I don't even try to muffle the sound of the headboard when I start pounding into her.

Chapter 13

Olivia

Talk about ups and downs. I shouldn't let Bryson and his plaything bother me but hearing them last night was brutal. Monday started out great and somehow ended up being one of the worst days I've had in a long time. Even headphones and the pillow over my head didn't work. I don't know why I expected it to when it didn't come close to drowning out the sounds of Bryson and that girl together the first time he brought her home. It went on for hours. Just when I thought he was done, and they would finally pass out, they started all over again. Her moans this time were real; not any of that fake shit from the other day.

Jealousy and unwanted arousal at being forced to listen to them all night still swims in my gut as I get up and head to the bathroom to shower. Anticipating them sleeping late, even though Bryson has class, makes me scramble out of the room, hoping to be finished before they wake up.

As soon as I reach the bathroom, Bryson's low moan sounds out from the other side of the door. I stand in the hall, foot tapping while I wait for them to emerge. Minutes later, I come face-to-face with Bryson and his plaything in the narrow hallway. Her giggle may be the same, but the realization that there's a reason she wears so much makeup makes me feel slightly better about myself. I shouldn't take pride in the fact that once her pounds of cosmetics are washed down the drain and the product is rinsed from her hair, she's nothing more than average. Splotchy skin and a rat's nest on her head is not how she looked when she sauntered in with him last night.

"Morning," he says as I flatten myself against the wall, waiting for them to pass. The post-orgasmic flush to his cheeks makes me envious of her for a split second.

He slaps her ass when she stops to talk to me, urging her back to his room without saying a word. I don't even bother gawking at him in nothing but a low-slung towel around his hips. Most of the appeal he had the last time I saw him in nothing but a towel is overpowered by disgust and pain. I'm more focused on my towel wrapped around her rail-thin body. I bite my tongue against the snide comments I want to make and close myself into the bathroom. The small room is complete mayhem. Her discarded lace panties on the floor are more than I can deal with right now. I immediately turn around and go back to my room, refusing to clean up his mess, as if the sex marathon last night wasn't enough to deal with.

Shortly after I return to my room, I hear both of them leave and a sense of relief washes over me. I specifically stated in my rules there would be no sex in the living room, but I didn't realize I needed to list all the common areas in the apartment. I make a mental note to send a revised list to him.

I pace for what seems like forever. Unable to forget about the condition the bathroom is in, I huff and leave the room, heading to the kitchen for cleaning supplies. After donning yellow kitchen gloves that go all the way up to my elbow, I attack the bathroom with a fury.

I toss her panties in the trash and break the rule about invading his space when I open his bedroom door and scoop my towel off the floor. Out of spite, I toss it into the trashcan along with her discarded lingerie. Who the hell leaves a guy's apartment wearing fewer clothes than they arrived in?

I'm on my knees, spray bottle of cleaner and scrub brush in hand, when I feel him in the doorway. Ignoring the fact that he's here when he should be at school, I continue to scrub the tub.

"What the hell are you doing?" His voice is gruff, the playfulness that usually marks it nowhere to be found. Why he's angry at me, I have no idea. I'm not the one who kept him up all night and left the bathroom disgusting.

"Cleaning the damn tub. I can't shower knowing you and that girl were fucking in here." The heat of my anger crawls up my neck, flushing my cheeks, and the tops of my ears burn as my blood begins to boil.

"That's ridiculous, Liv."

"Don't call me that," I snap, my back still facing him. Yesterday, the nickname was endearing. Today, it just grates on my last nerve.

"We didn't have sex in the shower, *Olivia*," he says, emphasizing my name in anger.

"Sure as hell sounded like it," I mutter, spraying more bleach in the tub.

"Why were you listening to what we were doing in here?" he spits.

"Kind of hard to miss, Bryson. The walls are thin. You know that as much as I do."

"I sure as fuck do!" His anger is misplaced. Maybe his plaything wasn't as good of a time as he had hoped. "I was forced to listen to you finger-fucking yourself minutes after spending the fucking day with me watching movies. You're not innocent in all of this."

My cheeks flush even more; this time from embarrassment. I didn't even take into consideration that Bryson could hear what was going on the other night in my room.

"Were you thinking of me while you were talking to him, obeying every dirty command he gave you?" I don't justify his question with an answer. "Have you even told him I'm here, *Olivia*? Does he know your eyes follow every move I make? Have you shared with him that you practically drool at the sight of me? Is he aware that I get hard every time you lick your perfect fucking lips? Have you shared all *that* with him?"

He gets hard around me? For some reason, the knowledge that I affect him makes me happy.

I inwardly chastise myself at the thought. All the things he just said, and that's the tidbit I hold on to?

I turn my attention away from the tub and stare at him in stunned silence, unable to formulate the words to explain things to him. My mouth opens and closes several times, but no sound comes out.

"Forget about it," he sighs. Pointing to the tub, he says, "You don't have to keep scrubbing the goddamn tub. There's nothing to clean. She swallowed every last drop."

He storms away, leaving me staring at the empty doorway until the slam of his bedroom door forces my eyes closed. That is not how I saw this morning going.

I'm still sitting on the floor watching the door when I see him walk by several long minutes later. The front door closes with a slam and strained silence fills the apartment. I only get up from the floor when my knees begin to scream at me. The hard tile is no place to wallow in my emotions.

After returning the cleaning supplies to the kitchen, I head back into the clean bathroom to shower. The hot water sloshing over my body helps relieve some of the tension in my stressed muscles, but it doesn't fully abate the rigidity that has been building in them since last night.

Coffee is next on my agenda, even though I want nothing more than to climb into bed and sleep until the frustration and confusion over my feelings for Bryson goes away. I've been alone for months, but today, for some reason, the pull of interaction is stronger than most. Guilt at how I spoke to him clouds my already depressed mind. It's apparent, on both our parts, feelings neither of us want for each other are there.

I carry my coffee to the living room and pick up my phone from the table. I turn it in my hands, over and over, until hitting the familiar number on my contact's list.

"Olivia?" her voice is near frantic, and that makes me even sadder. "Is everything okay?" Emotion bubbles in her tone.

"I'm fine, Momma."

Her sigh of relief makes me feel even worse. "You haven't called me momma in a long time. It's good to hear from you, baby. Are you sure everything is okay? You never call."

"I called last week," I correct.

"You only called because you didn't want Mr. Daniels living there. Is that what this call is about? I'm not breaking his lease unless he's done something reprehensible."

I'm certain her definition of reprehensible and mine aren't the same.

"Has he hurt you, Ollie?"

"No, Momma. He's fine."

As much as I don't want him pulling the crap he did last night, I don't want him gone. Given time, I can get over whatever this sick fascination is I have for him, and I pray he can do the same.

"I'm just super lonely today. I was wondering if you could grab some things from the store for me. I can text you a list."

"How about I pick you up and we go shopping together?" I hate hearing the hope in her voice when I know I'm just going to crush her excitement.

"Not today, Momma. If you're busy, I can just place the order online. They deliver pretty quickly at the beginning of the week." I'm not trying to manipulate her, but leaving the apartment just isn't an option. "Maybe we can watch a movie when you get here."

It's a consolation, but one I haven't extended in a long time.

"That would be wonderful, Ollie. Text me the list."

"Thank you, Momma. I love you."

"I love you, too," she says, the strong emotion still in her voice. I hang up before she can detect the same in mine.

Today, I hate that I've pushed everyone away. Tomorrow, may be a different story.

Chapter 14

Bryson

Even with the way my morning turned out, I should be walking across campus with a smile on my face. I'm not smiling, however, and my irritation must show. Everyone who's even so much as glanced in my direction has turned their backs to me and scuttled away.

I lost count of how many times I sank into Simone last night, each orgasm leaving me hungrier than the last. Fucking Simone, yet wanting *her*, left me unsatisfied and more annoyed every damn time I rolled the condom down my dick.

My actions were retaliatory, but fuck if I thought she would react the way she did this morning. The pain I normally saw in her eyes was replaced with a fierce hatred I didn't know she was capable of. I never should've said the things I did, but I let my emotions and the frustration over spending the night fucking a girl I didn't even want, control my mouth.

At the time, I thought she deserved it, but as I drove to class, guilt flooded me. It's not her fault that she tempts me so damn bad. She hasn't done anything to make me think she wants me other than the way I catch her watching me, but just being in the apartment makes me yearn to spend time with her.

I'm realizing very quickly this is my problem, not hers. This morning, I took that out on her, as if it's her fault she's beautiful beyond measure. As if it's her fault I crave to be Duncan, the man sharing the same air with her, not some voice from miles and miles away.

"How was last night?" Liam asks, slapping me on the shoulder.

"I've had better," I mumble, and immediately feel like an asshole. Simone was very attentive last night and this morning in the shower. She doesn't deserve my distaste.

"Of course, you have. Hell, we all have, but that chick is down for just about anything. Has no problem with a little anal when the girlfriend refuses." I look over at him, and chuckle when I see his eyebrows waving up and down.

"You seem like the type of douchebag who would cheat on his girlfriend just to fuck some other girl in the ass," I chastise with a smirk.

He holds his hand over his heart as if I've offended him, but the spark in his eyes tells a different story. "I've never cheated on a girlfriend."

It's my turn to raise an eyebrow, knowing he's full of shit.

"Scout's honor," he says, holding up two fingers instead of the traditional three. "I've never had a girlfriend to cheat on."

"Now *that* I believe," I agree as we walk up to the front of the baseball complex.

"Too much of an array of pussy out there to be tied down to one piece," he adds. "I'll be a bachelor until I get pudgy in about twenty years, then I'll find a good woman to take care of me."

"They won't even want your fat ass by then. Better grab one while you're still young."

"Nah, I'll find a young thing in my forties or fifties. Some chick with daddy issues who's down with anything."

I chuckle at how ridiculous his life plan is.

"Your dick may fall off before then."

"Not a chance, buddy. I keep that shit wrapped, all the time, every time." He slaps me on the back, as if he's just given golden advice.

"What's up with that?" I ask, pointing toward the small memorial I noticed after my first meeting with the team.

"Sad fucking deal, man. Kelly was like an honorary player. Played in high school, was good, too, but got sick before he could play in college."

"Sick?" I ask.

"Yeah, man. Cancer or some shit. Too weak to play, but his dad was a baseball alumnus. I'm surprised you didn't hear about it. That brave fucker committed suicide on a live social media feed." He holds the door open for me as he talks.

"No shit?"

"No shit," he confirms. "Brave motherfucker if you ask me."

"That would take some balls," I agree.

"Hey, fucker!" I look over and see another guy from the team walking over with a huge grin on his face. I watch as he and Liam do the bro-man, backslap thing. "The party this weekend is going to be epic! The Deltas are organizing a wet t-shirt contest. I heard the twins got tit jobs over the summer!"

"Sweet," Liam praises. He looks over to me. "You coming? The wet t-shirt contests get pretty fucking wild, as in they don't stay in the shirts very long. So, it's pretty much just wet tits."

"Wet new tits? Count me in."

***

My mood lifts once I hit the field with my teammates. Joking around and talking about the upcoming party while in the locker room is amusing, but the minute we hit the field, it's all business. These guys are as focused on getting ready for the season as I am. It's a change from the team at La Grande, but I guess when you're on a multiyear losing streak, it takes more than a pep talk to get you motivated.

We spend two hours running drills and hitting, and I let the excitement for the upcoming season fill my soul. The determination on the field is palpable.

Once we hit the locker room after practice, the playful banter and ass grabbing picks right back up.

"You heading to Cody's with us?" Liam asks as he pulls his shirt over his head.

"Not today. I have two classes left. I think I'll just head home after that." I stuff my dirty clothes in my gym bag and zip it up.

"You sure? It's two-dollar shot night," he tempts.

"If I keep skipping class, I'll get kicked off the team," I explain.

"Should've done online classes. That way you can party and do assignments whenever."

I smile at him. "I don't have the self-discipline online classes require."

He doesn't look like he has it either, but that's not my business to worry about. I'm concerned for myself, and if I can't resolve whatever the hell is going on with Olivia, I may end up falling behind even more.

Even though it's the last thing I want to do, I head back to the apartment after my last class. Leaving Olivia upset in the bathroom has worn on me all day. She can't control my appeal to her, and not being able to have her is no reason to take my anger out on her.

Laughter from more than one female greets me when I unlock the door. In the kitchen, I find Olivia and an older blonde woman who has many of her same features. I watch them, unnoticed, for a few moments as they unload groceries from reusable cloth bags.

Although she's smiling, Olivia looks tired and haggard, yet still as stunning and beautiful as ever. I want to laugh when I see her lining canned goods on the counter, straightening them before they even hit the shelf in the small pantry.

The other woman gasps when she notices me standing to the side.

"You must be Bryson," she says, walking closer and holding her hand out. "I'm Raquel Dawson, Ollie's mother."

I shake her hand. "Nice to finally meet you, Mrs. Dawson."

Her mother goes back to putting up groceries, and I can't pull my eyes from Olivia. The atmosphere changed the second she realized I was here. Her laughter faltered, then ceased altogether. The familiar hunch of her shoulders is back, and she refuses to make eye contact with me. I close some of the distance between us, needing to be closer to her, but also wanting to talk to her without her mother hearing—an impossible feat in this small kitchen.

"Can we talk?" I reach for her hand, but she pulls it away, fisting it at her side.

"Not right now," she says, cutting her eyes in her mother's direction.

"Bryson, we're having sushi delivered. Would you like to join us?"

I look at Olivia, trying to gauge whether the invite extends from her as well, but she turns her back to me and begins placing the canned goods on the shelf.

"No thank you. I have a ton of homework to catch up on," I decline.

"Are you sure? Olivia insisted we get enough for you too. She says you've been grabbing her meals while you're out." I continue to watch Olivia and notice her back stiffen as her mother confesses that they were talking about me.

"Maybe another time. You ladies have a good evening." I walk out of the room, refusing to stick around if she's going to give me the cold shoulder.

"He's cute," I hear her mother say.

"Yes, he's very handsome." Olivia's voice is resigned, as if she wishes I weren't good-looking.

"And nice. Very good manners."

"Yes, very respectful." I smile at her tone.

"Maybe you should—"

"Don't start, Mother," is Olivia's response.

I close myself in my room with every intention of going out and speaking to her the second her mother leaves, but homework and lack of sleep forces my eyes closed less than an hour later.

Chapter 15

Olivia

He already left for school by the time I woke up. My mother stayed much later than I'd originally planned. One movie turned into two, but I eventually asked her to leave. She always brings up subjects I don't want to talk about, and her opinions on how I should live my life are not the same as mine. When she began asking me about medication and leaving the apartment, I decided I'd had enough of her for one day. She left graciously this time; grateful I was the one who reached out to her.

I'm standing at the stove cooking chicken in a skillet when he comes in from school.

"Hey," I say over my shoulder before sprinkling seasoning on the meat. "I'm making stir-fry. Want some?"

He's silent for a moment, and I have to look over my shoulder to make sure he didn't walk away after finding me in here. Though, I wouldn't blame him. It's not like I ever start a conversation with him. But I've decided avoiding Bryson, pretending to still live alone, and being angry that he has a life outside of this apartment isn't helping anyone. As hard as it may be, I've opted to just let it go—turn over a new leaf, so to speak. He's living here to have a place to stay. He's not some friend put in this situation because my mother feels like I need a companion.

He narrows his eyes as he evaluates my offer. "Yes?"

"Are you asking?"

"Are you poisoning me? I'm hungry as hell and may even eat it knowing it'll kill me, but I'd like to make an informed decision." The apprehension in his voice makes me laugh.

"I have no reason to poison you." I turn toward him and narrow my eyes. "Did you leave a dirty towel on the bathroom floor?"

"No," he says with a smirk at my playfulness.

"Then, you're safe. For now." I angle my head to the fridge. "Can you grab the snap peas?"

"Sure," he says, his hand landing on my hip as he leans past me to get into the refrigerator.

I turn my body, forcing his hand to fall. I'm doing my best to start over without all the anger and hostility we spewed yesterday morning, but his hands on me is not something I can tolerate—especially not when they were on someone else a mere twenty-four hours ago.

"Tiny kitchen," he explains, backing away. "Want me to rinse these?"

"Yes, please. The colander is under there," I say, pointing my toe at the cabinet to the left of the sink.

"Any water chestnuts going in here?"

I crinkle my nose. "Not in mine, but I did have my mom pick up a small can for you."

"Ah," he says, his voice raising in excitement. "That's where the poison is."

"I wouldn't kill you, Bryson." He cuts his eyes at me in disbelief as he rinses the snap peas. "I never leave the apartment, no one really comes over, and your body would start to stink. I'm a depressed masochist, but I have trouble with dirty, stinky things."

"That's not remotely funny, Olivia." Today, I hate the way he says my full name. "I already hate that you never leave. I hate it even more not knowing why."

There's genuine concern in his eyes, but it's still not enough for me to open up to him.

He pulls down a paper towel and places the damp colander of peas on the counter. "I'm sorry about the things I said yesterday. I had no right to act that way."

"That," I say with a sigh, "was my fault. I shouldn't have gotten so upset about the bathroom being messy."

"The bathroom being messy?" He frowns. "That's all it was about?"

I turn my attention back to the chicken before it burns.

"Of course," I say with a quick lift of my shoulder. "What else would it have been about?"

How would I even begin to explain that the sight of another woman coming out of my bathroom with him pissed me off beyond belief? Answering his simple question truthfully would only bring a barrage of questions I'd never answer.

Silence fills the air, forcing me to look back over at him. He scrubs his hand over his face. "Yeah, sorry about the bathroom. I'll make sure to keep it clean from now on."

"Did you not want to eat?" I ask as he turns to leave the kitchen.

"I'm going to grab a quick shower. I'll be right back." He doesn't even turn his head to look at me as he leaves me standing in the kitchen, confused at his change in behavior.

Dinner is done and I'm plating our meals when Bryson walks back into the kitchen. He has a pile of laundry in one arm and is using the other to scrub his messy hair with a towel. He's also shirtless and the sweatpants hanging from his hips are riding obscenely low.

I swallow past the immediate dryness in my mouth as my eyes widen at the delectable sight of him.

"Sorry," he says when he notices my quirked eyebrow. "Laundry day."

I carry my plate to the living room while he starts his clothes on a wash cycle. I find it hard to believe he only has enough clothes for one load of laundry and know he's just toying with me. Two can play this game. I don't have any problem ignoring his insanely defined physique and chiseled muscles. I'm turning over a new leaf, one that doesn't include me drooling over Bryson Daniels.

Moments later, he joins me on the couch, touching my thigh with his, rather than sitting in the chair perpendicular to me.

"What do you want to watch?" he asks as I flip through shows on Netflix. "Oh, that! Since when is *Top Gun* on Netflix?"

"Are you a closet Tom Cruise fanboy?"

He grins at me, flashing his perfect smile. "Never been in the closet where Tom Cruise is concerned. Besides, this is the best bro movie ever."

I'm grateful he picked this movie. It keeps me from admitting my lifelong crush on Val Kilmer.

"Thank you," he says as the beginning credits roll. "Emerson would never sit through a movie like this for me."

"No big deal. I've seen just about everything Netflix and Prime have to offer. I'm not very picky," I admit.

"Is this all you do for fun? Watch TV? Surf the net?"

"Don't forget sleep," I tease.

"Can't forget that." After placing his plate on the coffee table, he says, "We forgot drinks. Want a beer?"

"No thanks," I tell him.

"Are you a wine girl?"

I crinkle my nose. "Ew, no. A water would be great, though."

I hit pause on the remote until he gets back.

"Don't tell me," he says, handing me a bottle of water, "you aren't a hard liquor kind of chick, are you?"

"I don't drink."

"At all? How is that even possible?"

I press play on the movie. "Just never been my thing. I figured drugs and alcohol are dangerous since I sort of have an addictive personality. I've always been afraid if I start, I may not be able to stop."

"That makes sense," he says, but the look on his face tells a different story.

"Tell me more about your sister."

"She's a huge pain in my ass," he complains, but the smile never leaves his face. "We have an older brother too, but there's a fourteen-year difference between us and Josh. He was in college by the time we were old enough to start school."

"Damn, it's like your parents started over from scratch."

He chuckles. "Yeah, my mom said we were the most exhausting surprise ever. Apparently, what happened in Tahiti didn't stay there. What about you? Brothers or sisters?"

"Only child."

"My dad is an antique dealer and my mom sells insurance. What do your folks do?"

"My mom is a housewife. That's code for she doesn't work and has hired help at home. My dad is a very lucky businessman. Everything he's ventured into has become insanely profitable." I shrug. "They're great people, but my dad traveled a lot when I was a kid, and my mother and I have grown apart over the last couple years."

"Did you guys have a falling out? You seemed okay yesterday."

"Twenty questions?" I smile at him. He watches me until I answer. "I think I was just tired of being at home. I was ready to spread my wings after high school. She blamed Duncan."

"What is he like?"

I shake my head. "I'm sorry. Duncan is not a subject I'm comfortable talking to anyone about."

"Is he abusive?" he presses. "Is that why your mother doesn't like him?"

"What? No!" I stand from the couch to take my plate to the kitchen. "Like I said, I don't want to talk about it."

I take a few minutes longer than necessary to clean up, trying my best to gain some composure before going back to the living room. The jolly mood I was pretending to feel earlier crumbled at the first mention of Duncan.

Even though I don't want to, I force myself to sit on the couch and finish the movie with Bryson. Thankfully, my alarm goes off.

"Do I need to leave?" Bryson asks as I stand to head into my room. I tilt my head in confusion. "You know, so you guys can have some privacy without being overheard?"

His mood has soured too. "That's not necessary. It's not that kind of night."

His comment about being overheard makes me wonder just how many of my chats have filtered through the wall.

Chapter 16

Bryson

She was mad because the bathroom was messy?

She was mad because the girl sucked my dick in the shower and not in the privacy of my room?

She was angry about seminal fluids in the community tub?

That's what she was angry about?

Her ire was due to the location of the blow job and not that I was getting one from another girl?

I had to leave her in the kitchen. If I hadn't, I would have said more things I'd regret later. I could see the jealousy in her eyes that morning, it was rolling off her in waves. I knew I had to test her. That's why I came back out still damp without a shirt on. Well, and because my ego took a massive hit with her words.

She tried to hide it, but I saw the slight drop of her jaw when I reentered, caught the tip of her tongue when it snaked out onto her bottom lip. With my ego restored, and only slightly bruised, I knew the rest of the evening would be great. It always is when she lets her walls down and actually sits and talks to me.

I can admit we're building a friendship. I'm also confident enough in myself to confess I seriously like this girl, and I can't even pinpoint the reason. She's beautiful, so that helps, but there are beautiful girls all over campus. For some reason, I'm drawn to her, but her having a boyfriend seriously puts a damper on my mood, especially when that damn phone alarm goes off and she leaves.

Duncan's raised voice echoes around the small apartment less than a minute later. Curious, I get off the couch and stand at her bedroom door. Normally, I would have to lean in closer, put my ear to the cold wood, but tonight, it's not necessary.

"Even your mother likes him, Ollie. That's saying something."

She *has* told him about me? Why didn't she just admit to that when I was clearly upset and assuming she hadn't?

"He's not who I want, Duncan. I want you. I need *you*. Not a stand-in." *Ouch.* Her voice cracks as she pleads with him, and the sorrow flowing out of her nearly breaks my heart.

"You know that's not going to happen. Don't cry, sweet cheeks. Your tears slay me." The way his voice is filled with emotion, his love for her is apparent, even though he's hurting her right now.

"I'll never recover from this."

"You will. I promise. You have to." Her sobs hit me right in the chest. "Everything I'm doing is for you. You have to move on."

"Fight, Duncan. Fight for me. Fight for *us*."

"Ollie," he says, an exasperated pain filling his tone. "I've been fighting for us for years. It's over, baby. You have to accept it."

"I won't," she sobs, and her pain nearly has me reaching for the doorknob. I'll make sure he knows I'll be here to catch her when she falls.

"No more video chats. I won't answer."

"No! You can't do that to me. Can't you see that you're breaking my heart?"

"I'm breaking my own heart, sweet cheeks."

I walk away from the door, unable to listen to her beg for him. Breaking up, I thought, would come as a relief for me, but it's clear she loves him and I wouldn't wish that kind of heartache on anyone.

Five minutes. Five minutes is all I can take of pacing my room, wringing my hands together before the sound of her muffled sobs through the wall destroy me. You'd think I'd be used to women crying, having grown up with a female twin, but I've never been able to tolerate tears without the urge to hold and comfort. I tug on a t-shirt and leave my room.

Not even bothering to knock on her door, I push it open and go to her on the bed. Curled up in a tiny ball, Olivia's shoulders shake as her crying continues. Closing her laptop, I place it on her bedside table before scooping her up in my arms. I position myself against the headboard and hold her to my chest.

She doesn't pull away from me, and I don't speak a word as she cries, her tears dampening my t-shirt.

She's heartbroken, yet clings to me, and I can't stop the way my body responds to her proximity. She smells amazing and the heat from her skin warms me to the point of arousal. There's no way to hide or stop my reaction, no matter how inappropriate it is right now.

I would prefer the first time she's in my arms to be about us, not *him*, but I'll take what I can get. The next time I hold her will be different—and there has to be a next time. She fits perfectly against me, and there's nowhere I would rather be in this moment than right here with her—even with her snot soaking my shirt.

After a few minutes, her sobs begin to weaken, and hope that I'm helping ease some of her pain by holding her swells within me. Her arms have managed to wind their way around my body, one behind my back, and the other around my neck. Stroking her hair, I whisper soothing words in her ear.

She pulls her head from my shoulder, and I immediately miss her body heat against me. The redness and swelling in her eyes somehow make her even more beautiful.

"Hey," I whisper, sweeping a lock of damp hair from her face. "You going to be okay?"

She shakes her head from side to side, lowering her gaze to my chest. "No," she sniffs.

I cup her face in both hands, urging her face up, and look into her eyes. "You will," I say, wanting her to really hear my words. My eyes dart back and forth as I will some of my strength into her.

Her eyes fall to my lips, and her pink tongue swipes at her bottom lip. My pulse pounds in my ears as I thicken further. Even though I know this isn't the time or place for an erection, I can't seem to control my body when I'm around her.

She leans in an inch closer. "Please."

I swallow past the lump in my throat as my thumb skates over her lip, tugging it softly. My mind and body are at war with one another, but whichever one I side with will only leave me with regret.

I rest my forehead against hers, relishing the way her breath gusts across my mouth. "I don't think that's a good idea."

Her hand releases my neck, lowering to fist the front of my shirt. "Please," she pleads, desperate, but her urgency isn't for me—it's a demand to ease the pain she's feeling.

I pull my head away and close my eyes against the need radiating from her. Any other time, I wouldn't mind being a rebound, but the rebound guy never sticks. They're tossed aside once the deed is done and remorse takes over, and I can't be that guy for Olivia.

"Bryson." She sighs as she shifts her hips, bringing my attention back to the fact that she's sitting on my lap. "Please."

She's said that word three times, and each plea breaks my resolve just a little more.

"I know breakups are hard, Olivia, but this isn't truly what you want right now." I kiss her cheek, already regretting not putting my mouth on hers. "If you still want me next week, I'm yours."

Fresh tears spring to her blue eyes and fight one another on the path down her cheeks.

My phone rings, echoing the song Emerson assigned as her ringtone around the small apartment.

"I have to get that," I say, holding in the sigh of relief at how thankful I am for the distraction. I place her back on her bed and stand with my back to her so I can adjust my erection. "Sleep well."

Before I make it over the threshold, she insists, "We didn't break up."

Anger sparks in fiery licks through my veins as my jaw tenses. Forcing myself not to respond, I pull the door closed behind me, shutting it with more force than I intended, but inwardly praising myself for walking away. Hundreds of retorts and thoughts war within my brain, but I keep my mouth shut. If she's delusional about the conversation I overheard, the last thing I need is to get tangled up in that situation.

I force my shoes on and grab my phone before leaving the apartment. Staying in that small living space with her while trying to process all of my emotions is not an option. Even with as angry as I am, I know I'll end up in her room, in *her*, if I sit and think about it too long, and that's not going to do anything for either of us but scratch an itch. I still have to live here, and some lines shouldn't be crossed.

Hitting the sidewalk in front of the apartment, I check the voicemail from Emerson and calm my breathing, forcing my body to relax after being so close to Olivia while my sister drones in my ear about wanting to come visit. Labor Day is next week, and she has no desire to stay at school. At least, that's what her message says. I can read between the lines, though. This is the first time we've been separated for this long since birth and she misses me.

I pause in front of the student union building and type out a text to Emerson. As much as I miss her, telling her I'd love for her to visit is double-edged. I'm also hoping having her around for a long weekend will help Olivia come out of her shell a little.

Chapter 17

Olivia

I stumble to the coffee pot, my head pounding harder than it has in some time. Ignoring the unwashed plate in the sink, I scoop double the amount of grounds into the filter and stand watch as the machine brews enough for my first cup.

Last night was brutal. Bryson's rejection, even though I know he did the right thing, hurt more than I thought it would when he walked out of my room. I wrap my arms around my stomach, remembering how I felt in his arms. Having gone so long without a masculine touch, I wanted to crawl inside him and live there. I felt protected, even though the pain in my heart was only eased temporarily.

"Make enough for two?" I jolt as Bryson enters the kitchen, startling me. He places a warm, comforting hand on my back. "Didn't mean to scare you."

I shift away from his touch and instantly regret it when his face falls at the rejection.

"Hungry?" he asks, not putting a voice to the elephant in the room.

I pour both of us a cup of coffee as he tugs open the refrigerator door and peers inside. He sighs out loud as he closes the door, still empty-handed.

"I need to go grocery shopping," he mutters before taking the cup I'm holding out to him.

"My mom got stuff to make sandwiches. You're more than welcome to any of it." I point to the plate left in the sink. "So long as you clean up after yourself."

"Old habits die hard," he mutters, stepping up beside me to wash the plate.

I shift away from him as a tingle of awareness washes over me. The heat of his body that close to mine is dangerous. The scent of his skin hitting my nose threatens the precarious hold I have on my emotions.

"My sister told me this place was the perfect fit," he says after rinsing the plate and putting it in the dishwasher. "She said it was messy, just like I tend to be."

I can't help but laugh, but don't regret trashing the apartment before Emerson came to look at it if it's what got him here in the first place.

"That would be my fault," I confess.

I smile at the look of confusion in his eyes as he brings the cup to his lips.

"Shit, this is strong," he says with a grimace.

"That's my fault, too. I needed something strong after last night."

He nods in understanding, but I'm grateful he doesn't bring up our almost kiss, or the fact that I begged him for it.

"I sort of trashed the apartment before she got here. I didn't want a roommate."

"I thought you just didn't want a guy living here," he says, a smirk on his perfect lips.

I drop my eyes, peering into my coffee.

"I didn't want *anyone* living here. My mother forced me to get a roommate. I was against it from the beginning."

He places his coffee on the counter before crossing his arms over his chest. "If you seriously don't want me here—"

I hold my hand up to stop him.

"Like I'll believe for a second you're willing to leave. You've mentioned more than once this was the only place you could find."

Amusement sparks in his eyes. "True. You're stuck with me, Olivia."

I tilt my cup up to hide my reaction at his words, reading into them more than I'm sure he means. Closing my eyes as the strong coffee infiltrates my groggy brain, I feel the air around us shift and do my best to ignore it. Having feelings for him does nothing to help anyone involved.

"Let's go to brunch," he offers.

My eyes snap open to find him directly in front of me. Shaking my head, I reply, "That's not a good idea. There's food here."

"There isn't breakfast food here. I can't start my day with a sandwich. I need bacon and pancakes covered in warm maple syrup." He pulls my coffee cup from my hands and places it in the sink.

My stomach betrays me, grumbling in protest at the mention of pancakes. "I can't leave, Bryson."

"You can."

I shake my head from side to side. "I haven't left in a long time, and I don't want to."

"Tell me why," he insists.

"I just can't leave."

"Not good enough, Olivia." He takes a step closer, and I take a step back, but my back makes contact with the counter, trapping me. "Tell me why you can't leave or go get dressed."

"An ultimatum? You may not know this about me, but I don't do very well with those."

A knowing grin marks his face as his eyes dart down to my mouth. "Oh, I know you're stubborn. So, what's it going to be?"

I watch his perfect lips turn up in a smirk without my responding until he clears his throat and steps away. I don't miss the subtle way he tries to adjust himself. He's wearing sweats, so hiding how he's feeling really isn't an option. A sense of feminine triumph I shouldn't feel sends shivers down my spine.

"Don't make me eat alone," he pouts, his bottom lip protruding in a cartoonish way.

I huff. "I'm sure you have a ton of friends already, Bryson. Call that chick who *swallowed every drop.* I'm sure she'd love to spend more time with you."

I regret the words as soon as they come out of my mouth and seeing his playfulness turn to disappointment makes me feel even worse.

"I'm sure she's busy with one of the other teammates. Besides," he says as he moves beside me, busying himself with washing our coffee cups, "I'd rather spend time with you over her any day. It's just pancakes."

It's just pancakes for you. For me, it's walking out into a world I deserted months ago.

"Don't you have school?" I bargain.

He shrugs, continuing to wash the dirty dishes. "I can go after."

My stomach growls again, and he turns, giving me a pointed look. My hands tremble just considering the idea, but the look on his face solidifies my decision. "Fine. But I need a shower first."

***

"This will be fun," Bryson says as he opens the door of his truck so I can climb in.

"Fun," I mumble as he closes me in. "More like torture and a futile exercise in trying not to freak out."

I fake a smile when he opens the driver's side door and climbs into the cab. He wastes no time putting the vehicle in gear and driving toward our destination.

"I love this song," Bryson says, turning up the volume when *My Wish* by Rascal Flatts begins to play.

Tears sting my eyes as he sings along. I make it to the first line of the chorus before I have to reach over and turn the radio off completely.

"Too early for music," I explain, trying to hide the emotion in my voice.

"We'll have to agree to disagree on that one." He grins at me, but leaves the radio off, and I turn toward the window, not wanting him to see how much it affected me.

Within minutes, Bryson pulls up outside a small diner. I've been here dozens of times before, but my whole body is shaking, knowing I'm about to walk into a place frequented by most students who go to Oregon State. I swipe at the few tears staining my cheeks and take in the biggest breath of my life.

Like a gentleman, Bryson gets out of the truck and opens my door for me.

"Come on," he says, offering his hand while I just stare at the front of the restaurant. His fingers open and close several times, urging me to get out and join him.

Relenting, I place my shaking hand in his.

"I'm thinking strawberry banana pancakes and thick cut maple bacon. What about you?" he asks, ignoring the tremor in my hand.

I give him a weak smile, but don't answer. Fear and emotion lodge in my throat, making it impossible to form words.

"You look like a blueberry pancake kind of girl," he continues, pulling open the door with his free hand.

"I'm allergic," I manage to say as my pulse pounds in my ears.

"That sucks. Blueberries are awesome." Bryson doesn't seem to notice the hush falling over the diners as they turn to see who's entering.

He gives my hand a reassuring squeeze when I try to pull it from his, refusing to let go. How I can be both grateful and annoyed at his insistence is beyond me.

The hostess seats us quickly, and Bryson chooses the seat with his back to the majority of the patrons, forcing me to face them. Whispers and darting glances are thrown my way by several people who recognize me, and I stick my nose in the menu to avoid the attention.

"The cheesecake crepes look really good. Want to try those?" I nod my head and hand him my menu as the waitress returns with coffee and glasses of water.

Bryson orders for both of us while I busy myself pouring coffee.

"This place is busier than I anticipated on a weekday," he says, looking over his shoulder.

"It's always busy," I say, keeping my eyes focused on him.

"Oh," he says, swinging his head back in my direction. "Emerson wants to come down this weekend. I know I should've asked first, but I already told her it would be fine."

I focus on his words, attempting to ignore the buzz in the diner that feels like it's directed only at me.

"That's okay, right?" he asks when I fail to respond.

"Sure," I answer.

"You don't sound sure," he teases. "If it's a problem, I can text and cancel."

Reaching out, I place my hand over his as he picks up his phone from the table. "Seriously, it's fine. Maybe you'll be cleaner while she's around."

"Doubtful," he says, twining his fingers with mine.

My phone rings in my pocket just as the waitress begins to pile our plates on the table, giving me the excuse I was looking for to pull my hand from his. After seeing it's Duncan's mom calling, I send it to voicemail, then delete that as soon as it dings the alert. I'm still angry at his parents and have absolutely nothing to say to either of them. I wish they'd stop trying to call me altogether.

Thankfully, brunch is uneventful, filled with small talk and warnings from Bryson about his meddling sister. I love how his face lights up when he speaks about her. He may pretend she's annoying, but the sparkle in his eyes is undeniable.

Things are going fine and the novelty of me sitting in the diner seems to be wearing off until the woman he brought home the other night saunters her lean body up to our table.

"Hey, handsome," she purrs, practically sitting in his lap.

"Simone," he says, a hint of irritation in his voice. "You remember my roommate, Olivia."

"Not really," she says without a glance in my direction.

I hate how his identification of me stings, even though I know it shouldn't bother me at all. I turn my eyes away from them and look out the window, but my awareness of their conversation never falters.

"We're having breakfast. Can I help you with something?" he bites out, the hint of annoyance in his voice turning to obvious anger. Well, obvious to me. Simone seems oblivious as she coos in his ear and rakes her fake nails over his chest.

"Don't," he says, his voice stern as he grabs her hand, urging her away.

"Fine," she says, her tone bitter. "Enjoy your breakfast."

A devious smile hits her lips. With a broad sweep of her hand, she intentionally tries to knock over my glass of ice water, but Bryson seems to have predicted her reaction and already has his hand wrapped around it.

"Enough, Simone," he warns.

She narrows her eyes at me, then turns back to Bryson. "Whenever you're over this little obsession with the hermit, you know where to find me."

He closes his eyes and takes a deep breath before turning his dark gaze back to me.

"Real winner you have there," I deadpan.

Ignoring my words, he pulls cash from his wallet, leaves it on the table, and stands from the booth. I grab my things and follow his lead. We walk to the truck in silence, but even in his annoyed state, he opens the door for me and closes it with a soft snick once I settle inside.

"I have a few errands to run before heading back," he informs me a few minutes later as he puts the truck in park in front of the student bookstore. "You coming?"

"Not a chance," I say, trepidation settling in my bones.

"I'll leave it running," he says before climbing out and walking away.

The perfect fit of his jeans does not go unnoticed by me or the small group of girls standing near the entrance. I chuckle under my breath when all four track him with their eyes until he disappears inside. Seems everyone on campus wants a piece of Bryson Daniels.

Chapter 18

Bryson

"Don't even start," I warn Liam as I walk up to the table he's sitting at with a couple guys from the team. I knew I'd find at least a few of them here.

When we got to the apartment earlier, Olivia was barely talking and seemed to shut down right in front of me—again. And while our outing appeared to do more harm than good, I knew it wasn't just that. There was something more brewing under the surface and I hated to admit how much it hurt that she wouldn't open up to me. Needing to clear my head, I went for a run, then headed to Cody's for a beer when that didn't work, instead of going to class. It would have been a waste of time anyway with how aggravated I was. With every step we took forward, it felt like we went back five, and I wasn't sure what to do anymore.

"Simone is floating around here somewhere," Liam says, looking to the front of the bar. "She says you dissed her in public. Mentioned something about fucking your roommate."

What is this, fucking high school? It hasn't even been two hours and his ass already knows what went on this morning.

"Fuck, Liam, why are you so worried about what I'm doing?" I ask, unable to hide my irritation. I flag down a waitress and order.

"If I recall," Liam continues, ignoring my outburst, "you did tell me your roommate was hot as fuck, but you also said she had a boyfriend. You dipping your stick in someone else's pussy?"

I clench my fists in anger and one of our teammates places his hand on my shoulder. "Ignore Ashford, man. He's pissed off and taking his anger out on everyone."

"Yeah, herpes will do that to a dude!" another guy chimes in, holding his beer up in a mock toast.

A smile spreads over my face. "Serves your ass right. All that whoring around." I kick at his foot on the barstool.

"It's crabs, you pieces of shit!" He tilts up his beer and takes a long pull before turning his attention back to me. "Do you know how bad your nuts hurt from using that tiny little comb?"

I hold my hands up. "I've got no clue, man. I don't sleep with questionable women."

He huffs. "You fucked Simone."

"Everyone here knows she's waxed smooth, dude!" Joey says from across the table. I look over to see him fist bumping another player. "I told you to stay away from that damn freshman." Liam hangs his head, mumbling something incoherent under his breath.

Her overpowering perfume hits me before I feel Simone walk up behind me. I turn in her direction, needing to apologize for earlier, but the smirk on her face annoys me, and her words piss me off further. "I knew you'd get tired of the roommate. Her pussy isn't as good as mine, is it?"

"I haven't touched, tasted, or stuck my dick in her pussy, Simone, but I can tell you, I'd choose hers over yours any day of the week," I sneer, my jaw clenching. *So much for apologizing.*

"You haven't tasted mine either, handsome. If you did, I can promise you'd never taste another one."

"That's because he'd be dead," Joey adds.

A smile splits my face at their antics, calming my anger just a bit.

"Listen, Simone, we had fun together, but it's not going anywhere."

"Fun?" she hisses. "That's all I was to you?"

I take a step back. "Don't show any fear," Liam whispers in my ear. "She can smell it."

I want to ask him why he didn't warn me about her being crazy, but the fire in her eyes is more imminent.

"You threw yourself at me," I remind her. "Not the other way around."

"I sucked your dick."

"You sucked my dick," Joey says.

"Mine too," Liam adds.

I roll my lips between my teeth to keep from smiling. I'm not trying to be an asshole, but she knew the score. Even if I wanted to keep something going with her, the way she acted toward Olivia earlier would have put an end to that.

"You're an asshole," she spits. "Forget the offer from earlier. Don't come crawling back when you want more of *this*," she hisses, adding extra emphasis, and I cringe as she grabs at her crotch like a man.

"Nasty bitch," Joey mutters as she walks away.

"You could've warned me that she gets crazy," I say, taking a sip of my beer after the waitress hands it to me, pointing my eyes at Liam.

"Don't look at me," he defends. "She's never acted like that before. You must have a special cock or something."

"Lucky me," I mutter, falling onto the empty chair beside him.

He winces as he shifts in his seat, and I can't help but laugh at him. "Why didn't you just shave that shit, man?"

"I asked the same thing," Joey says. "Says his garden is a delicate area and it should grow freely."

"Well," Liam says with another groan, "next time, I'm shaving."

Joey laughs. "How about staying away from the nasty ones so there isn't a next time?"

I nod my head in agreement.

"The nasty ones are the most fun," Liam explains on a whine, and we both throw wadded up napkins at his dumb ass. In an attempt to change the subject from Liam's seafood nut salad, we focus our attention on one subject we'll never get tired of talking about—baseball.

"I don't know about Jason, though," Joey says, shaking his head.

"How did that base clogger even make the team? If he could hit it over the wall, his slow-ass run wouldn't be such a problem," Liam adds.

"But he can't. I hope coach keeps him benched," Joey mutters, turning his beer up to his lips.

Red flashes in my periphery as a high-pitched giggle reaches my ears. I look over to see Simone sitting in some love-drunk dude's lap. She has his rapt attention, his bright, glossy eyes gazing up at her. Simone, on the other hand, only has eyes for our table. Indifferent to her performance, I turn my attention back to my teammates.

"Which one is Jason?" I ask Joey.

"The ginger with the scraggly beard," he explains.

Commotion from Simone's direction draws all of our attention again, just in time to see her slap her enamored suitor's cheek and storm off.

"Asshole," she seethes as she walks by me.

I watch her walk away, hoping she'll leave, but she posts up near the bar and looks over her shoulder at me. I chew at the inside of my lip as dread washes over me. Cold fingers reach out and grab my beer, the desire to wash away the sour taste in my mouth hitting hard. This isn't going to be the last I hear from Simone.

***

"I'm not going to give you these notes until you swear I'll get them back before class tomorrow," I tell Liam as I stick my key into the apartment door.

"Calm down, dude. I won't forget your notes," he agrees.

"That means you actually have to go to class tomorrow."

"No shit," he mutters as we step inside.

When I see Olivia sitting on the couch, my smile grows. My eyes skirt over her, and I blow out a relieved breath, grateful she's back in her sweats and hoodie. Walking in with Liam and finding her in those little shorts she's so fond of wearing would have more than likely ended with me kicking his ass.

She grins back, seeming to be in a much better mood than when I left her, but just as fast as the smile came, it drops, and all the color drains from her face.

"Olivia?" Liam says, stepping farther into the apartment. "I thought you moved home."

Her eyes dart between Liam and I, but no sound comes from her mouth. My brows furrow at her visceral reaction to the sight of Liam, and I gaze back to him before shutting this shit down. Grabbing my bag from beside the door, I pull out all of my economics papers and shove them at Liam while pushing him out the door.

"Dude, we have to talk," he insists, his voice low.

"Not right now," I say, dismissing him.

"Seriously, Bryson. That's—"

I shut the door in his face and turn my attention back to the quaking woman on the couch. She's staring off into space as if she's seen a ghost, her body trembling. I sit beside her and pull her against me, much like I did last night, trying to calm her.

"What's wrong?" I ask into her hair, my voice soft.

She shakes her head no, but doesn't say another word, and I comfort her without drilling her for information. I don't want to cause more stress, and I certainly don't want her to leave my arms.

Before long, her breathing slows to the point that I know she's fallen asleep, which I'm okay with as well.

***

The third episode of *Survivor Man* plays on the television, the sound almost muted. Over the last two-and-a-half hours, she has managed to shift her body to where she's lying stretched out on the couch with her head in my lap. I started to stroke her long, blonde hair the second she fell asleep.

I want to touch her all the time, but the only time she allows it is when she's upset and distraught. It's not the best-case scenario, but I'll take every opportunity I can get. I continue to stroke her hair like I have been for a while when she stirs, sighing.

"I missed you so much," she mumbles, the words almost incoherent as she nuzzles deeper into my lap. "I knew you'd come back."

My hand stills on her hair when I realize she's either talking in her sleep or thinks I'm *him*.

"Olivia," I say in a hushed tone, not wanting to startle her, but needing her to know Duncan isn't the one comforting her right now. He broke up with her, tossed her aside, and left me to pick up the pieces.

She stiffens and jolts up, pulling her head from my lap. Her eyes lock with mine, and for the briefest of moments, I realize she's disappointed I'm the one holding her on the couch. Fire sears my veins as my breaths come out fast and short.

"Why'd you let me do that?" she all but hisses at me. Her eyes dart around the room and her hands fidget as if she's been caught doing something wrong.

"Do what? Hold you when you're upset? Comfort you when you need a friend?" I reach out to touch her face, but she whips away, scooting farther from me on the couch.

"That," she spits, pointing to the erection in my jeans from her grinding her head on my cock. "That's not comfort."

"It's not like I unzipped my pants and stuck my dick in your ear, Olivia. I can't help how my body responds when you're close," I say, adjusting myself into a less-conspicuous position. I don't have it in me to feel embarrassed by my spontaneous hard-on.

"You need to learn, Bryson. And you never should've let me fall asleep on you like that." I want to reach for her again when she stands from the couch, but there's only anger on her face, drawing in her brows and forcing her nostrils to flare.

"You just seemed so upset and exhausted," I explain, scrubbing my hands over my face, confused by her swift change in mood. "I don't... fuck. Sorry."

She shakes her head in disgust and walks out of the room, the lock on her door clicking into place a second later.

Chapter 19

Olivia

"You seem sad. I don't want you to be sad, sweet cheeks."

I peer across the room, sighing and refusing to look at the computer screen.

"Look at me," Duncan whispers, urging my eyes to meet his.

He pauses, waiting for the response I deny.

"It's not fair that you call and then ignore me. I get that you're upset, sweet cheeks, but acting this way isn't doing anyone justice. We can't work it out if you don't tell me what's wrong."

"You know what's wrong, Duncan. I shouldn't have to rehash it every time we talk." My voice echoes from the small speakers on my laptop.

"This isn't my fault. Do you know how many times I've prayed and hoped for a different life? I didn't ask for this." Tears glisten in his sunken, tired eyes, forcing the same from mine.

"I know you didn't."

"I hate seeing you upset and in pain when I'm unable to fix things. Some days, I wish we never met so you wouldn't have to go through this with me."

"Don't ever say that!" A violent sob escapes my lips as resignation clouds his face.

"It's true, sweet cheeks. I found a doctor willing to help," he says with a rough swallow.

"I can't talk about it. That's not the answer, Duncan. Please."

"You know as well as I do it's over. I've been telling you for weeks. Your denial doesn't change the future." The sudden drop in his shoulders is a clear sign of defeat, and my chin trembles at the wave of emotions passing over his face.

"I've already filled out the paperwork, sweet cheeks. It's done."

I slam my laptop closed, unable to listen to another word.

With a parched mouth and sore throat from crying, I leave the room in search of cold liquids and Hershey Kisses. Bryson stormed out shortly after I bit his head off for comforting me, leaving me alone in the apartment, and I haven't heard him come back yet.

Natural instinct took over when I woke and realized I enjoyed his touch a little too much. He didn't deserve the wrath of my guilt even though I gave it freely. I was angry that I *wasn't* upset at his hands being on me.

Liam showing up threw me for a loop, and the anxiety and emotion that racked my body at seeing him hit like a blow. None of this was Bryson's fault. He's unaware of my history, even though he's tried to pull the information from me numerous times.

And instead of grilling me this time, he offered his arms and calm, patient voice, only to be paid back with anger and disrespect. I hate that he's not here and I can't apologize for overreacting, but I also don't know how to do that without giving a voice to my demons. Opening the gates of hell isn't something I want to do—ever.

I grab a cold bottle of water from the fridge and down more than half before pulling it from my mouth. Soft pants escape my lips as my body attempts to adjust to the influx of frigid liquids. Reaching to the top of the cabinet, I pull down the almost empty bag of Kisses and resolve to finishing off the remaining handful. After tossing the empty bag in the trash, I head back to my room.

Fighting the allure of my comfortable bed, I sit at my desk and let the emotions of the day wash over me. Internal heaviness pulls my shoulders down and indecision concerning my slippery feelings for Bryson exhausts me.

Unsure hands pull open desk drawers, looking for something, anything, to keep me busy. Wishing I still had friends to talk to is futile. They couldn't handle my emotional outbursts and self-loathing after Duncan left. Sure, they stuck around for a while, but over time, they allowed their own lives to take over, and I can't fault them for that. I'd like to think I would've been different, but I'm not sure that's the case.

Tucked back in the corner of my top desk drawer, my fingers graze the full orange bottle of antidepressants my mother insisted I get months ago. I live in my pain now, just as I did then.

Slamming the drawer closed, I push away from the desk. My eyes dart around the room, only to land on the bed—my go-to when my emotions run high. Giving in, I lie down, plug my earbuds in, and select the same playlist that tortures me daily. I twirl the ring on my left hand, allowing the music to wash over me, pulling on the same desperation the video chats with Duncan do. I'm only three songs in before my phone rings, interrupting my emotional distress.

Sitting up in bed, I tug the headphones from my ears and answer, grasping at any outside distraction I can get.

"Olivia?" My mother's voice is a soothing balm to my broken soul.

"Hey, Mom." I attempt to sound upbeat, not wanting to concern her with my current mindset.

"I haven't spoken to you in a few days. Just calling to check in," she says, reservation in her tone as she tries to determine my mood.

Guilt washes over me the same way it did before I left Bryson alone in the living room. I hurt everyone I come in contact with.

"I'm doing well," I tell her in a cheerful voice, hoping the anguish isn't evident.

"That's great to hear, Ollie."

"I had brunch with Bryson earlier," I offer, unprompted.

"Really?" A lightness I haven't heard in a long time fills her voice.

I shift on the bed with conflicted unease at pretending to be happy as a tear rolls down my cheek.

"Did he cook for you? A man who can cook is a valuable thing to have around."

"We actually went to the little diner near campus."

Silence falls down the line.

"He brought you back food? That was sweet of him."

"I went *with* him to the diner, Mom."

She tries to clear her throat, but the sob escapes anyway.

"Why are you crying?" I bite the back of my hand, attempting to keep my own emotions in check.

I want to cry and beg my mother to come hold me, to lie and tell me everything will be okay, but we're past that now. She hates how much I'm hurting but feels it's time to let Duncan go and move on.

"I'm just happy you got out for a little bit. How was it?" she sniffs, and her tone lightens as the first wave of sobbing passes.

"Uneventful," I lie.

If I relay the details of that woman coming up to the table, I'll give a voice to the jealousy I'm struggling with, and I refuse to give my mother that carrot of hope. She's already trying to push Bryson and me together, she doesn't need any more fuel.

"I had crepes and he had pancakes," I say, keeping the conversation simple.

He held my hand when I was upset and defended me in front of a woman he screwed less than ten feet from my head just days ago.

I close my eyes, remembering the disgust in his gaze when she dismissed me at the table. I'm thankful he's never turned that searing glance my way. Even when he's been angry with me, he's never looked at me with revulsion.

I realize I've turned my thoughts inward when my mother's voice breaks into my reflection.

"I'm sorry, what?"

She sighs, just like she always does when I lose track.

"I asked when are you guys planning on going out again?"

I shake my head even though she can't see me. "I don't think we will."

He hates me and probably thinks I'm a psycho.

"Maybe we can go out soon then?" Hope fills her voice.

I'm torn between letting her think there's a chance and telling her I hated leaving and don't plan to do it again anytime soon.

"We'll see," I lie, opting for the former to ease her concern.

I drop my phone to the bed, the slam of the front door surprising me. Knowing he's back sets me on edge, and the bravado I tried to build up to apologize escapes me. I pick my phone back up and bring it to my ear.

"I have to go, Mom. Bryson just got home." I may not have the courage to apologize to him right now, but I've met the limits of conversation with my mother. If we stay on the phone any longer, the discussion is going to head toward topics I refuse to participate in.

"Oh, do you guys have plans?"

Does groveling and begging for forgiveness count?
"Maybe watch a little TV. Talk to you soon, Mom. Love you."

Chapter 20

Bryson

"Shit," I mutter as I stumble and hit my shin on the entryway table. Maybe running until almost muscle failure wasn't the brightest idea.

I take a calming breath, resisting the need to kick or punch something. Living with Olivia and dealing with her mood swings has been great for my physical health. I haven't worked out this much during the off season since freshman year in high school when I had something to prove to the varsity team I somehow managed to get on. Emotionally? That's another story. My mental health is spiraling, but I just can't let her go. Knowing she's bringing me down doesn't stop my need to attempt to lift her up. The hints of happiness and occasional laugh that escapes when she lets go for a minute keeps me trying. The blackest of clouds follow her daily, but the tiny rays of sunshine that break through leave me thirsting for more.

I tap on her door before heading to my room. I don't want to end the day on such a sour note, and if going to her and begging her to talk it out with me is what it takes, it's a tiny sacrifice I'm willing to make. I know she's on the other side of the door, but my attempt to get her to answer doesn't work.

Hanging my head in resignation, I grab clean clothes from my room and hit the shower. Hot water would soothe my tight, overworked muscles best, but my already heated skin insists on water temps bordering frigid.

I moan and hiss in unison when the first arctic splash hits my chest, fighting the urge to increase the hot output. Exhausted fingers flex against the tile wall as I lean in and let the water flow down my back, only turning up the heat when my teeth begin to chatter.

Toweling off, I dress fully, not needing another half-naked run-in with Olivia in the hallway. I give her door another try on my way into the kitchen for something to eat, but it once again goes unanswered. Hiding out and avoiding each other may have worked when I first got here, but I refuse to let it continue that way. I'll give her tonight, but I'll force her to talk to me tomorrow, even if I have to tie her down to get through the conversation.

She offered the sandwich ingredients earlier, so I take her up on it now, opting to use a paper towel rather than a plate so I don't have to come back and wash it later.

Setting my sandwich on the bedside table, I plug my earbuds in and load my favorite playlist. I crack my neck, reach into my backpack, and pull out the assignments I've been dreading for days. I know baseball is my backup plan and school is my number one priority, but I wish I had the talent, or money, for it to be the other way around. School is vital for my future, but I hate it with a passion. I alternate bites of sandwich with paragraphs of text I don't absorb until the music is interrupted by a text alert.

Liam's name flashes on the screen and I roll my eyes, knowing he's going to have some damn excuse about my economic notes for tomorrow.

I open the text and a video clip appears. Narrowing my eyes to get a better look at the tiny screen, I debate whether to open it. The last thing I need with my already wavering attention span is porn.

Curious, I tap the video and watch, confused.

The camera pans around a baseball diamond, landing on the haggard face of a man who looks about my age as he watches a performance on the field. The bill of a baseball cap doesn't hide his weak attempt at a smile, but his eyes brighten marginally when a wisp of golden hair flies across his face. A soft, familiar laugh makes its way to my ears, forcing me to look over my shoulder at the wall I share with Olivia. It takes a second before I realize the sound, *her* sound, is coming from the video and not somewhere in the apartment.

I focus back on the video just in time to see Olivia's face on the other side of the man, love and concern marking her brow and dulling her eyes.

The camera turns back to the dance routine and ends abruptly. My face screws up, wondering why Liam would send me some shit like this. I don't need to be reminded that she's taken. She does that herself every damn time her phone goes off. I was made well aware of her relationship status when I heard her fingering her damn self at his command.

Bryson: WTF, dude? I get it, she has a damn boyfriend. Fuck off with that shit.

Watching the tiny text dots appear and disappear for a long moment, I wonder if he's going to pop off with some asshole bullshit about poaching another guy's woman, or worse, encourage me to fuck her since her boyfriend is so damn far away—not that I haven't considered the notion myself.

I don't get words from him the second time either. Another video clip pops up. It takes forever to load, and I almost refuse to open it when I notice it's close to twenty minutes long. Apparently, I'm a glutton for punishment. The second it's fully downloaded, I tap the triangle for it to play, praying to everything that is holy he's not sending me some sex tape they made—hearing that shit through the wall was bad enough. I consider the possibility since she refuses to leave the apartment. Extreme embarrassment like that would make me question staying in the same town.

I still when the video begins and the soft intro music to *My Wish* by Rascal Flatts plays in the background. It seems the video is being recorded on a laptop with the top only partially open.

The lid lifts and a man with sunken cheeks and lifeless eyes faces the camera.

"I'm ready," he says to someone off screen.

His voice. I recognize it from listening at Olivia's closed door. It's the same timbre that comes from Duncan, only weaker, raspier. This is a shell of the man I'd seen just moments ago.

I watch with rapt attention as he reaches for something off screen before popping medicine in his mouth and taking a swig of water from a bottle.

Sad eyes face the camera once again, and I'm immediately drawn to his pain. His illness and long battle are apparent in the deep-set lines of his forehead and hollowness of his cheeks. My heart begins to hammer in my chest.

"Five minutes?" he asks, looking away from the computer for a moment.

"Maximum," a male voice off camera confirms.

"Many will think this is a fucked up way to do this, but a lot of you have been there for me through all of this, and since secobarbital works so quickly, this is the best way I could think of to reach out to everyone and say goodbye. I'm terminal. I have been for a while. While fighting AML day in and day out for years, I've prayed I wouldn't have to exercise the rights provided by the Death with Dignity Act, but here I am."

Messages begin to flash at the bottom of the video, having been written while the video was still live. Dread and nausea wash over me when I realize this is the fucking video Liam was telling me about. He referred to the guy as Kelly, which I grasp must be Duncan's last name.

Several messages flash until one name stands out like a beacon.

Olivia Dawson: Please, God, no, Duncan. What did you take? Where are you?

The shrill ring of Duncan's phone echoes around the room he's sitting in, but he reaches down to silence it. It has to be her calling, freaking out at what she's watching.

"Mom, Dad, I know you supported me with this decision, but I didn't have it in me to watch the pain in your eyes as I took my last breath. I'm doing this here with the help of a medical professional, so you don't have to suffer any longer. I chose this way to remove your struggle of begging me to fight longer. I'm so tired of fighting, so tired of the pain and inability to help myself. It's not getting better for me, and there's nothing that can be done. It's time."

Several names I recognize from the team roster flash at the bottom with words of encouragement and goodbyes. Hearts and tear-stained emojis float across the screen.

Olivia Dawson: Don't leave me, Duncan. I need you.

My throat clogs and my hands begin to tremble, shaking the screen, but I force myself to keep watching.

"Sweet cheeks, my beautiful, precious angel. I'm going to miss you the most. You are my soulmate, my fairy-tale ending. You are my ultimate fantasy and wildest dreams, but I need you to realize I'm not yours. My final chapter, my ever-after, is over, but yours will continue. It has to continue. You have to accept that I'm merely a placeholder for the man who will come in and sweep you off your feet. He'll love you the deepest and help you forget the pain you're feeling right now."

Olivia Dawson: Never! I choose you, Duncan. Please, I choose you!

My heart breaks, and his voice cracks as her message joins the others.

"This is going to hurt for a while, but you have to let me go to find him. I need you to find him, Ollie. Please, baby. Tell me you're going to love again. Please. Swear to me you'll open your heart and live your life to the fullest."

Olivia Dawson: Duncan…

"I'm at peace with my decision, sweet cheeks. I need to know you're going to be okay. Swear you'll eventually be happy. That you'll move on."

His eyes cast down, watching the same comments roll so fast, it's almost too quick to read them fully.

Olivia Dawson: I swear, Duncan.

His eyes meet the camera once more. *"That's my girl. I want you to keep going to school. Make new friends. Laugh when you feel like crying. Never give up on your dreams, Ollie. Have babies and love with every molecule in your body. I'm in your heart, beautiful. Take me everywhere you go."*

His head nods forward and he barely catches it.

"I love you. Chat soon, sweet cheeks."

Olivia Dawson: Never goodbye.

The video continues to roll as a man in a white medical coat helps Duncan lean back, situating his weak head on a pillow. It isn't until Duncan begins to hum along with the video that I realize the same song has been playing on repeat in the background this whole time. The same song Olivia turned off in the truck—a freak out over morbid memories from a horrible time in her life.

Rogue tears spring from my eyes and land on the screen of my phone. Messages continue to stream on the bottom of the video even as the humming ceases and labored breathing takes its place.

Not one more message from Olivia comes across the feed. I can't even begin to imagine what she went through watching that live.

A ragged final breath echoes in my head and I regret not turning off the video sooner.

I watch with soaked eyes as the doctor steps back up to Duncan. Placing fingers on his neck, he checks his watch, and announces, *"Time of death, twelve fifty-two p.m."*

Chapter 21

Olivia

I clasp my chest when I open the door to the bathroom and find Bryson leaning against the wall, waiting for me to exit. The apartment had been quiet for a while, giving me the opportunity to dart across the hall for a shower without running into him. I'd hoped it would stay that way, that maybe he had fallen asleep.

"Sorry," I apologize. "I didn't know you were waiting. I wouldn't have taken so long."

"I don't need the bathroom, Olivia." His tone is flat, as if trying to cover some unnamed emotion and struggling to do so.

I do my best to step around him, but his body lines up flush against mine, almost pinning me against the wall.

His eyes search mine, for answers or an explanation, I can't tell which.

"I'm sorry for how I acted earlier. I shouldn't have blown up at you like that. You didn't deserve it. I'm just..." my voice trails off. I've said too much already.

"You're confused about how you feel about me." I nod, unable to lie. "You want to act on it, but you don't."

I drop my head when his eyes shift lower, focusing on my mouth.

He tilts my chin up with the tip of his finger, and my eyes squeeze shut, refusing to meet his eyes. Warmth flows over me as his breath ghosts over my cheek.

"I can't, Bryson. It's not fair."

"To Duncan?" he sighs but doesn't pull away. "It's not fair to Duncan?"

"It's not fair to you either, Bryson," I say, finally opening my eyes to face him, showing more courage than I actually feel. I choke on a swallow as my throat tries to close and tears sting the backs of my eyes.

"You love him." His words are resolute, not a question.

"More than anyone can understand. My mom, my friends—none of them understand."

"You miss him."

"Every second of every day," I confess.

"I'm here, Liv." He leans in another inch, his breath warming my trembling lips.

I allow the smallest of brushes before I push on his chest. He backs away instantly, rejection clouding his dark eyes.

"I can't," I repeat as I step past him and head into my room.

I lean against the door, trying to calm my panting breath and raging heartbeat. It doesn't work. I attempt pacing in the small area at the foot of my bed, but resilience still eludes me. When I close my eyes, I feel the whisper of his lips on mine. I hate that I walked away. I know I can't lead him on, not after begging him to kiss me at my lowest point, but I have nothing left to give. My heart belongs to Duncan, but I can't keep images of Bryson out of my mind.

I want him on a base, carnal level, but it's the emotional attachment to Duncan I can't let go of—the young love I've held on to for so long.

Giving in to the pull of my laptop, I scoop it up, place it on my lap, and log in.

After selecting the folder I click more often than I should, I pull up the video I watch every time I catch myself thinking of the man who lives ten feet away. It has nothing to do with Bryson, but a guy my mom tried to set me up with when Duncan found out he was no longer in remission the second time. He began to pull away from me, insisting I would be better if I let go of the idea of us.

"Hey, baby." Even over a year after the video chat was recorded, I hear the strain in my voice. *"I miss you."*

"I miss you, too, sweet cheeks. How's school?"

The girl in the smaller window, a shadow of who I once was, shrugs. *"I haven't been this week."*

"It's Thursday, Ollie. You promised last week you'd make every class. This isn't healthy. You have to live your life."

I remain silent, just as recorded Olivia does.

Duncan sighs in frustration.

"Your mom sent me the link to Jacob's Facebook page. He seems like a pretty decent guy."

My mouth turns down at the mention of the man my mother thinks is an appropriate replacement for the love of my life. She gave up on Duncan long before his suicide video went viral. Even after all this time, I'm still bitter about her abandonment.

"Not going to happen." The words streaming from the video make me look up to my bedroom door, torn between wishing Bryson would knock like he did earlier and praying he stays away from me.

"Even your mother likes him, Ollie. That's saying something." He's pretending to be okay with me moving on, but there's a battle in his eyes. I can't imagine how difficult it was for him to say those words.

"He's not who I want, Duncan. I want you. I need you. Not a stand-in." Tears stream down my cheeks. I've watched this video hundreds of times, but the pain hits me in the chest with just as much force as it did when we were chatting in real time.

"You know that's not going to happen. Don't cry, sweet cheeks. Your tears slay me." I shake my head, mimicking the girl in the smaller video window. I hate his parents for forcing me away. They claim they did it to make it easier on me.

"It'll help in the long run," his mother whispered before he got on a plane and headed out of state for treatments from the best doctors in the country. *"Don't show him how sad you are. He can't fight if he's worried about you."*

I squeeze my eyes closed, willing away the heartache. Had we known the experimental, last-ditch-effort treatments were going to do more harm than good, we would have rather spent his last days together. Well, I would have. Duncan started pulling away the minute he boarded the plane, no doubt letting his mother's words sink into his own head.

"I'll never recover from this, Duncan." I still haven't.

"You will. I promise. You have to." I can't. *"Everything I'm doing is for you. You have to move on."*

"Fight, Duncan. Fight for me. Fight for us." He fought long and hard, but the leukemia won. A horrible disease took over his body and turned a vibrant, amazing man into a shadow of himself.

"Ollie, I've been fighting for us for years. It's over, baby. You have to accept it." I didn't know this then, but he'd already spoken with his doctors. They gave him four months max; he was gone in two.

"I won't." I don't even bother to wipe away the tears falling from my eyes.

"No more video chats, sweet cheeks. I won't—"

My bedroom door flies open and I slam my laptop closed on instinct, glaring at Bryson in the doorway. As long as he's been here, he's never just barged in—except the last time I watched this video.

"What are you doing?" I finally ask when he just stands there, eyes darting from me to my laptop and back again.

"How long?" he asks, holding his hands palm up by his sides.

"Wh-what?" I stammer.

"How long are you planning on lying to me? Fighting what you feel for me? I need a timetable here, Olivia. I can wait as long as you need, but I need you to give me something, anything," he says with a strained voice, taking a step closer to me.

"I can't," I repeat the words from the hallway, lowering my head as I twist my fingers together in my lap. "Duncan—"

"Is gone, Liv. Duncan is gone." My eyes snap up to his as renewed tears force their way from my tired eyes.

I shake my head, not because I'm denying it—I know full well my beautiful man, my best friend, is gone; I live the pain every day—but the barrier of Bryson not knowing the truth has protected me. I haven't intentionally lied to him, but when he assumed I had a long-distance relationship, I didn't correct him.

I've been confronted more than once about how I have chosen to grieve. I've dealt with frustration, misunderstanding, and criticism for months from people who insist I get over it. Bryson, however, is sad for me, not angry.

I shake my head to ward him off as he steps closer. Undeterred, he squats at the edge of the bed and clasps my shaking hands in his.

"Stop pretending, Liv."

I'm here.

His words from the hallway rattle in my head. He knew then. He was giving me an opportunity to admit what I've been hiding since the day he showed up.

This is more than I can handle. My emotions are all over the place. I'm relieved, yet apprehensive now that he knows. The cocoon I've built around myself has split open with the revelation of Duncan's death. The layer of protection that's kept him at arm's length, the only boundary between us, is now gone. My heart aches for my loss, but my brain keeps reminding me Bryson may be able to help ease it somehow. I allow the anger to take over, reacting the same way I have numerous times—what caused my friends and family to walk away and never look back.

I pull my hands from his and shove at his chest. Catching him off guard, his balance sways as he lands on his butt on my carpet. He looks up at me, confusion and dejected pain in his eyes.

I steel my spine and look at him. "I need you to leave."

Chapter 22

Bryson

"Not gonna happen, Liv."

I pick myself up off her floor and stand over her. I'm not trying to intimidate her, but I refuse to allow her to push me away. I cup her cheek, only for her to jerk back from my touch.

"Don't," she says, her voice quivering.

"He wouldn't want this."

Swollen eyes stare up at me. "You don't have a damn clue what he would want, Bryson. Don't talk to me about things you can't even begin to understand."

"Liam sent me the video," I confess.

"That's not..." she shakes her head violently. "That's not any of his damn business. It's not any of *your* business."

"They were friends, Liv. *We* are friends," I say, keeping my tone soft. "He mentioned Duncan when I first got here and saw the memorial outside the baseball complex."

"There's a memorial?" Confusion marks her brow.

I nod. Has she not been out of this apartment since it happened? She's only left with me once, and that was almost against her will.

"I didn't understand why you reacted the way you did when he came over earlier. At first, I thought maybe you guys had a fling or something." She looks into my eyes, checking for the emotion evident in my voice—jealousy. I know she finds it, because I'm doing nothing to hide it. The thought of her messing around with one of my teammates makes my blood boil, even though I have no right to be angered by anything in her past.

She huffs an incredulous laugh. "That would never happen."

Good to know.

"He sent the video to my phone. I watched the entire thing, listened to the words he said to you. He wouldn't want you like this, curled up every day, refusing to have a life. He wanted you to live."

Her broken mood shifts at my words. "I am living," she spits.

"You're not. You've convinced me for weeks Duncan was alive."

"I never lied to you, Bryson."

"Your omission of the truth is the same thing. We've talked about Duncan on more than one occasion, yet you never told me the truth. You knew I thought you guys were in a long-distance relationship. Allowing that is the same as lying."

"I don't owe you anything. The truth about my situation isn't your concern."

"You couldn't be more wrong, beautiful. I refuse to allow you to keep living this way. It's time you started moving on." I take a step closer, only for her to retreat farther from my touch.

"I can't do this," she says, scooting back on the bed. The distance, both physically and emotionally, between us, kills me. "I want you to go."

"You can't just push me away. You don't have to fight what you feel for me. He wanted you to move on." My eyes plead with her to realize I'm putting myself out there for her, that the love she holds so dearly for Duncan isn't enough to keep me from her.

"I don't feel anything for you, Bryson. Please leave." The tremble in her voice betrays her lie. "Besides, you have that super classy Simone woman. She can give you want you want. I'm not on the menu."

"Don't do that. I'm not your friends, and I'm not your mother. I'm not just going to walk away because you want to wallow in your pain. I'm here, and I'm not going anywhere."

She curls her knees to her chest, burying her face, and doesn't acknowledge me as I climb in behind her, wrapping my arms around her small frame. Relenting marginally, she sinks into my embrace.

Resting my head on her shoulder, I close my eyes and breathe her in. Silent sobs wrack her body, and I don't know whether she's responding this way because she feels guilty for being in my arms or finds comfort in my touch.

"I never wanted any of this," she mutters without lifting her head.

With tender lips, I kiss the side of her neck. "Even as much as I'm drawn to you, Liv, even as much as I imagine you being mine, I wish he were still here too. I'd rather meet him on the ball field and obsess over you from afar if it meant you had a smile on your face instead of the tears in your eyes."

She softens against me, relaxing further as I speak the truth.

After a while, her tears begin to slow and she shifts her closed-off posture until she's lying back against my chest. Her hands cling to my arms as they remain wrapped around her. She may not give me much, but the soft touch of her fingers is more than I can ask for right now.

Needing her to open up to me, I run my nose along the soft column of her neck. "Let me show you what living really is."

I pull her hair from her face and neck so my lips have better access.

She stiffens. "I'm not going to sleep with you, Bryson."

I chuckle, shaking both our bodies. "That's not what I'm talking about."

Turning her head so she can look into my eyes, I can't help but drop my gaze to her lips. Her breath hitches at my perusal and my lips tingle to feel hers. The light brush in the hallway was torture to walk away from.

Clearing my throat in an attempt to pull us out of a moment she's not ready for, I say, "I don't expect all of my dreams to come true in one night."

She frowns at my refusal to let the subject go, but I won't lie to her. I need her to know exactly where I stand, and although getting her beneath me isn't on the top of my list, it's definitely within the top ten. Feeling like I'm losing her, I get off the bed and hold out my hand.

"What?" I smile at the quizzical look on her face.

"Let's go for a drive."

I expect the immediate shake of her head. "It's late."

"And tomorrow, you'll complain it's early. Now is as good a time as any."

"I can't."

"You can," I insist. "If we stay here, I'm going to want to kiss you."

She frowns.

"Fine," I say with a shrug, climbing back onto her bed.

She shifts her weight until she's lying on her back and I'm positioned to her side. I'm only doing it to force her hand to leave the apartment with me, but I end up testing my own willpower as her lips tremble and her gorgeous blonde hair fans out, a contrast to her dark comforter.

"I'd rather stay here and make out with you anyway," I admit, wagging my eyebrows up and down. I pucker my lips in an exaggerated way and lean into her. Her hand shoots up and I laugh around her fingers when she uses it to cover my mouth.

"Stop," she says, a lightness in her voice I haven't heard in days.

Keeping with her playful mood, I stick my tongue out, wetting her fingers.

"Gross." She pulls her hand from my lips and scrubs it on the bed before turning her eyes back to mine.

Even though it's not what she wants right now, I hate that my body is beside hers rather than lined up between her legs. Sex wouldn't solve a damn thing, but I'm pretty sure an orgasm or ten would lift her mood some. Feeling like an asshole for wanting her so fiercely while she's in so much pain, I smack a kiss to her forehead, climb off the bed, grab her arm, and pull her up with me.

"Come on, Liv. It's just a ride and grabbing a bite to eat."

She shakes her head. "First it was a ride and now you want to eat?"

I pat my stomach. "I'm a growing boy. I'm always hungry."

"There's nothing *boy* about you, Bryson," she mutters under her breath.

I grin at her as she turns her face away in embarrassment, hating that her cheeks are already red from crying. I'd love nothing more than to see them flush pink from her slipup.

"We'll get drive-thru. How long has it been since you've had fresh French fries?"

Her face softens. "Too long."

"Now's the time then." I pull her toward the bedroom door, our hands still clasped.

"Maybe tomorrow," she says, tugging her hand from mine.

"Nope. Strike while the iron is hot."

"I'm not dressed," she complains.

"It's a ride around town and a drive-thru window. Who cares what you're wearing?"

She looks down at her sweats and tank top, forcing me to notice her hardened nipples for the first time since we stood in the hallway earlier. My mouth waters and my tongue tingles for a taste.

"Maybe throw this on," I say, picking up her hoodie from the floor and offering it to her.

Turning my back to her, I adjust myself in my own sweats, doing my best to keep in mind she's not in the same place as I am in our mutual attraction.

I wait for her near the door and she eventually walks out of her room, a scowl on her face. Once she's standing in front of me, I reach out and force the corners of her lips up.

"No frowning or I won't let you get a cookie for dessert."

With a resolved sigh, she follows me out of the apartment. Reaching down to her fisted hand, I pull it to my mouth and kiss her knuckles. She eyes me but doesn't pull her hands from mine. The smile on my face as we walk to my truck couldn't be forced away even if someone tried.

Chapter 23

Olivia

"So, we're just going to hit the drive-thru and head back home?" I ask, eyeing the crowd loitering outside the hamburger joint Bryson just drove up to.

"That's not what we discussed," he says, giving me a side-eye.

"What the hell are they doing out?" I ask, looking at the time on my phone. "It's three in the morning on a school night."

Bryson pulls his truck into the line for the drive-thru and turns his attention to me, frowning as I cower lower in the seat and pull my hood up until it's almost covering my face.

"Why are you hiding?" he asks with a chuckle.

"I recognize half of these people."

His face falls as he looks over to the outdoor seating area filled with college students. "You don't want to be seen with me? That's kinda fucked up, Liv."

I roll my eyes at him. "It's not that at all. I just don't want to be seen."

His face shifts. "Did they hurt you? Were they mean… you know, after?"

I shake my head. "Nothing like that. I just can't stand the pity. It's in their eyes, in the way they act around me—like I'm a fragile piece of glass that will break if they act normal. Duncan was very well known around campus, everyone was so generous, but then…" I tuck my chin to my chest as my voice trails off.

"I'm here to support you while you work on healing and moving on, but I'm a full disclosure type of guy. Some of the things I'm going to say are going to upset you, but I want you to know that's not my intention. I'm not going to walk on eggshells around you. It won't do either of us any good."

"Hell of a preamble there, Bryson. Is this where you yell surprise and push me out of the truck into the middle of the crowd all sink or swim like?"

I expect him to laugh, but he doesn't give in to my attempt at distraction. *Not in a playing mood.*

"If you don't want people to treat you like glass, you have to stop acting like glass. Getting out this evening is the first step. Take this off," he says, reaching over and pulling the hood from my head. "Sit up and be strong."

"I don't feel strong," I tell him, keeping my eyes on him and refusing to look out at the people only a few feet away. My skin burns from their stares, from their judgment.

He reaches over and takes my hands, resting them on my thigh. "Pretend until you do."

"Fake it 'til I make it?" He nods as I look out at the small groups of people. "I can do that."

As we pull up a couple feet over the next fifteen minutes, I realize no one is looking in our direction, and I'm thankful for the dark tint of Bryson's truck windows.

"That's all you're going to eat?" he asks, angling his head toward my large fry and chocolate chip cookie.

"No judging," I chastise. "You don't see me asking about the three meals you ordered."

His smile gleams at me. "I got one of those for you. I know you'll get hungry, eventually."

We drive around town for half an hour, eating in companionable silence before I grow weary and wonder if he's being quiet as a way to get me to talk. If he is, it's working.

"Just gonna drive around all night? You have class in the morning," I say, as if he's not aware of his own schedule.

"We can head to Wal-Mart. Get a little grocery shopping done. I ate all the lunch meat," he says as we pull up to the same red light we've seen a half dozen times already.

I shake my head, still looking out the window. "I don't want to be around people."

"Okay," he says, simple as that.

"Hold on. You ate all the lunch meat? There was over half a pack left."

He gives me a mischievous grin. "Growing boy, remember?"

I cringe, thinking about my comment earlier. He's caught me staring at his chiseled body more than once and seems to remember every reaction and word I say. A man who pays attention even when you don't want him to is a novelty.

I lift the straw to my diet soda to my mouth, finding it empty as the echo of my futile suction rings in the cab of the truck.

"Here," he says, holding his chocolate shake toward me. "You can suck on mine."

I feign disgust but feel my lips twitch as I look at him. "You'd like that, wouldn't you?"

His eyes glass over for a second. "More than I could ever verbalize."

I hate the serious sexual direction our conversation has veered toward, even more so when my body responds to his suggestion.

"I'm not Simone," I say, turning my attention back to the window.

"What's that supposed to mean?" His tone has changed as well, marked with mild irritation.

"It means," I say, my gaze shifting back to look him in the eye, "I'm not going to be sucking you off in the shower anytime soon."

The glint in his eye is the last thing I expect. "Not anytime *soon*, but someday?"

"You're incorrigible, Bryson." I shake my head and pull my eyes from him, but the twitch in my lips is now a full-blown smile.

"I am not. I'm just a man who goes after what he wants, and I've got my eyes set on you, Liv."

The truck begins to roll forward once more. "So, I'm a challenge then."

It's not a question, he's made his intent very clear. I'm just not sure of his end game.

"Oh, you're challenging," he says with a quick laugh, "but you're not a plaything, beautiful."

I stew in the silence that falls over the truck for a long while before looking back at him. "Is this where you claim you can see us growing old together? That I'm the most special girl in the world? That, even depressed and standoffish, being around me is the highlight of your day?" I hate the sarcastic tone in my voice, but I'm not a fan of being placated or dished empty, meaningless promises. I've had my fair share of those.

He shakes his head, calming my nerves a bit. Pulling into a park, he cuts the engine to the truck and turns to face me. "But only because you're not ready to hear it yet."

***

"What is this place?" I ask, thirty minutes after sitting in complete silence.

"A dog park," he explains. "I found it on one of my morning runs. People get up pretty early to run off their animals' energy before leaving them alone for the day."

I beam as the first car pulls in and the owner leads a large collie to the fenced in area.

"You like dogs?" Bryson asks, noticing my smile.

"Love them," I tell him, never taking my eyes from the playful pup.

"We should get a dog." That simple. He notices I like something, so he feels like I should just have it.

"Dogs have to be walked."

"Good thing your legs work then, huh?" His look is a challenge, an ultimatum of sorts.

I shake my head and turn my attention back to the park, noticing several more people have shown up with their beloved dogs.

"They're here so early," I say as the sun puts off the first light of morning. "Too early for me."

Bryson's hand brushes across mine again. "How many early mornings and sleepless nights did you have when Duncan was sick?"

"Too many," I whisper without meeting his eyes. A tear falls down my cheek. "Not enough."

His thumb sweeps the tear from my chin. "We do what we have to for the things—the *people* we love. It's a sacrifice, but one we'll gladly make if it makes someone smile. It shows them we're invested in their happiness."

"True," I agree.

Silence fills the cab as I look down at the hand he's stroking. The small band of diamonds on my finger catches my attention.

"I don't know how to live in a world where he no longer exists."

"None of that sad stuff, Liv. Look at me," he says, lifting my chin. "You get better, stronger, one day at a time, but you have to keep moving forward."

That's so much easier said than done, but I can admit I haven't even thought about trying until now. Bryson gives me hope. Someone willing to stick around and fight with me may be what I need.

"I'm sorry I didn't correct you when you assumed he was just away. It was easier after the way you looked at me."

"How did I look at you?" he whispers in my ear, having scooted closer.

I raise my head and catch his eyes with mine. "The same way I look at you."

"Oh, beautiful," he says, resting his forehead against mine, his warm breath gusting across my lips. "I sure hope I don't lick my lips as often as you do."

"Jackass." I slap his chest and pull my head from his. I love how he can make a serious conversation light and playful. It's exactly what I need since I'm warring internally over my emotions.

"Want to play with some dogs?" he asks, opening his door.

"Of course," I answer, climbing out behind him.

Chapter 24

Bryson

"You forgot, didn't you?" Confusion runs across my face when I answer the door and find Emerson standing on the other side.

"No?" Running my hand over my face isn't helping to ring any bells.

"Is that a question?" she huffs, kicking out her foot, her hand on her hip.

I raise an eyebrow at her ridiculous pose. I'm in no mood for Diva Emerson today.

"It's Labor Day weekend, Bryson. We scheduled this."

I nod and let her step past me into the apartment. What she's saying sounds vaguely familiar. "I haven't slept since yesterday morning, Emmy. Not really firing on all cylinders here."

I rub at my tired eyes, attempting to force them to wake up, but the urge to still close them is strong. Being up all last night, and most of today, comforting Olivia has exhausted me. I know she's tired as well, but we've opted to hang out on the couch and spend time together versus splitting into our separate rooms to sleep.

"I guess that means you haven't changed your sheets yet," she sighs as I close the door.

Of course, that's the first thing she would think of. "I just got back from class. I was going to change them."

"Doubtful," she says, calling me out on my lie. "You didn't even remember I was coming. That gorgeous roommate of yours keeping you up all night? I'm not sleeping on sheets you've been banging her on, Bry. I refuse."

"Will you keep your damn voice down?" I whisper-hiss.

I hang my head as we walk into the living room where Olivia is curled up on the couch. I never regret seeing my sister, but I had just settled in beside Olivia and her head was on my shoulder. It's not often she initiates contact, and Emerson showing up has ruined that. I can't help the irritation beginning to seep into me.

Looking at Olivia, my eyes beg for forgiveness at Emerson's brashness. As much as Emerson's feminine shit has rubbed off on me, her masculine side is much bigger. She can hang with the guys and do laps around them on a bad day.

Embarrassment washes over Olivia's face at hearing my sister's words. I cringe, knowing she's going to invert on herself again because of it.

"I..." Olivia pauses as she gets up off the couch, the blanket we were about to share wrapped all the way around her body, covering up the tank top and tiny shorts she's wearing—covering up the warm skin that was against me only moments ago.

"We don't... I mean, we haven't..." Her head tucks against her chest, blatantly refusing to make further eye contact with either of us.

If Emerson were my brother, I'd smack her upside her damn head. My stomach falls as I watch Olivia scurry to her room. Seeing her waddling down the hallway like a penguin wrapped in that blanket would almost be comical if my frustration level wasn't through the roof.

"Damn it," Emerson says on a sigh when Olivia's door clicks shut. She spins on her heel and glares at me. "You could've told me she was sitting in the damn living room!"

"You didn't give me time! You just barged in here and started running your damn mouth!" I hate nothing more than raising my voice to my sister, but this time, it's warranted. I drag my hands through my hair to keep them from wrapping around her thin neck.

"She doesn't have to be so touchy either. It's a simple thing to clear up." It's just like Emerson to turn defensive when her actions cause someone else discomfort.

"We need to go, now," I hiss, grabbing her arm and urging her toward the door.

"Stop!" she says, pulling away from my grasp. A twinge of guilt hits my gut when she reaches up to rub the soreness I just caused on her arm. "I just got here."

"I'm hungry," I lie. "Let's go."

Once we're standing outside the door, I turn to her. "I forgot my keys. Be right back. Oh, and, Emerson? You can hear every single word said in that apartment, no matter where the people are. Watch what you say, at all times."

I feel like an ass, but I lock the door, leaving my twin standing outside while I head back inside and knock on Olivia's door. It goes unanswered, just like I knew it would, but I couldn't leave without trying.

***

I watch with an odd happiness at the tears falling from my sister's eyes. No matter how brash she can be, her empathy for others knows no bounds. Normally tears would make me uncomfortable, and I'd do anything in my power to make her smile again, but I know she needs to realize how tentative Olivia's moods are, how her words affect others. The tears rolling down her cheeks are evidence that she may think before she speaks next time there's even a remote chance Olivia could hear.

"That poor girl," she sobs as the video ends.

During the ride over, I filled in Emerson on what Olivia has been through because I wanted to prevent her from saying something that could trigger a depressive mood. I also told her everything Olivia and I have been through up to now—the video chats, the lies of omission. It wasn't my intention to actually show Emerson the video—I didn't want to put her through that—but after mentioning it and talking about Olivia, she insisted.

"She's been through a lot," I concede.

"You like her. I could tell the second I was in the room with both of you. The change in atmosphere was damn near palpable." My ever-observant sister cuts to the chase as usual.

"She's incredible," I admit.

"She's broken, Bryson. Right? I mean, who wouldn't be? She still watches their recorded videos... she can't let him go."

I gauge my words carefully, wavering between telling my sister to fuck off and admitting the truth as she pulls a napkin from the dispenser on the diner table and tries to fix her smeared makeup.

"He's a part of her, Emerson. I'd never ask her to give up on that. Expecting her to forget something so profound is unreasonable. He's part of her past." My eyes plead with her to understand and the softness in which my words flow reveal a devotion to how serious I've become about the woman I share an apartment with. I lower my head to my hands, the exhaustion from earlier taking hold once more. If thinking about all of this drains me, I can't imagine what it does to Olivia.

"And what?" she says, staring across the table. "You want to be her future? Bryson, from what you told me, she wants to wallow in her grief until it fully consumes her."

I raise my head, meeting my sister's eyes. "Not forever, Emmy. I see sparks of life, moments where she's happy and not miserable about her loss. I see hope in her eyes sometimes."

I don't even attempt to hide my emotions from her. I'm an open book as she looks at me, searching for a reason to continue trying to convince me to let it go—to give up on pursuing Olivia.

"And that's enough for you?" She sounds doubtful, but it's to be expected. Emerson is even less open to love than I am—*was*.

"For now? Yes. Later on, down the road..." I scrub my hands over my face, not wanting the fingers of doubt to creep in. "Can you imagine being loved by someone as much as she loves Duncan? If I could have a fraction of that, I'd be a very happy man."

"Love? Seriously, Bry? You've known this chick for a couple weeks and you're already talking about love? Did you get hit in the head with a ball at practice?" she asks, gawking at me like I've grown three heads.

"I'm not saying I love her, Emmy. Shit, you're so oblivious sometimes. I'm trying to tell you when she loves, she loves hard, and that would be something I'm interested in."

"You want to love her?"

"I'm saying, I can see myself loving her but being loved *by her* would be beyond amazing." A faint smile crosses my face at just the idea of it.

"You have one tough uphill battle, brother. I hope you're up for it."

"Me too," I mutter as the waitress comes to the table to drop our orders off.

I know then and there, I'm willing to do something I've never done before. If chasing her, fighting for her, and proving to her that I will to go the extra mile to earn a fraction of that love is what I need to do, then I'll do every single bit of it with a smile on my face.

***

"I know you heard me when I said I was giving up alcohol this weekend," Emerson complains as we pull up to the house party that's looking more like a block party right now.

"You wanted to hang out this weekend. This is what I had planned. You don't have to drink." I cut my eyes to her as I put the truck in park and open my door.

"Booze and boys? Bryson, you know I can't turn those down," she whispers, as if her confession is a secret, disappointment clear as day in her voice.

"We can leave," I say as I climb back into the truck.

Reaching out a hand, she grasps my arm. "Who is that?"

I follow her finger and whip back around while shaking my head. "No. Not a chance. Rule number one—no hooking up with my teammates, Emmy. Hard limit, seriously."

"He's a ballplayer?" she coos, making my stomach turn.

"Liam Ashford isn't someone you need to even talk to. I hear he can charm the panties off a nun." Looking over, I see her brow furrow at my words. I've done my due diligence by warning her. Emerson has a bad taste in her mouth for playboys. It's the reason she left La Grande the same time I did.

"Good thing I'm not wearing panties," she says absently, never taking her eyes off my teammate.

"What the fuck, Emmy?" I say as I scrunch my nose, flabbergasted. "Don't say that type of shit around me, and don't even think about it. I already want to throat punch him and he hasn't even met you yet."

She finally pulls her eyes off Liam to look over at me. "You want me to be supportive of your grandiose dreams of Olivia, the least you can do is let me have a little fun."

I shake my head. "Not the same. He's a dog. I'm the one left on this campus after you leave and the last thing I need is him bragging to our team about how he bagged my fucking sister."

She doesn't look convinced, and I hate when she gets that determined gleam in her eyes. I never should've told her to stay away. Now she'll want him even more just because I did. She may be over bad boys and players, but forbidden fruit is a whole other story.

"Besides," I add, "he has crabs."

"Has or had?" I glare at her as the truth about the Deltas hits me in the chest. Who is this woman and what has she done with my sister?

"Like it fucking matters."

Her laugh makes my skin crawl.

A knock on my window pulls my attention from my disgusting sister, only to find the man of the damn hour looking through the glass.

I open the door and he crowds in immediately.

"Hey, man." He peers over my shoulder and I recognize the second he sets eyes on my sister. "I'd ask who the hottie is, but you guys look so damn much alike, I already know the answer."

"Good," I hiss. "Since she looks like me, you can stay away."

"Hate to break it to you, bro, but if I were a chick, I'd be all over your ass—and I'm not even a little gay. Liam," he says, not bothering to let me get out of his way before reaching into the truck and shaking Emerson's hand. "You, beautiful thing, look a lot like my next girlfriend."

Emerson giggles like a fucking schoolgirl and my hands clench into fists.

"I don't do the boyfriend thing," she tells him.

"Perfect," he says with a glint in his eye I don't like.

I know there is no way to stop this train wreck even if I wanted to, so I slide out of the truck and head into the house. Maybe after a couple beers, life will seem less fucked up.

Chapter 25

Olivia

My heart slams in my chest when feminine giggles wake me from a deep sleep. The second I allow images of Bryson and some floozy slut making out in the hallway to filter in, tears spring to my eyes. After Duncan passed, I swore I'd never put my heart through that kind of pain again, but somehow, Bryson found a crack and maneuvered his way inside. It's the only explanation I have for the way I'm feeling right now.

More giggling. More tears.

They fumble, trying to make their way to his room, and bang into my door more than once—as if him saying the sweet things he's proclaimed the last couple days didn't even happen.

"Damn it," he mutters as she giggles. "Emerson, I swear to fuck, if you don't get in there and lie down, I'm going to make you sleep in the damn tub."

Emerson?

The tears fall harder as relief overwhelms me. I listen to him bicker, finally making their way into his room. My door creaks open a few minutes later, but I don't move. I continue to face the wall, no plans to even acknowledge him. How would I explain my jealousy at hearing another woman in the apartment? Expressing that emotion will bring on questions I don't even have the answers to right now.

My bed dips behind me and I stiffen. "I know you didn't sleep through that."

Although he's on top of the covers, his breath tickles the tiny hairs on my skin. Pulling my hair out of my face, he notices the tears on my still wet cheeks.

"Olivia," he says, his eyes as soft as his voice, "I didn't mean to wake you up."

I shake my head. "I thought you... I thought you brought someone else..." my words die off on my lips as I hiccup in a small breath.

He tugs my shoulder and forces me onto my back. I expect frustration, but only find compassion as my eyes meet his, searching.

His thumb whispers across my cheek as his eyes move to my lips. A light flicker of arousal sparks inside me and I lift toward him, meeting him halfway as he leans down.

Warm lips find my forehead, several inches above where I'd anticipated them. I sigh my disappointment. His touch is brief before he pulls away and stands to the side of the bed. Of their own volition, my shoulders slump forward and I tuck my head lower, hoping he can't read the fading desire I harbor for him to kiss me.

"I'm sorry," I whisper into the darkness.

"For what?" His voice is just as low as mine, maintaining the intimacy of the moment.

For thinking I meant more to you. For having unwarranted emotions, you clearly don't return. For letting myself hope you would kiss my lips rather than a friendly peck on the forehead.

"Everything."

"Olivia? What are you—" He turns on the bedside lamp, momentarily blinding me. My hand moves to shield my eyes. Sitting up on the bed to avoid the direct glow from the lamp light, I blink to adjust my sight. "What are you apologizing for?"

"I just read everything wrong, I guess." I wring my hands in my lap. "I was sort of confused where you stand, but now it's clear."

"Is it?" My eyes lift to his at the mirth in his tone. "Are you saying you're confused about what I want?"

"It's clear what you want. I've tried to kiss you more than once and you've backed away each time."

His eyes soften at my confession.

"So, backing away means I don't want to kiss you?" I nod. "Liv, I've been drinking. If I kiss you now, I may never be able to stop."

Sincerity is written all over his face as he reaches his hand up, his thumb stroking over my bottom lip. He wants his lips on mine just as I want his. He's trying to be a gentleman, which I can appreciate, but it's not what I want right now.

I hitch a shoulder. "I like kissing. You wouldn't have to stop."

"Yeah?"

I smile. "I mean, I think I'll like kissing you."

"Kissing me would be awesome, beautiful, but it's the keeping it at kissing that will be difficult, and I don't want to scare or upset you."

"So, no kissing tonight." He smiles bigger when I frown.

"What about one tiny kiss tonight, Liv? Tomorrow, I'll make out with you for hours, but I have to sleep off my buzz first."

Heat washes over me at the idea of his mouth on mine for any length of time but knowing he's promising hours of attention makes my body hum with anticipation.

"One kiss," I confirm as he moves closer to the bed.

My eyes flutter closed when his big hand cups my jaw. The contact lights a fire in me that has lain dormant for so long, it's almost unidentifiable.

"Liv," he whispers right before our lips meet.

Flutters assault my tummy as he slips his tongue past my lips, tangling it with mine. A decadent shiver races down my spine and goose flesh covers my exposed skin. Flexing fingers gently hold my face in place as the kiss deepens.

When he groans into my mouth, it's the same noise I know I'd make if I were capable of sound. My hands find the soft fabric of his t-shirt and fist the material, but he pulls back when I try to tug him closer, breaking his lips away from mine.

"Bryson," I plead.

He meets my lips once more, this kiss more chaste than the tantalizing one before it.

"Tomorrow," he promises. "Get some sleep, Liv. You'll need the energy for my crazy sister."

When the door opens, the beam of light from the hallway flashes over the closed laptop on the end of my bed, and shame washes over me when I realize I don't regret his mouth on mine.

***

The smell of rich coffee fills my nose as I roll over and stretch. Sleep was elusive after Bryson left my room last night, but I finally managed to drift off as the first rays of sun reached my window.

Knowing I'll find him in the kitchen, I throw on sweats, but leave the hoodie on the floor. My tank top should be a tease enough this morning.

Finger-combing my hair as I make my way down the hall, I wonder when I even started caring about how I look. The change seems so gradual, I can't pinpoint the exact moment. I duck into the bathroom before meeting up with the handsome roommate I never wanted. A few minutes later, I'm walking into the living room with an empty bladder and fresh breath.

"Wow," I mutter when my eyes find Bryson sprawled out on the couch.

I trace his carved abdomen with my eyes, following them until they V off at his waist. The blanket from the back of the couch is wrapped around his legs but has been kicked down enough that there's no missing his dark boxer briefs or the thick erection testing the strength of the fabric.

My mouth goes dry and my hands tremble.

"Gross, isn't it?"

I gasp when I realize Emerson is standing right beside me, watching me gawk at her brother. The sound forces Bryson's eyes to drift open. A seductive smile spreads across his face when he notices me, only to fall the second he sees his sister in the room as well.

"Emmy, will you make me a cup of coffee?" He's speaking to his sister, but his eyes never pull from mine. The sleepy gruffness of his voice does all sorts of things to my body.

I know I should look away, but that's a skill I can't seem to manage right now.

"Yeah. If you put some damn clothes on. No one wants to see that shit!" She turns her back and heads toward the kitchen.

"No one?" he asks, a hint of challenge in his voice. Raising a brow, he moves his hand from behind his head and glides it down his stomach. My mouth begins to water as he pauses briefly over his erection before reaching for the blanket over his legs. A low hiss escapes his mouth when he makes contact with himself, the sound echoing in my core.

With a slack jaw and probably drool hanging from my chin, I watch with regret as he covers himself up to the chin.

"Morning," he says in a still sleepy voice, as if he didn't just put on an erotic show for me.

I shift my weight on unsteady legs, forcing myself to finally blink.

"C-coffee," I stammer before hightailing it to the kitchen.

Emerson has three coffee mugs out on the counter, which I find rather generous of her.

"I don't know how you like your coffee," she says, pointing to the empty cup.

At this point, I'd consider mainlining it.

Warm arms wrap around me from behind without regard for Emerson standing in the small kitchen. I was wondering how today was going to go and assumed we'd pretend nothing happened until the attraction built up to the point where we were forced to act on it. Clearly, I was wrong.

"Yuck," Emerson says, scooping up her cup before walking out of the kitchen.

"That couch seriously sucks," Bryson says near my ear as he pulls my hair back, opening the expanse of my shoulder to him.

"Mmmm." The sound falls from my mouth when his lips meet the juncture of my throat and shoulder.

"I liked the way you were looking at me a minute ago." Teeth meet skin and I tremble in his arms.

"Like a deaf mute who doesn't understand social cues?"

He smiles against my neck. Placing his hand around my waist and flat on my stomach, he urges me back until I'm flush against his body. I moan again as his fingers dig in deeper.

"You looked as if you liked what you saw," he murmurs.

"You're very fit," I pant. "Lots of muscles."

"And I have a big cock." As if to prove his very apparent point, he grinds harder against me.

I somehow manage to keep a lock on the whimper that almost falls from my lips at the contact. "I hadn't noticed."

He nips my neck, forcing me to squeal. "Liar."

"Jesus Christ, Bryson. Just last night you were refusing to kiss her and now you're dry humping her in the kitchen. Talk about one extreme to the other."

I squeeze my eyes shut and turn to face him, my cheeks on fire. I'd completely forgotten she was here.

"Thin walls," we both mumble at the same time.

He reaches out and brushes his fingers down my cheek before leaning in and giving me a quick kiss, his teeth tugging on my lower lip before pulling away.

I immediately regret not throwing on my hoodie when Bryson swaggers down the hallway and his twin sister's eyes land directly on my hard nipples.

Embarrassed, I hang my head and start to walk away.

"Nope," she says just as intrusively as her brother. "Get dressed. I have a full day planned for us."

I shake my head and look up at her.

"Don't give me that," she says, one brow arched, leaving no room for discussion. "I had to watch you make out with my brother. You owe me."

My eyes widen and the all too familiar tremble begins in my fingertips. She must see the terror in my eyes, because as I'm walking by, she whispers, "Don't worry, Olivia. We'll go to a different town."

Thankful for her foresight, I don't even let it anger me that Bryson must have told her my pitiful story.

***

"See, that wasn't so bad, was it?" Emerson smiles over her iced tea and nods toward the floor full of bags at our feet.

"I haven't been out in a while. I actually forgot how much I enjoy shopping."

"You put a hurtin' on that credit card."

I smile at her, but don't respond. My finances, or abundance of money, isn't something I readily discuss with anyone. Money doesn't buy everything, and my life is daily proof of that.

"I can see what he sees," she says with an odd wonderment in her voice.

"What do you mean?" I almost whisper as I smile inwardly. I know who she's talking about, but it's the vagueness that has me curious.

"It's not only that you're beautiful, because you are, but it's like this sense of... I don't even know. Gravity? Urgency, maybe? I'm just drawn to you. It has to be the same for him."

I clear my throat and dart my eyes away from her. "I don't know if that's what Bryson feels."

Horny, maybe, I add in my head.

"You have that man on a leash, Olivia. Don't fool yourself. I've never seen my brother soft for any woman."

I give her a weak smile because I have no idea how I'm supposed to react to her words.

Chapter 26

Bryson

"Stop looking at me like that. It wasn't so bad." I juggle the bags of groceries and try to unlock the door at the same time but can't reach my keys without putting the bags down. Like an idiot, I didn't want to take more than one trip into the apartment. I angle my hips toward Liv, indicating the keys in my pocket. "A little help please?"

"I told you I could help carry the groceries," she chides as her hand slides in to grab my keys.

Once she's close enough, I run my nose up her cheek. "But then you wouldn't have your hand in my pocket."

My cock thickens, immediately seeking out her touch, but her hand pulls free before he can reach his destination.

For weeks now, this woman has tempted my resolve, provoking my ability to keep a handle on my willpower. We've kissed—oh God, have we kissed—until my muscles ache from the strain of keeping my hands to myself, but things haven't progressed past that. I'm constantly on edge, suspended in a perpetual state of arousal.

Something changed in Olivia when Emerson was here two weeks ago. I don't know if it was that first delicate kiss we shared in the lamp light of her room, or the mini-shopping spree she had with my sister, but the differences are evident in how she talks, how she responds to my touch, and her willingness to be more open to ideas of living again.

Even though our physical relationship hasn't progressed much, she's changing every day. I've managed to get her out of the apartment more and more, even up to an every-other-day arrangement. Today was the grocery store. The day after next, we've planned for another visit to the dog park. Early of course, when most people are sleeping.

"Your muscles sure do look good under the weight of all those bags, though." I beam at her compliment as she slips the key into the lock.

"Just give the word, beautiful, and I'll strip down and flex like I'm in the Mr. Universe competition."

She bites her lip as she mulls over the idea, her eyes scanning over my body. I flex deeper for her enjoyment. Not to be outdone, my dick stands at a full salute as well.

"I may have to take you up on that." She ducks her head, trying to hide the sudden blush on her cheeks and walks into the kitchen.

Soft touches and light grazes have become one of my favorite things, and today is no different. I skim my hand over her back as she bends to organize things in the fridge. I stroke her arms while she pulls groceries from the reusable bags. I feed the fire, giving life to the fantasies I'll satisfy later when I'm alone in my room.

"How do you know the manager from that store?" I query.

"Owner," she corrects. "Her daughter and I were friends."

"College friends?" I know her mother doesn't live far, but we've never talked about where exactly she's from. I just assumed they moved closer to her apartment when she refused to leave.

"High school. Kacie and I graduated together. We weren't best friends but ran in the same circles."

I take the bottle of salad dressing from her hand and place it in the door of the fridge.

"Top shelf," she instructs and I pull it out just as fast.

We haven't discussed a lot of things, including her OCD and germaphobia, but that will end soon. I'm torn between talking about it while she's in a good mood—afraid it will bring her down—but it doesn't feel right bringing it up when she's upset either.

"Where did you go to high school?" I move the bottle to the designated spot without a word. One disclosure at a time is probably best.

"Here. My parents live across town. They wanted to move to an area with more sun, namely the beach, but after Duncan..." her voice trails off, just like it always does when the subject leads back to him.

"Duncan was from here as well?" She nods. "Makes sense. Liam mentioned everyone loved him. Explains the outpouring of support if the kids in college also went to high school with you guys, and why everyone seems to know you everywhere we go."

"Small-town living," she mutters, folding the bags and storing them under the cabinet.

Her good mood is dissipating rapidly, and that's not something I'm going to let happen—especially on a homework-free, practice-free Sunday. I haven't been busting my ass all week with schoolwork so I could free up today for her to close down and shut me out.

"How about," I begin, wrapping my hands around her waist and pulling her against my chest, "we make quesadillas and watch a movie?"

She leans her weight against me, relaxing into my embrace as some of the tension leaves her body.

"Sounds perfect," she rasps.

Thirty minutes later, we're climbing on the couch with a pile of chicken and cheesy goodness.

"What are we going to watch?" She lifts the remote and logs into Netflix.

"Well, we watched *Hope Floats* yesterday," I remind her.

She sighs. "So, it's your turn. What'll it be?"

The screen flashes row after row of movies; most we've watched together over the past couple weeks, the others we've watched on our own.

"*Savages*," I say when the highlighted square passes over it.

She takes a minute to read the synopsis, then eyes me warily. "Pot growers with a shared girlfriend?"

"Loads of action and steamy sex scenes. It has everything a great movie needs."

"Is that something you're into?" she asks with caution.

"Drugs?" I ask, avoiding her true question. "Not my scene."

She rolls her eyes but selects the movie anyway. I could speak the truth. I could put a voice to the fact that, although I may not be her boyfriend, I'm sharing her daily with a man who wanted nothing more than for her to be happy and get on with her life.

A short time later, Olivia is squirming in her seat, quesadillas forgotten on the table.

Blake Lively has nothing on Olivia Dawson, but it's not a hardship to watch two incredibly sensual sex scenes with the Hollywood starlet in the first fifteen minutes of the movie.

Wrapping my arm around her back, I pull her closer until her body is against mine. Within seconds, her hand is on my thigh, so close, but seemingly miles away from where I want her—where I *need* her to be.

"So violent," she whispers.

"Is that why you're trembling?"

She pulls her eyes from the movie, raises her head off my chest, and looks up at me. With an almost indiscernible shake of her head, my eyes fall to her perfect lips. Short, harsh pants of breath rush from her mouth, lighting me on fire. She's seriously turned on, and there's no way I'm wasting this moment.

Shifting my weight, I pull her until she's straddling my lap, and groan when the heat between her thighs rests against my straining erection.

Her hands find my hair as my lips hit her neck. Tracing the raging pulse at her throat, my hands snake under her tank top, spanning across the delicate flesh of her back. She arches, forcing her magnificent breasts harder against my chest.

"Olivia," I plead against her throat before seeking out her mouth.

She whimpers, her hips rotating on their own volition, searing my blood with the contact. I despise whoever created the very first strip of fabric right now but want to hug the person responsible for yoga pants and thin basketball shorts.

My hands wander down until I'm gripping both cheeks inside her yoga pants and guide her grinding hips.

Pulling my mouth from hers, I look into her hooded eyes.

"Please," I whisper, realizing I'm not above begging.

She swallows, her throat working up the ability to speak. "I can't."

I nod in understanding. She's not ready. "It's a big step," I placate.

Her eyes dart from mine and my chest falls, imagining she's thinking about Duncan and the times she was with him, but she blows me out of the water with her next words. Nodding, she says, "The biggest step—one I've never taken before."

Sweet hell.

I shake my head in disbelief, my eyes nearly bulging out of their sockets. "You're not saying you're a... you and Duncan never...?"

She refuses to meet my eyes, but answers with a nod of her head. My cock strains even harder inside my shorts at her confession.

"Hey," I say, reaching up and cupping her cheek after regaining some composure, "I understand, Liv. I'm not here to pressure you, but I want it out in the open that I'm ready for that next step whenever you are. Have no doubt about that."

I grip her neck and pull her back down to my mouth, knowing we aren't taking this much further, but not wanting to stop.

"Is this okay?" I ask, sliding my hands back along her ass and rotating her hips on me.

"So very okay," she pants against my mouth.

Lips, hands and hips work together to build me up to a point I never thought imaginable. Her whimpers and coos of satisfaction nearly force me over the edge.

"Fuck, Liv. You're gonna make me come."

"Me too," she confesses.

And damn if that isn't my undoing. I grip her harder and shift her weight faster as we both climb.

Her body stiffens and then begins to tremble as my sac draws tighter. I rotate her hips once more before spurts of cum soak the inside of my shorts. I kiss her through it, calming her pulse with slow, passionate licks inside her mouth.

"W-wow," she sighs against my lips.

I smile against her mouth. "Your lips are swollen."

"I think my butt is bruised, too. Hell of a grip you have there, short stop," she throws back with a wink.

"When I find something worth holding on to, I seize it," I say, then my eyes narrow on hers. "I never told you what position I played."

Guilt tints her cheeks as she bites her lip, mirth swimming in her beautiful blue eyes.

"Did you google the roster?"

"Maybe," she teases, getting up from my lap.

I want her to stay on me forever, but there is one hell of a mess we need to clean up.

"Shower with me?"

She freezes. Okay, maybe not.

"Too soon?"

"Sorry, Bryson."

"Don't apologize for that, Olivia. You grab one first and then I'll go."

A short while later, after toweling off and opting not to wear a shirt, I find the living room empty. The fact that she pulled away from me a little bit ago when I tried to kiss her while we were switching out positions in the bathroom sat heavy in my gut during my entire shower. She's slipping away from me again and I'm not sure how to stop it. I may only be holding on to her with the tips of my fingers, but I won't sit idly by as she closes in on herself—especially not after the fun on the couch.

I knock on her door, but turn the knob immediately, not giving her a chance to deny me entry.

"Nope," I say, walking toward her bed and grabbing her hand.

"I'm tired, Bryson. I just want to take a nap."

"You're sad. There's a difference."

"I can't help it, Bryson. It's not about you. I promise." Her words gut me. I know it's not about me. It's about him and that makes it even worse.

"You can be sad with me. Living room, come on." I tug her hand again, but she refuses to budge. I lift the covers off her and press my knee into the mattress, threatening to slide in next to her. "Fine. We can be sad in here, but I'll warn you, having you horizontal in a bed is the epitome of my wettest dreams, so I'm bound to press my luck. I apologize in advance when you get angry at where my hands may wander."

She looks over her shoulder at me, gauging my seriousness. "Fine. Let's go to the couch."

"Perfect," I tell her, backing away so she can climb out of bed. "Do I still need to keep my hands to myself?"

She gives my chest a playful smack as she walks by. "Yes, but my hands have free rein."

I'm totally down with that plan. I give her ass a sharp smack on the way down the hall, thankful I was able to ward off another bad mood.

Chapter 27

Olivia

"You're up early."

I look away from the stove and over my shoulder. This time, I'm not even shy about staring at Bryson without a shirt. He knows full well how attracted I am to him.

"Out of clean shirts?" I tease.

"No. I just like the way you look at me when I don't wear one," he confesses, wrapping his arms around me.

The scent of his masculine bodywash fills my nose as I lean back against him. I cherish the way he holds me—unexpectant, yet fully in the moment. I relax into his embrace, sighing with contentment.

"You have an amazing body, Bryson. I sometimes lose the power of speech around you."

"You should try it sometime."

I tilt my head to the side. "Try what?"

He chuckles, the warm air hitting my cheek, heating me further.

"Walking around without a shirt on. I imagine all sorts of responses I'd have if you went shirtless." He waggles his brows up and down playfully.

"Stop it." I swat at him with the spatula in my hand.

He takes a step back and looks into the skillet. "Making breakfast? Smells wonderful."

"You're distracting me. Put on a shirt and I might feed you."

His eyebrows pop up, as if he's considering staying half naked to get more of a response.

"Go." I encourage him out of the kitchen with another wave of the spatula.

By the time he makes it back, regretfully fully clothed, I'm plating an omelet for him. Sitting down at the small table, he wastes no time digging in.

"What are your plans for the day?" I sit in the other chair with a cup of coffee.

Please say you've quit school and plan to just stay home all day like I do. I know it's unreasonable, but I love the little bubble we lived in this past weekend—at least until I got to my room and my phone vibrated with my video alert. That popped my bubble and allowed the guilt to sink in.

"Class this morning, practice this afternoon. Want to grab lunch with me in between?"

I give him my best *have you lost your damn mind* look, but he ignores it.

"Seriously, Liv. It'll be fun."

I roll my eyes. "You said that about grocery shopping yesterday. Don't even pretend you weren't uncomfortable talking to Kacie's mom."

He shrugs and finishes chewing before replying, "Didn't bother me."

"You looked bothered when she started talking about Duncan, and the way she was looking at me, judging me for shopping with another guy so soon..."

His hand covers mine. "Liv, she wasn't judging you. I never once got that vibe from her."

"Seriously? Her *'good to see you moving on, Ollie'* was filled with judgment."

"It wasn't," he argues.

I huff. "Then how did you interpret it?"

"Exactly how she said it. I promise I didn't see judgment in her eyes or hear it in her words." His thumb rubs over the back of my hand, calming my nerves a bit.

"I guess," I murmur, my eyes focused on the table.

He continues to eat while I reflect back on yesterday. Encounters like that are the main reason I stay home. Not many people have been where I am, suffered what I have, but they all seem to have an opinion on how I should handle things, how soon I should "let it go", and the timeframe to do it in.

"I have an idea!" He claps his hands together as if he's been hit with brilliance. His smile is jovial as he looks over at me with a hint of mischief in his eyes.

"That doesn't sound good at all," I mutter, bringing my coffee to my lips.

"I'll bring you lunch from campus and we can eat together. When I leave for practice, you can come with me. Cheer for me from the stands. Lots of people have been showing up lately."

"Did you slip in the shower? Bang your head on your headboard?"

"You sound like Emerson," he chides. "Besides, if there's any headboard banging, you'll know because you'll be in the bedroom with me."

His wink is sweet, but not enough to make me forget his suggestion.

"I probably know every one of the people coming to those practices, Bryson, so my answer is a big fat no."

I get up from the table, pour out my coffee, and begin to wash my cup.

"We can skip the dog park tomorrow," he offers. "In exchange for you watching me practice."

"I'd rather see the dogs," I complain.

Finishing off his last bite, he gets up from the table and walks over to me. I take his plate from his hand and begin to wash it. He finds his place behind my back and wraps his arms around my waist.

"It would really make me happy, Liv... to know you're in the stands, cheering for me. Live in the now with me, please."

I shake my head. "It's practice, no one cheers. If they do, they're idiots."

"Cheer for me in your head. I bet I'll be a rock star on the field if you're there."

I shake my head again. The thought of sitting in those stands makes my stomach turn with more than just fear—it's longing and loss, and knowing I've spent time with Duncan there makes me feel uneasy. "I'm just not comfortable with that."

"Getting out of your comfort zone is exactly what you need. You'll thank me later."

***

"I can't believe I let him talk me into this," I mutter as a small horde of girls file into the stands.

Bryson and I got to the field early and I prayed to be the only one here today, but apparently those prayers went unanswered.

The group of four are loud and obnoxious, not following the proper etiquette—obviously freshman. Anyone who's been around a baseball diamond knows practice, especially pre-season, is important, so the silent rule is to... well, remain silent. These women are acting like they're at a bachelorette party and the players are their personal strippers. I don't know if I've ever been to a practice where the women catcall and threaten to take their shirts off for a foul ball. Ridiculous. The freshman players are eating it up while the upper classmen seem annoyed.

"Idiots, aren't they?" I look over, torn between smiling and running when Ainsley, a friend from when I was actually social, sits down beside me.

I look back over at the girls now passing around a flask and back to my former friend. "Coach will straighten them out."

She gives me a knowing look. Coach Finley pulls no punches. If these women remain a distraction, he'll ban them from practice. They'll eventually calm down. Getting ejected from the sports complex is detrimental for a cleat chaser—ultimate death.

"Can I hug you?" she asks, her eyes wary and tone cautious, as if she's unsure of my reaction even though we were pretty close friends in another life. Her hands flex at her sides, waiting for the go ahead, but unwilling to reach for me until she gets my approval.

I open my arms to her and melt into her embrace. I never knew such a simple gesture, a single touch from another person, could feel so good. Bryson cradling me in his arms is of course different from this, but as Ainsley squeezes me a little tighter before letting me go, I realize I needed her touch as much as I need every one of Bryson's. "It's good to see you, Ollie. I've missed you. Lots of us have."

Guilt hits me hard. Ainsley and a few of the other girls who hung around the ball players and I became pretty good friends last year. Right now, I realize I abandoned them more than they did me. I pushed them away and practically locked myself in the apartment. My self-imposed isolation is one hundred percent my doing. I felt like it was what I needed, but as time went on and I pulled further away, it just became habit, a way of life. Sitting here beside her now makes me wish I'd opened my eyes a lot sooner.

I've missed this, even with as uncomfortable as I am being here. I missed friends, the sound of practice, and the earthy smell of the field as the guys work through fall training.

"Missed you, too," I say as she pulls away and takes a seat beside me.

"Those girls are out of control." I follow her eyes back to the rambunctious group and shake my head.

"Freshman," I mutter. Realization hits and I look back to Ainsley. "Scott graduated last year. Who are you here to watch?"

Her brother, Scott, pitched for Oregon State all four years of his college career and I read online that Dallas drafted him last season.

She gives me a shy grin. "Wanna play this game? I could ask you the same thing."

My cheeks heat. I walked right through a door I opened myself.

"I'm here watching my roommate." Confusion crosses her face, so I point out on the field between second and third base. "Bryson Daniels."

She rolls her lips between her teeth to keep from smiling, but her eyes shine with amusement.

"That's very... supportive of you," she finally manages. "*Just* roommates?"

I look back to the field, finding Bryson looking in our direction. He gives me a goofy grin and a thumbs up. Shaking my head at his silliness, I look back at my friend and shrug, unsure how to answer her honestly.

How do I begin to explain to someone who knew Duncan that I've started to develop feelings for another man? I'm not ready for the judgment and opinions everyone will have, especially someone I once considered a close friend.

But at the same time, I don't want to hide behind my grief any longer. I feel it every single day, like a slap to the face, but there are moments when Bryson and I are together that things seem like they're getting better, that there is life and happiness to be found outside of Duncan's memories.

"Word on the diamond is he's the one to catch. Queen Simone already had her claws in him, but that's to be expected."

My jaw clenches, and I'm certain she can hear my teeth grinding. "We met a few weeks ago."

I don't mention I haven't seen her since she was put in her place at the diner, or how Bryson spends almost every free second with me.

"I don't remember her from before." My voice drops at the last word. *Before*. Such a simple word that holds so much power. *Before* feels like yesterday for the pain, but a decade for the loss.

"She stuck to upper classman, mostly. She didn't bother Duncan because she knew she wouldn't have a chance."

My eyes close at his name coming from someone else's lips, a harsh reminder that he's still on the minds of others. I wish I could be more like Ainsley, able to mention his loss without my stomach knotting and heart tightening in my chest.

"Sorry," Ainsley says, her tone soft. She places her hand on my shoulder.

A weak smile is all I can manage. I grip the edge of the seat, a way to hold me in place, ground me in the moment when every instinct says to get up and run. I want to run from Ainsley and her mention of Duncan and Simone—run from the feelings I can't seem to control around Bryson, run from the ever pressing knowledge that my life has changed and I'm still incredibly bitter about my story being changed.

"I'm here to watch JJ," she confesses with a conspiratorial whisper. She must notice my shift in demeanor, and I'm grateful for the topic change.

I pull my head back and look at her with surprise. "JJ, as in Joey Jessup? No way!"

I'm genuinely shocked at her admission, and I know she can read as much on my face. My lips turn up into a smirk when I see her eyes glittering with adoration as she watches JJ on the pitcher's mound.

It's her turn to blush.

"You're together?"

She shakes her head, her lips turning down at the corners as an emotion I can't name passes over her eyes. "He doesn't even know my name."

"Sure he does. He and Scott were thick as thieves, if I remember correctly."

"Best friends," she confirms. "Still are, but Scott's Little Sis is all he ever calls me."

"Oh God. Immediate friend zone."

She huffs. "More like surrogate older brother."

I cringe. "Sorry. Maybe with Scott gone this season, he'll see you in a different light."

"Fingers crossed," she mutters, looking out on the field, mild disappointment in her eyes.

I know the feeling. I'm just glad I never had to look out on this field and see Duncan. It's the only reason I agreed to come today. His memories here are with me in the stands. Ainsley showing up is a blessing because she doesn't allow the wallowing I was sure to do today.

Chapter 28

Bryson

"On your period?" Liam asks, popping me in the back with a rolled-up towel.

I sneer at him, rubbing the burning spot on my skin. "Asshole."

"It's the only reason I can explain the half-assed job you did out on the field," he complains, scrubbing water from his skin.

I relaxed a little when I noticed Olivia smiling and talking to another girl in the stands. As far as looking like a rock star? Let's just say, I hope she was paying more attention to her friend than my shitty attempt at baseball.

"Olivia was in the stands." I tug my t-shirt over my head, wanting to get out to her as fast as I can.

"Ah," he says. "That explains it. Distracted by the gorgeous girl. She needs to stay home if you can't play with her here."

My hackles immediately go up. I know what he's getting at, but it doesn't piss me off any less. "She's at home too much. I guess I was just worried about her."

"Worried?" He looks over at me before I can school my face back to passive. His eyes narrow as he reads my protective stance of Olivia clear as day on my face. "Fuck, Daniels. Don't tell me you're getting tangled up with her."

"You should stay out of it," I sneer. I shouldn't react this way. He's not approaching this in a disapproving way, but more like a hopeless, cautious concern.

"I knew her before Duncan died. No one loves someone that hard and survives losing them the way she did. I saw her at the funeral, she was a shell of her former self. She was an amazing woman and—"

I close the distance between us. "Is, Ashford. She *is* an amazing woman."

He holds his hands up in surrender. "I don't mean anything negative. I just mean I'm surprised she's not institutionalized."

"She's not fucking crazy," I hiss. I run my hands through my hair, trusting it's enough to keep from ripping his throat out. *Does he know about her watching the recorded videos? Staying locked in her apartment for the last eight months?*

My hand is around his throat before I even give it a second thought.

"Damn, man," he gurgles around my fingers.

I release him and take a step back. I've never been a violent man, but this asshole talking about Olivia in any way but positive makes me want to bash his head in.

He rubs at his neck, the look on his face softening.

"I was about to do the same to you, asshole. I didn't like the idea of you sniffing around her after seeing the way you fucked and then treated Simone, but it's clear the situation with Olivia isn't even remotely the same."

"Since when are you worried about how women are treated? I've seen you go through girls like water in a sieve." I lower my indignant eyes, forcing him to look directly at me. Contempt washes over me at the hint that he thinks I'm anything like him, that what I feel for Olivia is even remotely similar to the situations he gets into with women.

His face grows serious. "I don't treat women like shit, Daniels. I may not call them the next day, but they understand where I stand before I pull my cock out. Which reminds me, can you give me Emerson's number? She forgot to give it to me after the party."

This motherfucker.

My fists clench at my sides.

"Joking, dude. Fuck, seriously, let me go hit Coach up for some Midol." He grins and starts to get dressed. "Do you need a heating pad too?"

"I don't even want to know why you know so much about periods, man. You sure you got a dick in your pants, or are you hiding a clam to go along with those crabs?" JJ breaks into our conversation, smacking Liam upside the head. "Don't let Seafood Platter over here get you riled up. He knows as well as I do that little sisters are off-limits."

"Sounds like there's a story there." I turn my attention to JJ, if anything to keep from laying out Liam.

"Our boy here," Liam says, walking up and wrapping his arms around JJ's shoulders just to be shoved off, "has had a hard-on for Owens' little sister for the last two years. I swear, his cock gets stiff every time he sees her."

"Owens? Pitcher for Dallas?" I ask with a smirk.

"And best friend," Liam adds, looking at JJ.

"Fuck off, asshole," he says, walking away.

"Just so you know," I say to Liam, "I treated Simone like shit because she disrespected my girl at the diner."

"Your girl, huh?"

I shrug before bending down to tie my shoes. It isn't a lie. If I had it my way, Olivia would already be mine.

"Does she know she's yours?"

"She will."

"Well," Liam says, slapping my back, "let's go get your girl out of the stands before the cleat chasers run her off."

I laugh. "You just want to go score with one of the freshman girls."

"You gonna give me Emerson's number?"

"Not a fucking chance," I say.

"Then don't worry about the freshman chicks." He gets a mischievous gleam in his eye. "Hopefully one of them is Catholic."

"You looking for a religious experience?"

"No, just a tight ass to fuck."

"And they have to be Catholic for that?"

He laughs at my question.

"It's not religious, man. You know, a butt slut, a Mormon virgin?"

I shake my head.

"Seriously? The Missouri compromise? The Christian side hug? A thirty-three percenter?"

I shake my head again and keep a straight face, just fucking with him at this point. I knew what he was saying at butt slut—it's what we called them in high school.

"Fuck! Do you live under a rock! A girl saving her vaginity? The fucking poophole loophole?"

"Sorry, man. Not a clue," I deadpan, having a hard time not smiling at his ridiculousness.

"Forget it, man. Look that shit up on Urban Dictionary," he mutters.

"Hey, guys," JJ says, running up to us, "wait up."

"He saw Ainsley in the stands," Liam whispers before JJ makes it across the room. "Could he be less obvious?"

My laugh echoes off the walls as we make our way to the waiting women.

***

"Hi," a tiny girl, who I know is a freshman but looks twelve, says as soon as I enter the stands. My skin crawls at the idea of anyone being attracted to a girl who looks so young.

"Hey," I answer, walking right past her to the blonde beauty a few rows up.

We look at each other for a long moment without even speaking. Her hair whips in the gentle breeze and the thin strap of her tank falls off of her shoulder, revealing the added color to her skin from the sun. I want to trace the line with my tongue.

"Have fun?"

She grins. "It wasn't absolute torture."

"Good to hear."

"Hey, SLS." JJ's voice comes from my left. "Didn't see you up here."

"My ass," Liam mutters on my right.

"SLS?" I ask with confusion.

"Scott's Little Sister," the redhead says from beside Olivia, a frown marring her pretty face. "Most people call me Ainsley."

My eyes widen in understanding when she looks at JJ the way I imagine I look at Olivia. I don't know if their situation is any better than the one we're facing.

"Olivia," JJ says, stepping past me and wrapping his arms around her in a brotherly way. "You look great. It's good to see you."

When he pulls back, their voices lower, I watch my teammate comfort the girl I'm falling for, wiping a tear from her cheek and hugging her a second time. I clench my fists at my side, my fingers twitching at their familiarity.

Hating that he's the one touching her and not me, I pull on his shoulder until he releases her. "Paws off, Jessup."

He laughs, but steps away so I can wrap myself around her from behind. She stiffens, her reaction a contradiction to how she acts when we're alone. Remembering what she said about the lady in the grocery store and feeling judged, I step back. I don't release her fully, keeping a hand on her lower back.

She glances up at me in a silent thank you.

"You guys want to grab something to eat?" JJ asks, standing awkwardly beside Ainsley, arms down by his side like a pole.

I smirk at the way her pinky finger twitches as if she wants to reach out and touch him but won't because of the unspoken law of sisters being off-limits. I almost feel sorry for them but remembering the way Liam was sniffing around my sister, I let go of it real quick.

I look over at Olivia, judging her mood. The faintest of nods tells me she's had enough for the day.

"Nah, man," I answer. "We ate lunch before practice and I have a ton of homework. Think we'll just head back to the apartment."

"Ashford?" JJ says, getting the tomcat's attention. "Wanna go eat?"

"No thanks, man," he answers, never taking his eyes off the tiny girl who spoke to me earlier. "Lining up my next meal right now."

"Gross," Ainsley mutters.

"On that disgusting note, let's get out of here."

"I agree with JJ," Olivia says, leading the way out of the bleachers.

"You hungry, SLS?" JJ's voice floats up from behind as we make our way to the parking lot.

"Sure," comes the meek reply.

The girls hug at the truck, Olivia promising to attend more practices and get together with Ainsley soon. My heart grows just a little more at how much my girl is breaking out of her shell right in front of me.

"You have a ton of homework?" she asks fifteen minutes later as we step into the apartment.

"Nope. I was hoping for more baseball," I say, gently pinning her to the closed door.

"You should've stayed at the field if you wanted more baseball." Her head tilts to the side as my nose drags up her neck.

"I was hoping for first base right here, possibly stealing second," I whisper in her ear.

"If you play the same way you did at practice, you won't even get your cleats on first, buddy."

I smile against her skin, loving that she actually paid attention today while regretting her seeing me in less than top performance.

"Let me try," I say against her lips.

Her content sigh gives me the opening I need and I slip my tongue against hers. Kissing Olivia Dawson has easily become one of my most sought after means of entertainment.

"First," I whisper, breaking from her mouth momentarily, only to dive right back in.

Her small hands grip my shirt, pulling me closer, and I have to bend my knees to get the contact I truly want. Whimpering, she deepens the kiss, angling her head to the right.

Agile fingers work her shirt up until they're on the warm skin of her stomach, itching to go further.

"This okay?" She doesn't even bother opening her eyes as she gives an affirmative nod.

Both thumbs stroke over her ribcage, catching the bottom of her bra. My hips bolt forward of their own volition, meeting the heat emanating from the apex of her thighs. Fuck, do I hate denim right now.

Lowering my mouth to her shoulder, I allow my tongue to swipe at the skin there, and her moan forces me to nip. I could spend the rest of my life tasting this woman.

Erotic pain washes over me when she takes my hair in her grip and urges me down. I take a step away, forcing her hands from my head. I understand getting carried away—usually, I'm a fan of it, but only if both parties are all-in. I search her face for doubt, a hint of unease, or discomfort. I find swollen lips, pink cheeks, and heavy-lidded eyes.

"You putting the brakes on, short stop?" Her playful tone is the only answer I need.

"Not today, Liv." I close the distance between us. "You're the one driving this machine."

She yanks at the front of my shirt again, and I gladly fall against her.

Lips crash, tongues tangle.

Her hands, mercifully, reach down and tug my shirt up and over my head, so I do the same with her tank top. Standing in awe, I stare at her cotton-covered globes. My eyes travel over the milky white flesh just above the cups of her bra. Sweeping an eager tongue over my bottom lip, my cock thickens further. "You have amazing breasts."

"They're practically covered," she smirks. "You should remedy that."

My eyes pull from the gray cotton for the first time since it made its appearance to look into hers. "Liv, I don't—"

My words fall away when she reaches behind her and flicks the clasp open. A second later, the fabric falls from her skin, exposing her dusty pink nipples. My mouth waters and I grow infinitely hard in my basketball shorts.

I look back into her eyes—if she's offering, I'm sure as fuck not squandering this opportunity—and find nothing but the same arousal I feel.

"Hell yeah," I pant, reaching and clasping her small rib cage in my hands. I lower my mouth to the perfectly puckered pink flesh and her body melts against me.

Her head tilts back, causing a soft thud to echo through the otherwise silent apartment. Soft, panting breaths escape her lips as I tease her with my mouth.

"Second base," she whispers.

Chapter 29

Olivia

The foreign feeling of heavy warmth startles me when I wake to the sun streaming in through my bedroom window. However, it's the fact that the heaviness is a hand cupping my bare breast that makes me freeze.

"Don't freak out," Bryson mutters against my neck.

"We slept together." I freeze at my own words and the way they sound. We didn't *sleep* together; we closed our eyes and passed the night away in slumber.

"We did," he confirms. "It was amazing. You're easy to snuggle with."

"I fell asleep on the couch. How did we end up in here?" I shift my weight and turn over to face him.

The sleepy, disheveled look first thing in the morning is seriously working for him.

"I carried you, but I was a good boy. Even though your jeans probably weren't the best option to sleep in, I didn't even attempt to make you more comfortable." The bright smile on his face shows me he's quite proud of himself.

"Such a gentleman," I praise as his hand reaches up, pushing my long bangs behind my ear.

"Not exactly," he confesses, running his thumb over my naked breast.

I follow his gaze, needing to see his hand on me.

His long finger traces over a strawberry-shaped hickey an inch above my nipple.

"You marked me," I whisper.

Cupping my chin, he says, "You marked me, too."

"Where?" My voice is low, almost seductive in the early morning light.

His hand clasps mine and he raises it to his chest, covering his heart. I swallow roughly as a riot of emotions bombard my head. I didn't expect the tender sentiment, but damned if it doesn't confuse me with the other things bouncing around in there.

I close my eyes, unable to handle the adoring look he's giving me.

"Don't close me out, beautiful. I'm here." His words are strained, full of emotion and rejection.

A tear rolls down my cheek. All I seem to do around him is cry, but the alternative is trying to put into words what I'm feeling, and since I don't understand them fully, it's an impossible task.

"I didn't mean to upset you. I'll go, give you some space."

I shake my head, clinging to his hand. "I want you here, Bryson. I'm trying."

He pulls me against his chest, but his bare skin against mine doesn't hold the same comfort it did last night.

"I've got class." Grateful for the temporary reprieve, I nod against his chest before he gets up, leaving me alone in my room with a soft click of my door.

Waiting until I hear the shower turn on, I throw on a t-shirt and finger comb my hair in the mirror. Once the hiss of the water starts, I head to the kitchen—coffee always makes things clearer.

Shortly after I've filled my cup and taken my position on the couch, Bryson comes out dressed for school. His distance doesn't go unnoticed when he sits in the armchair rather than beside me. I know I'm not being fair to him, but I warned him before the truth about Duncan was brought to light. I just never anticipated hurting myself when I couldn't let him in.

"Want me to grab you for practice this afternoon?"

I shake my head. The last thing I need is to be around other people.

He nods as if he knew the answer and was only asking out of courtesy. He gives me a chaste, emotionless kiss on my forehead and then he's gone. He deserves more than I can give him, but I also don't want to lose him. I'm having a day today, but before him, they were all bad. He's brought light in my life and I'd be a fool not to grab that while he's still offering. My brain understands the reasoning, if only my heart would get in line.

I sit in contemplation until my coffee turns cold. Not solving a damn thing, I finally go to the kitchen and notice the coffee still sitting in the pot. Bryson didn't drink any this morning either, I realize, my shoulders drooping under the weight of exhaustion and guilt.

"He couldn't get out of here fast enough," I mutter, cleaning my cup and the coffee pot.

Dishes lead to wiping everything down, which begins the spiral into an all-out cleaning frenzy. Cabinets are emptied and rearranged, only to be changed again. Floors are scrubbed by hand, and pristine walls are wiped down. I know none of it needs to be done, but the minute my hands stop cleaning, they'll reach for the computer. Bryson deserves better. Duncan deserves better. *I deserve better.*

Forcing my hand still when I begin to scrub the counter tops for the third time, I rest my head on my forearms and let the tears fall. Trying to stop them now will only give me a headache, which will lead to the migraine medicine, and that ends in sleep.

Surrendering to the emotions, I slide down the cabinet and cry, each tear that falls another crushing defeat. I weep on the kitchen floor until my sobs are waterless and the migraine I was hoping to avoid is battering against my skull.

I claw my way up the cabinet, knowing there's no way to avoid the medicine, computer, or bed. With a small sliver of hope, I opt for Tylenol instead of the prescription meds that will knock me out with certainty.

Holding a cold bottle of water against my forehead, I sit on the couch and thrum my fingers on my laptop. As much grief as the videos of Duncan bring, the joy at seeing his face, hearing his voice, is equally present. It's that comfort I'm seeking when I yield to the pull and log in.

Picking the most lighthearted one I can find; I click play and let my fingers trace his handsome face. I appreciate the healthy look in his eyes, the fullness in his cheeks. His remission didn't last long, but the bounce back his senior year in high school was remarkable—it gave us hope.

"Show it to me again," he insists.

I twirl the small band of diamonds on my left hand as the recorded Olivia holds her left hand up in front of the screen, a proud look on her face.

"You don't think it's too soon?" she asks as I swallow down my *tears.* Not as lighthearted as I remember.

"I don't want to waste another second of our lives, sweet cheeks. It's already too short as it is. Leukemia has made me realize I have to live in the now. Are you having second thoughts?"

"Never," she says with such devotion. *"My parents will never let me get married before I finish high school, though. They love you, but not that much."*

I close my eyes, letting his laughter wash over me, sink into my soul, and repair the damage I've been causing myself these last few weeks, only to find the pain is not as deep as it has been.

"I love you, sweet cheeks. Talk soon."

"I love you, too," I whisper as the video ends. Opening my eyes with renewed hope, I find Bryson standing across the room.

I close my laptop on instinct. I've felt guilt over how I feel about Bryson almost since the day he moved in, but when did that shame shift?

He frowns but doesn't get angry like I expect. He doesn't act the way my mom does when she knows I've been watching the videos. Instead, he sits at the end of the couch and strokes the top of my foot absently with his thumb.

"Will you ever share those with me?" His focus is still on my foot, and I appreciate the privacy he gives me as I struggle with his request.

"They're private."

"I understand." The words are his, but the stutter of his hand betrays his placation. "You don't have to love him in secret, Liv. Maybe if he was a part of us and not just a part of you, it would be easier for you to…" his voice trails off as he stands from the couch.

"Bryson," I say, reaching for him.

"Never mind." Frustration radiates off him as his hands rake through his hair. "A couple guys from the team are going to grab a few beers at Cody's. Wanna come?"

"I thought you had practice." I know he's missed more than one class while keeping me company, but practice is never something he misses.

"It's six in the evening." Annoyance marks his tone. "Have you eaten today?"

"I'm not a child, Bryson. I'll eat when I'm hungry." I hate speaking to him this way, but I'm not infirm and helpless.

"Right. Cody's?" I'm amazed he's even bothering to ask again when it's clear he wants nothing more than to escape. It serves as a bitter reminder that people don't stick around. They didn't a couple weeks after the funeral. I should expect no different from Bryson. His words are sweet and nurturing, but his actions are what speak the loudest. Disappointment in him for being so quick to leave hits me.

"No, thank you."

He walks away without another word and I want to beg him to turn back around, to hold me, but to what end? I'll let him comfort me tonight, only to push him away tomorrow.

He deserves better. I lay my head back on the arm of the couch, refusing to let the tears fall as they begin to sting the back of my eyes. I've cried almost all day to no avail, no sense in wasting more, especially on a man who's so quick to walk away from me.

Chapter 30

Bryson

"A beer. Whatever you have on tap is fine," I tell the waitress when she walks up to the table.

"ID," she insists, her hand out.

I raise an eyebrow at her. "Seriously? It wasn't an issue last week."

"Oregon Liquor Control is here," she informs, hitching her head toward the bar where a paunchy man in a bad suit is talking to the owner.

"Fuck," I mutter. "Coke is fine."

"Sorry, honey," she whispers before heading back to the bar. "Things will be back to normal next week."

First walking in on Olivia, hearing her say I love you to him, and now a twenty-year-old can't get a damn beer—what kind of college town is this?

"That sucks," Liam says, angling his beer up and taking a long pull. "Eventually, you'll be a man."

I grab my nuts over my jeans. "I'm all man, asshole."

He grins around the mouth of his beer. "Shitty mood? I've got whiskey in the truck."

"Not the best idea right now. Thank you," I tell the waitress when she places my Coke on the table in front of me.

"Whiskey is always a good idea," he corrects. "Trouble in paradise?"

"I'm not talking to you about Olivia," I warn.

I look away from him, contemplating going back to the apartment and taking whatever scrap of attention Olivia is willing to give me. Seeing JJ walk in, I tilt my head up in acknowledgment.

"I'll tell you about that gorgeous little freshman," he bargains. "You'll want to hear about this thing she does with her legs behind her head."

"Keep your sex stories to yourself, dumbass," JJ says, walking up and clapping me on the back while looking at Liam. "This isn't the fucking locker room."

"Yeah?" Liam challenges. "Where's SLS?"

"Not today," JJ warns.

Liam's eyes dart around the bar before standing up. "You two pussies are ruining my buzz. I'd rather hunt for hot chicks than sit here and listen to your sob stories about chicks you can't have."

"Jackass," JJ mutters as Liam leaves us for a small group of girls near the jukebox.

"Coke?" he asks, looking at the untouched glass in front of me.

"Alcohol Commission is here," I complain.

"Gonna be a sucky week around campus," he says, holding his hand up to the waitress to order a beer.

"No doubt," I agree. The waitress brings JJ's beer as I watch the condensation drip down my glass, puddling at the base.

"Vulture, six o'clock," he cautions around the lip of his bottle.

I groan when I see Simone sauntering up with what I used to see as a sexy smile on her face. This woman cannot take a hint.

"Boys," she purrs, wrapping an arm around my shoulder.

I shake her off, forcing her to take a step back. My lungs burn from her overuse of perfume. How was I ever attracted to her? Caked on makeup, hair so full of product it's more like a helmet, and a dark soul— all things I didn't bother to see before opening my eyes and actually looking at Olivia. Things I took for granted until I had the opportunity to run my fingers through her soft, wavy hair and breathe in her delicate, feminine scent.

"That's not very nice," she pouts at my rejection.

I hitch a shoulder.

"Hey, JJ." She turns from jilted at my rebuff to angry when JJ flat-out ignores her.

Simone sniffing around is the perfect way to round out my day. Yesterday was perfect—Olivia at practice, her lips on mine later at the apartment, my lips all over her. If I concentrate hard enough, I can still feel her pebbled flesh on my tongue.

Five minutes against the door led to a half hour on the couch— mouths tasting, hands exploring, hips grinding. We kept it above the waist—second base, as she called it—but it was absolute bliss and pure torture. Exhausted from the crazy day, she fell asleep in my arms, only to wake up and regret every second of it.

Refusing to take the hint, Simone continues to stand beside me. Advice from my mom and sister wage war in my head as I try to decide between mom's, *'always be respectful'*, and Emmy's, *'some bitches deserve to be treated like shit'*. Granted, my sister's ire was mainly for the girl she caught her high school boyfriend fucking when she wouldn't give it up, but still, seems fitting.

Fortunately, Simone makes the choice for me.

"I thought I recognized that girl from the diner but couldn't place her. I realized the other day, she's the crazy chick whose boyfriend offed himself on social media." She smiles as if she's just solved some big mystery rather than revealed how sick and twisted she is.

I sense JJ stand up from his chair just as Liam cages her in over her shoulder.

"I have the patience of a damn saint," Liam whispers into her ear, just loud enough so our group can hear. "I let a lot of shit just roll off my back, but your dirty ass has crossed a line."

JJ steps in closer, and I've never been prouder of my teammates. I only wish Olivia were here to see them come to her defense.

"Big mistake," JJ taunts, a depraved look in his eyes I've never seen before.

"Daniels mentioned you disrespected Ollie the other day, and I was going to let bygones be bygones since I wasn't there—was just going to stay away from you, but then you come in here and spew even more trash." The calmness Liam is displaying is more concerning than a raging bull, and Simone feels the same way standing with wide eyes like a deer caught in headlights.

"Could have just kept your mouth shut," JJ adds.

"But no," Liam says. "You come in here and not only disrespect his girl, but you try to put a negative spin on the bravery Duncan Kelly showed? Tsk-tsk, little girl."

"Bad move, Simone," JJ cuts in.

I can't find an ounce of concern for the tremble in her shoulders. She took it one step too far.

"So," Liam continues, "here we are with a situation that got out of control and a decision on how it should be handled. Should be a tough choice."

Her eyes widen, as if she realizes what's going to happen. Apparently, I'm the only one in the dark.

"Not a tough choice at all," JJ says.

"Nope," Liam agrees. "Wanna give her the good news, Captain?"

"Love to," JJ begins. "No ball players."

"You wouldn't!" she cries, stomping her foot like a petulant child who's been grounded from her favorite toy.

"No cleat chasers," JJ continues.

"I take it back!" she screeches, her wide eyes full of regret and fear. The tremble in her overdrawn lips is a plus.

"What's done is done," Liam finishes.

"Listen up!" JJ bellows, grabbing the attention of everyone in the bar. "Simone is blacklisted. Any guy caught messing with her and any girl caught hanging out with her is out!"

His umpire like voice echoes off the walls as Simone wails beside me. I huff an empty laugh.

"Time to move on, Simone," Liam declares. "Your old ass was getting tired anyway."

Cheers erupt around the bar when she scurries out alone.

"Now," Liam says with a slap to my back, "back to looking for some freshman pussy."

I shake my head while watching him walk back to the same group of girls he was speaking to before Simone lost her shit.

"That was intense," I mutter, picking up my Coke and taking a sip for the first time.

"It was a long time coming. She's been harassing the other girls, threatening them to stay away from the players, staking her claim," JJ explains. "Today was just the tipping point."

"Tainting the fish in your pond, huh?"

He shakes his head and looks away. "I don't have fish or a pond, man."

I leave it alone. The last thing I want is someone asking me about my situation with Olivia.

It doesn't take long before I'm ready to leave the bar. My mood and no alcohol make staying pointless. I grab cheeseburgers and fries for both Olivia and me before heading home, knowing she probably hasn't eaten all day because of her mood.

She's in her room when I walk in, asleep in her bed. I head back to the living room, making quick work of my food and putting hers in the fridge.

Even upset and unsure about where we're heading, she told me she wanted me with her this morning. That's the hope I hold to when I go back into her room, kick off my shoes, and climb in behind her on her bed.

I pull her against my chest, hating that I spent the evening without her.

"I missed you," she mumbles, her voice thick with sleep.

I hold her closer. "I missed you, too."

She stiffens suddenly and tries to wiggle out of my arms. I clench my eyes closed, immediately preparing myself for the rejection that follows when she thinks she's talking to Duncan in her sleep.

"You smell like a slut," she hisses, scampering away from me.

I lift my shoulder and turn my head to smell my shirt.

"Fucking Simone," I mutter, pulling the offending garment over my head.

"Please leave," she begs. Sighing dejectedly, she lowers her dull eyes, refusing me the gorgeous blue I've sought out for weeks now.

I shake my head back and forth, hating that she's pushing me away once again. Always thinking the worst and pushing me away.

Her back against the wall, she hangs her head low, her disappointment clear in the dim light.

Two steps forward and ten steps back, jumping to conclusions, never wanting to let me explain—it's getting out of hand.

"What's wrong?" I ask, my brows furrowed. "Wait—you think I fucked her?"

"You did fuck her!" she roars, pain from my previous actions floating in her eyes. Her lip trembles, breaking down the wall I can't seem to build where she's concerned.

"That was one night, Liv, and I've regretted it every single day since. You make me wish I've never touched another woman before you, but I can't change my past any more than you can change yours." I reach for her, only to catch empty air as she scoots farther down the bed, out of my reach. "Simone was at the bar tonight, spouting evil shit. JJ and Liam tore into her, then blacklisted her. She managed to put her arm around my shoulder once before I pushed her away."

Her eyes widen and she finally makes full eye contact with me. "Blacklisted?"

I nod. "Listen—"

She holds her hand up, halting me. "You don't owe me an explanation."

"I do," I insist. "If you crawled into bed with me smelling like some other man, I'd lose my shit. You are the only woman I see, the only woman I want to spend every waking hour with. I don't want you to doubt that. I don't want you to doubt me. I'm here, Liv."

Her eyes dart between both of mine, searching for truth, deception.

"I'll go," I say, getting out of the bed. Why would I think such an incredibly shitty day would turn around and end on a positive note?

"Come back after you shower," she murmurs, her eyes lifting to mine.

Relief settles in my belly, and the tension in my shoulders slowly melts away at her words—an olive branch after such a stressful day.

I've never showered so fast in my life.

Chapter 31

Olivia

"You're back." I smile at Ainsley as she sits down beside me in the stands.

"Small doses of socialization seem to work best for me these days."

She nods. "I understand. Maybe next time, it won't be weeks before I see you again."

I turn my head back to the Beaver's practice without answering her. When I was here two weeks ago, I promised I'd meet up with her, only to turn around and avoid her calls and make excuses about leaving the apartment. When I said the words, I meant every one, but it's been too easy to fall back into the routine of staying home and only leaving when Bryson offers.

"Any progress with JJ?"

She huffs an incredulous laugh. "Only in my dreams."

"Sometimes, that's the best place for them," I reflect, my gaze remaining on the field.

My dreams have actually been calm—innocuous most nights. On nights when the memories are too strong, Bryson is there to comfort me because I haven't slept alone in my bed since the practice I attended. Sleeping in his arms has become one of the things I look forward to each day. Physically, our relationship hasn't progressed... but emotionally, I can feel myself opening up to him more each day. It's growing organically in a way I never imagined possible at my age.

"He's not blind. He'll come around, eventually."

"Doubtful, but it's not going to keep me from being around all the time, reminding him of my presence." She leans back on her elbows and tilts her face to the sun, trying to catch the limited rays. October is coming to an end, and heat from the sun is sparse these days.

"I'm pretty sure he doesn't have to be reminded, Ainsley. He's well aware of you."

She looks at me with hope, gearing up to ask questions about my comment, but stops short when the same group of loud girls from last practice stumbles into the stands.

"Ugh," she groans.

"Ignore them," I say.

Ten minutes later, I'm wishing I could take my own advice.

"Number two is seriously hot," one girl pants. "I'd love to grip that dark hair while I face-fuck him."

I cringe at her brashness. Where do these nasty girls even come from?

"That's Bryson Daniels," Ainsley pipes in.

The girls turn en masse, looking up at where we sit only two rows higher than them. From the looks on their faces, they didn't even realize we were up here, but with the way they stumbled into the stands, it's clear they're not firing on all cylinders.

"*The* Bryson Daniels?" the face-fucker asks.

"The one and only," my friend confirms. They all smile from ear to ear, privileged to information I'm not. My skin crawls and I rub at my forearms, trying to will the unease away.

"This is Olivia, his girlfriend." My head whips around and I glare at her, finding her thumb hitched in my direction.

I do my best to keep from narrowing my eyes. I know we need to be a united front while speaking to these women, but it doesn't keep me from wanting to pull handfuls of hair from Ainsley's perfect little head for outing me.

"He's yours?" the young girl Liam was hanging all over a few weeks ago asks.

I have no clue how to answer her question. I can't make claims on the man, but it doesn't stop me from wanting to claw these girls' eyes out and stomp on their heads.

"He is," Ainsley confirms for me. "You know what happened to the last girl who tried to pilfer her man, right?"

They shake their head in unison, like kittens watching a red laser dot on the wall.

"Simone was the last one who tried to *tramp*-ple in her territory."

I chuckle at the emphasis while the four girls in front of us turn around and slink lower in their chairs. Oh, the power of a blacklist.

"That's fine," the face-fucker whispers. "I have eyes for the pitcher anyway."

"Uh-uh," I say, loud enough for them to hear.

They turn back again, their eyes narrowed.

Ainsley leans forward, a harsh sneer on her face. "Mine."

"Better stick to the pimply freshman," I suggest. "Or Liam."

The girl from a few weeks ago shakes her head violently. "He's too big for anal."

Her friends grab her hand and drag her out of the stands as confusion races across my face.

"Why the fuck would she share that shit?" I ask, my nose scrunched.

"Saddlebackers," she mutters.

"What?" I turn my face to her.

"They think only having anal sex keeps them virgins," she explains.

"Wow," I mutter.

"Yeah, they're complete idiots." She flops back in her seat. "JJ's going to kill me."

"For claiming him?" I do my best not to smile.

"Yeah," she sighs.

"I think you'd be surprised."

She doesn't respond and spends the rest of practice in quiet contemplation.

***

"Why are you so quiet?" Bryson clasps my hand in his and settles both of them on this thigh as he drives us back to the apartment.

"It's nothing."

"It's something," he persists.

"Just the saddlebackers in the stands."

His eyebrows scrunch together in confusion. "The what?"

My cheeks flush. Explaining it is much worse than using the slang term. "You know, chicks who have sex but not… you know, vaginal sex."

His eyes cut to me, then back to the road. "Butt sluts?"

I can hear the mirth in his voice. "See, that term makes sense."

"Saddlebackers," he whispers. "That's one Liam didn't use. I'll have to let him know he needs to bone up on his research."

"I don't even want to know."

"Believe me, I'm not going there."

"You're not interested in anal sex?" I tease.

He waits until we're at a red light before turning his grinning face to me. "You offering?"

"Ha! You wish, Casanova."

"What did they say to upset you?"

I purse my lips, trying to find the right phrasing. I'm no longer upset after our banter, but I do have questions and need answers.

"They questioned what we were," I reply, my voice low, unsure if I stepped over a line.

"What did you tell them?" Hope with an edge of caution fills his voice.

I shrug. "I couldn't answer them. We haven't defined this—us," I say, waving my hand between us as I watch his face for a reaction.

"You need a definition?" he asks with a smile.

"I need to know what to say when people ask. Roommate doesn't feel right considering the only thing staying in your room is your clothes."

He squeezes my hand harder on his thigh.

"Just tell them the same thing I tell the guys."

"What do you tell them?" I ask, arching a brow as we slow for another red light.

Releasing my hand and cupping my cheek, he says, "That you're mine."

When his eyes go back to the road, I turn my head, looking out the window to hide the smile on my face.

***

His.

We've hardly spoken since we returned to the apartment. Other than deciding on tacos for dinner, we've just operated around one another in routine silence until the meal was prepared. He's giving me space, probably wondering if he went too far with his proclamation, but space is the last thing I want right now.

"You're not leaving any room for lettuce and tomatoes," I chastise as he fills his taco shells with seasoned meat and cheese.

"Vegetables are for losers," he advises, stuffing more cheese inside one shell until it cracks.

"Says the insanely fit guy who juices kale."

"Aw, beautiful, that's sweet. Are you worried about my health?"

I freeze at his words. His health will always be a concern for me. Surely, he knows that.

"Fuck, Liv. I'm sorry," he apologizes, noticing the shift in my mood. "I'll eat it on the side."

I clear my throat as he piles diced tomatoes and shredded lettuce beside his tacos.

"You don't have to do that," I whisper.

"Look at me." He gently grips both sides of my face. "I'm as healthy as an ox."

"I know." And I do. He's in prime, top physical shape, but Duncan was healthy too... until he wasn't.

"I'm not going anywhere," he promises, pulling me against his warm chest. His strong heartbeat pounds against my ear, and I sigh, leaning closer into him, ease settling over me as some of my anxiety washes away.

It isn't until this moment that I realize the distance I've been keeping between us has had a lot to do with my fear of losing him, too.

"Let's eat and watch a movie," he offers, stepping away from me.

"My turn to pick," I taunt as we grab our plates and head to the living room.

"It is not," he argues. "We had to watch that damn Legally Dumb movie the other day."

"*Legally Blonde*," I correct, ignoring the mix up between my hair color and the insulting word. "And you forced me to sit through almost three hours of football."

"The Raiders were playing," he responds, setting his plate down on the table and grabbing the blanket off the back of the couch.

I sit down, holding my plate high while he covers my legs. "It's not like they're from here, Bryson."

"Oregon doesn't have an NFL team. You should know that."

"Really? Please tell me why that's a requirement for me."

He faces me, his dark eyes serious. "I play baseball."

Shaking my head, I give him a dubious look. *As if that explains a damn thing.*

"And I can name all MLB teams in both leagues and more stats than most men, but that doesn't have any bearing on football. Baseball requires skill and planning. Any big brut can run down a field and plow over people."

His eyes soften as his lips turn up into a grin.

He leans in to kiss me, and I wait for it almost impatiently.

"You make me hard when you defend my sport, beautiful," he groans against my lips.

"You're always hard," I correct. I press a gentle hand against his chest, forcing him to take a step back. "Let's eat."

Thirty minutes later, my alarm goes off. We're spooning on the couch and I feel him stiffen at the sound and what it represents. Without a second thought, I reach over and silence the phone before snuggling back against his chest.

Chapter 32

Bryson

"See, that wasn't so bad."

Glassy-eyed, I stare at the credits scrolling on the television.

"Yes, it was," I argue.

"It was an action movie. I thought you loved action movies." She frowns, looking from me to the television and back to me again.

"*Miss Congeniality* is *not* an action movie. *Transformers* is an action movie. *Deadpool* is an action movie. That," I wave my hand at the screen, then pull out my phone, "was a chick flick."

I find the IMDB app on my phone, type in the title, and grumble incoherently when the movie pulls up.

"What does it say?" Mischief fills her voice. "Give it to me."

She yanks my phone from my hand before I can close the app.

Holding it up, she waves it in front of my face. "Action, comedy, crime. I was right! What do I win?"

"Me?" I offer with a shrug.

She contemplates my offer, nibbling at the skin of her lower lip. My cock thickens when naughtiness fills her eyes. Hope fills my gut when her hands find my chest and she shifts to straddle my lap.

Her trembling fingers find the hem of my shirt, and a second later, she's lifting it over my head.

"What are you doing?" I ask, needing to know where her head is at.

Her hot mouth finds the skin on my neck, pulling a groan from my lips.

"Baseball," she whispers in my ear.

My lips lift. "I like baseball."

"I like baseball with you." The brush of her hair against my chest as her mouth tastes my throat ignites my skin, the soft waves flowing over my chest and down my abdomen. I resist the urge to grab a handful and direct her mouth south.

My fingers flex, gripping her ass, forcing her against me as her mouth finds mine. The kiss is searing and passionate, different from every one before it. It's sure and needy as she demands more from me.

I've restrained myself every other time her mouth has been on mine. I can easily go from playful banter to balls deep fucking in the blink of an eye, but Olivia isn't a quick fuck. I don't see her as a means to an orgasmic end.

She's more.

I've waited, prayed, and bided my time until she was ready to take that next step, so her hips flexing against my shaft and soft moans rising up from her throat is confusing. For the first time in my life, I think about the aftermath, what tomorrow will bring. Each and every time we get close physically, she pushes me away and closes off emotionally. As much as I would love to sink inside of her, as much as I would enjoy my mouth on every inch of her delicate flesh, I hesitate.

It suddenly becomes clear that the end game with Olivia isn't conquering her body, but rather occupying her heart. Knowing this, I push her back slightly, my grip still on her hips.

"Olivia," I pant, breathless from our kiss.

"First base," she coos, taking off her tank top and revealing her perfect and blessedly braless breasts.

"Jesus," I mutter. Relenting to the need that's been building for weeks, I release her hips and taunt her puckered nipples with my thumbs.

Leaning forward, she presses one breast to my lips and I peer up at her, watching for her reaction when my tongue swipes at her offered flesh. Hooded eyes regard me with sultry desire, driving my hunger as my cock demands attention below her.

I release her breast and lavish the same attention on the other while pinching and toying with the wet flesh of the breast I just released.

Her hands find my engorged length peeking out from the top band of my shorts and I freeze.

"Olivia, no," I say with newfound willpower.

"I want this," she whimpers, her eyes pleading with me as the tip of her finger brushes over my erection.

"We don't have to do this," I say, stilling her hands and bringing them to the safety of my chest.

Her lips find mine again, desperation radiating off her.

I pull my head back.

"I want this," she repeats as her eyes grow bleary with tears.

Without a word, I lift her at her hips, stand from the couch, and carry her into her room, laying her down on the bed. Positioning myself over her, I push her blonde waves away from her face.

"I don't want to waste my life, Bryson."

"Hey," I whisper, sweeping my thumb over her cheek. "There's no rush. I'll still be here tomorrow, next week, next year. You don't have to live like it's already over." Truth spills from my mouth as I picture a life with her.

"Tomorrow is never promised."

Now we get to the root of the issue. Does she want this from me because she regrets never taking this step with him? Will she picture him when I sink inside her?

"I want this with you," she says, bringing her hand up to my face as if she can read my mental struggle.

Pulling away, I stand at the side of the bed.

"Bryson?"

"I have to get a condom," I mumble before walking out the door and heading to my own bedroom. Once inside, I rest my head against the coolness of the wall separating our rooms instead of retrieving the latex I used as an excuse to catch my breath. I argue with myself that no matter how upset she gets, no matter how much she pulls away, I'm still able to bring her back around. My reasoning is solid, but taking her virginity is not something that can be forgotten tomorrow or the next day. That act is life changing. That regret can be long-lived.

Still undecided over how the night will end, I grab a condom and go back to her. Covered to her neck in the sheet, I register her shock at seeing me back in her room. I must have been gone a while for that amount of doubt to set in.

Placing the condom on the bedside table, I climb back into bed. She reaches for me the second I get within touching distance, and I decide to throw my doubt into the wind and leave it up to her to pump the brakes. She will if she's not comfortable, and I have to trust that.

I groan as I pull back the covers and find her naked. The glorious sight of every inch of her milky flesh exposed makes my mouth water.

"You need the condom."

"Not yet," I say as my mouth finds her breast. "Let me please you."

A hand grips my hair, and nails scrape my back as I kiss down her body and dip my tongue into her bellybutton. Whimpering moans escape her lips as she opens her legs wider for me.

"Beautiful," I praise, working my thumb over her clit in a slow, circular motion.

Her hips buck as both hands lock into my hair, and my control snaps. Soft, easy, and slow are no longer part of my vocabulary as my mouth closes over her silken, heated flesh, my tongue performing an un-choreographed dance against her clit.

Her hips buck against my mouth while her hands attempt to pull me off her as her body fights opposing forces—too much, yet not enough. My own body is familiar with the sensation every second I'm near her.

I grind my cock into the mattress as I continue to work her over the edge, needing her as wet and turned on as possible. Taking what she's offering won't be completely pleasant for her, but I'm going to do my damn best to make it as pleasurable as possible. A voice inside my head cheers at the knowledge of being her first, but I quiet it, knowing I won't last long at all. It's not the norm for me, but I haven't been inside a woman in weeks—my longest dry spell since hitting puberty.

I sweep my finger at her entrance and dip inside, testing her. She quivers at the attention, her body clamping and gripping, begging for more.

I close my eyes and devour her, my cock so hard, it's almost painful. Her moans echo off the walls as my tongue lashes at her and my finger delves deeper. Back arching off of the bed, she gasps sharply as her body begins to convulse. I never take my mouth from her but watch as her eyes squeeze shut and her teeth clamp her bottom lip so hard, I expect to see blood. She tugs on my hair, forcing my head away, and with one last lick, I stop and lift onto my arms.

Running my hand over my mouth, I crawl up her body, feeling like a hero at the satisfied smile on her face.

"Third base," she says breathlessly.

I grin at her continued baseball analogy. "That's plenty for tonight."

She shakes her head as her eyes find mine.

"Home run," she insists.

"I think this is too serious of a situation for you to use baseball to ask for something so precious. A home run isn't what I want from you, Liv."

Her smile falters momentarily until a mischievous glint sparks in her eye. "Fuck me, Bryson."

The pulse in my cock pounds at her demands, but my head knows that's not what this is.

"I don't want to fuck you either."

"Then, what...?" her voice trails off when she notes the look in my eyes.

Her eyes soften immediately, only the faintest of nods granting me permission.

My weight shifts from one side to the other as I push my shorts and boxers off my legs. Looking up, I find Olivia waiting with the condom between her fingers. Her active involvement in preparing me for her means more than she could possibly know. I open the foil packet and work it down my length, the feel of my own hand almost too much at this point.

"This is going to hurt, Liv," I warn, positioning myself at her entrance and rubbing over her clit.

"I know," she whispers, closing her eyes.

"Don't," I beg. "I need to know you're with me."

Her eyes find mine as I push the first thick inch inside. I lean forward to kiss the pained grimace from her face.

"Are you sure? It's not too late."

She gently shakes her head.

"No, beautiful. I need the words."

"Please, Bryson. I'm ready."

I take her at her word, pushing in and not stopping when I meet the thin barrier. I hold her tighter, whispering assurances in her ear as I claim the one thing no other man will get. Her body clamps down, tiny muscles rippling along me. I fight the need to speed up, to push deeper, until I'm covered in a sheen of sweat and my body trembles from my restraint.

I kiss her tears away and swallow her cries when I pull out and slowly thrust in again. Fingers dig into my back, and her leg wraps around my hip, urging me on.

"I won't last," I confess, searching her eyes for remorse.

"That's okay," she says with a short, pained laugh.

My hips jerk forward one last time before I groan my release. With my eyes closed, my mouth seeks hers, praising her for her surrender. I kiss her forever, refusing to pull my mouth from hers even when she winces against my lips as my body leaves hers. Keeping my mouth busy is the only way to keep my words inside—words I so desperately want to say... words she's not close to being ready to hear.

Chapter 33

Olivia

"Hey." Bryson's husky voice pulls me from a deep sleep as his reverent touch pushes hair away from my face. "I have a meeting with the team before class."

I roll closer to him, wincing from the soreness.

"I'm sorry." His look is sincere, but he's still a man, so the glint of triumph is still in his eyes.

"No, you're not." I slap at his chest.

He clasps my hand and holds it to his mouth. "I hate that I hurt you. Seeing you in pain is the last thing I want."

I close my eyes at his sweet words. "I'd go through it every day if it means you never stop looking at me the way you did last night."

It's true. The sting and ache from his body pales in comparison to the joy that took over my heart.

His big hand brushes over my cheek as I try to express without words how special last night was for me. Appreciation at his tenderness, euphoria at the way he handled my body, and mental acuity at wanting to do it again is all there on my face.

His face softens, his mouth tilting up in a small smile and eyes filling with promise. His lips find mine in an unhurried, passionate kiss—a kiss that translates into a promise of more. Sexual tension is on the edge as it always is, but this kiss is gracious, humble, and filled with assurance, quelling any doubts I may have had before today.

"You're going to be late," I mutter against his mouth after the kiss slows to soft pecks and nips.

He groans in aggravation and shifts his hips against me. The heat of his erection stokes the fire always present when he's nearby.

My pulse increases as he presses harder against me, a need building from some place so deep it almost scares me. The fear of the unknown, however, isn't enough to keep me from wanting him again.

"Fuck," he hisses when I open my legs for him. "I'm going to quit the team."

With wide eyes, I stare back at him. "You can't."

"If I did, I could spend so much more time with you, in you." His mouth finds mine again, licking, biting, and toying before he pulls back on a defeated groan. "I have to go."

He jerks back and stands, as if he's fighting invisible forces pulling him to the bed. His erection stands proud, jutting out below his naked hips. In the darkness, it seemed less daunting, but seeing it now, it's no wonder I'm a little sore this morning.

He leans in one last time. "Take a hot bath, beautiful. It'll ease some of the soreness."

"I will," I promise. A hot bubble bath and relaxing music sounds like the perfect way to start my day.

Tugging the corner of the sheet, he surveys my exposed flesh. Gripping his length tightly, he strokes up and down at a leisurely pace. The fire in his eyes combined with the movement of his hand makes me squirm.

"Take the bath, Olivia. I'm going to need you again when I get back."

I nod in agreement, hating baseball today as he leaves the room.

Exhaustion, emotional overload, and the exertion from last night drags me back under. I wake hours later, slightly less sore, realizing I fell back asleep before I even heard Bryson leave the apartment. I reach to the bedside table, searching for my phone to check the time when my eyes land on a sticky-note with a heart on it. Beside the thoughtful note are two painkillers and a bottle of water.

I consume his gift and scoot off the bed. The sting when my body hits the hot water quickly abates, and before long, I'm in heaven. Muscles ease their tension as tiny bubbles pop against my skin. The ringing of my phone destroys my little slice of heaven. I ignore it, letting it go to voicemail, only for it to blast through the bathroom again a minute later.

Sighing, I shake a cloud of bubbles from my hands and grab my phone.

"Hey, Mom." I close my eyes again and slink lower in the tub.

"Hey, Ollie. You sound tired. Are you getting sick?" She's so invasive.

"No, I'm in the bath."

"You shouldn't have answered if you were in the tub, dear."

"I let it go to voicemail and you called right back. Is it important?" I hate rushing my mom, but a relaxing bath is anything but relaxing with her concern in my ear.

"There's been some fraudulent activity on your credit card. I just wanted you to know your new one should be here in a week or so."

I sit up, water sluicing around me. "Fraudulent activity?" I shop online, so someone getting my information if I made the mistake of purchasing from an unsecure site isn't a far stretch.

"Yes. Someone must have gotten your card. I'm concerned about Bryson, Ollie. Has he had access to your purse?"

I bristle. "He's not like that, Mom. Why are you even suspecting him?"

He's not the type, right? He wouldn't just get close to me to use me, would he? Last night flashes through my head. He wouldn't steal *that* from me, would he?

"All the purchases were made in a two-hour time span," she informs.

"Sometimes I go a little crazy when shopping online." My pulse pounds in my head at the possibility of Bryson being that guy and my hands tremble to the point where I'm afraid I'm going to drop the phone.

"This wasn't you. These purchases were made in person a couple weekends ago. The card was used locally, Ollie. Now, I've contacted the police and they are working on getting video from the stores. We'll know then."

I sigh in relief and sag against the back of the tub.

"Those are my charges, Mom."

"Don't protect him, Ollie."

I can't help but laugh. One second, she's talking him up and trying to shove me onto him, and the next she's accusing him of credit card fraud.

"I'm not," I snap. "His sister Emerson came to town and we went shopping. We went to Trader Joe's and the outlet mall, so there will be numerous charges from there, and we ended up at that cute little sandwich shop on twenty-third."

"Really?" Her voice cracks and I can all but see the tears welling in her eyes. "You went shopping?"

"I did," I confirm. "Had a lot of fun. I've gone out several times recently. Lunch, the dog park, even tagged along to a few baseball practices with Bryson."

"You don't know how happy I am to hear that!" Of course I do, I can hear it in her voice. "So, are you and Bryson, you know...?"

I groan into the phone, resisting the urge to sink below the water line and let the bubbles swallow me up.

"Don't you need to call the police and cancel their investigation?"

"Oh, damn! Yes, I do. Love you, Ollie."

"Love you, too." I disconnect the call before she can ask any other intrusive questions.

A bathrobe is all I bother putting on. I bounce around the apartment practically on the tips of my toes, ecstatic about his promise and what the plans will be when he gets back.

I'm going to need you.

Not want—*need.*

That word is so powerful to me, and every time I think about the way it fell from his lips in his husky voice this morning, my body responds differently than it ever has. I'm flying through the clouds by the time the afternoon rolls around, the smile that was on my lips when he kissed me this morning never really dissipating. I feel weightless, and I'm in desperate need of grounding myself.

Call it a character flaw but reading too much into situations has always been an issue with me. Last night was amazing, as I hope every night from now on will be, but that doesn't keep me from wondering where it's all heading or when it will inevitably collapse. It doesn't prevent the insidious doubt from creeping in, the voice that constantly tells me to open my eyes and quit dreaming like a little girl when she thinks about her future and the fairy tale she wants her life to be. I dreamed of that fairy tale once, and in the end, it left me broken, a partial shell of who I once was.

I don't open my laptop out of spite or some negative emotion. Regret and guilt almost didn't even register when I woke up in his arms this morning. There was a twinge, but not the torrential onslaught I imagined it would be. Had we taken that first step the night I begged him to kiss me, the morning-after chain reaction of going all the way when I knew I wasn't ready would have been destructive to the bond we've been forming. I was ready last night.

I pull up a video and hover the mouse over the play triangle. The guilt I feel now is for Bryson, not Duncan. I can tell, little by little, I'm moving on. I know what happened last night was meant to happen exactly like it had. I can admit I have serious feelings for Bryson without hating myself for it, but today, I miss Duncan.

Even with all of that info, I still hit play.

"You look better."

"I still feel like shit."

"You're gorgeous. Even better looking than the day I fell in love with you."

"And what day was that, sweet cheeks?" I smile, watching his eyes lighten up. It's my favorite part of this video. He'd just started his first round of chemo, so the drugs hadn't destroyed him yet.

"First day of freshman year."

"I was covered in acne and had braces."

"Like I said, even better looking than the day I fell in love with you."

A heavy thumb forces me to jerk my chin up. My eyes land on Bryson's backpack on the floor and travel up his legs until landing on his gorgeous, but extremely exasperated face. His eyes dart from mine to the laptop as Duncan's voice tells me he loves me. I close the lid on the laptop, my eyes never leaving his face. No sense in trying to hide it now.

"Bryson, I—"

His hand flips up to silence me and I'm grateful for it. I honestly didn't even know what I was going to say. I watch him pace, my heart rate increasing with each heavy step.

He turns his back to me, his hands plowing through his hair. Denying me the look in his eyes is more painful than I ever thought it could be. The lack of insight to how he feels guts me, causing my stomach to flip with unease, and I have to wonder if it's intentional, a way to hurt me like I've clearly hurt him.

"Am I just a placeholder? A surrogate because you can't have the man you truly desire?" The pain is evident in his voice without even having to see the same reaction on his face. Defeat slumps his shoulders as he takes another step away.

I shake my head no, even though he can't see my face. "No," I sob, hanging my head in shame for making him feel this way.

"I let it go before, Liv. It cut me deep the day I came in here and you were watching those damn videos, but I figured you needed more time, so I gave it to you." He spins around, and the tears on his cheeks slay me. "It's always one step forward and ten steps back with you."

Jerky hands swipe at the tears rolling down his cheeks. His heavy breathing fills the small room as his hands clasp the back of his neck, tugging to ease the tension I've brought on. It's clear he's upset with me, and possibly even more furious that he's so emotional over it.

"I'm here, Liv. Me! I'm more than a memory." He pounds his hand against his chest, his lips working into a tight line to control his emotion. "We made love last night. When you gave me… fuck! I lost myself to you in this bedroom. How fucked up is it that I come home and realize I've lost you to him?" He jabs his finger at the laptop still sitting on my lap. "No, fuck that," he continues. "It's apparent I never had you."

The tremor in his last words and dullness suddenly hitting his eyes all show his defeat. Tears fall, but it's the slam of his bedroom door a few seconds later that breaks me. My lips quiver uncontrollably as resignation that I've lost him too descends on me. Unsure what to do, I gather my laptop and hide away in my room, hating that I need Duncan more now than ever.

Chapter 34

Bryson

"Fuck!" I bellow, loathing the way my frustration is bouncing off the walls.

I didn't think getting Olivia to care for me was going be easy, but I sure as shit never thought it would be this hard. I felt like we crossed over into new territory last night. I saw the affection in her eyes, felt it in the way she clung to me. It was with reverence, not desperation and despair. I had her last night. She was one hundred percent with me in that bed. I had every piece of her. There was no room for Duncan there, but that didn't last long.

The grin on my face was so wide, the stars in my eyes so bright, people even commented on how happy I looked, and I was—until I got home, expecting her to be as elated to see me, only to find him right back between us. I had my doubts; it's her pattern. We get closer, then she pulls away—I don't know why I let myself hope for anything different.

I squeeze my fists tight at my sides, trying to talk myself into keeping them from slamming into the thin walls.

Am I pissed? Fuck yeah, I am. Did she deserve to be yelled at when I've known the score all along? Part of me thinks so, but the section of my heart that sees only her knows better.

I resolve myself to apologizing, but pace my room for a few more minutes, trying to calm down so I don't explode again and giving her time to absorb my words and frustration.

I take a final deep breath before lifting my hand to knock on her door. For weeks, I've just walked right in. We've spent every second of our time together, but this evening, it doesn't feel right. Before my knuckles can land against the wood, I hear *his* voice, and any calm I'd managed before this second vanishes as if it never existed. My jaw clenches so hard, my teeth hurt. Lowering my hand, I take a step back, resisting the urge to kick the door in and demand she never watch the videos again. How can she start a life with me when she's living in the past?

The insidious doubt snakes up my spine and settles like a boulder in the pit of my stomach. Maybe I misread her. Damn, maybe she was faking it. Can passion and something akin to love look the same? Was she imagining it was Duncan she was with?

Her sobs break my mental battle and I reach for her door handle, hating that she's hurting, hating that I may have been the one to cause some of that pain, but once again, his voice seeps through, oozing like a virus around the frame. Her pain becomes less of a concern when my heart is practically shattered, circling the drain. The faith and hope I'd allowed myself to build drains out of me. I leave it at her closed door and escape the apartment. Staying here will only lead to more words and sacrifices falling on deaf ears.

I don't even bother with my truck, needing the cool fall air and expulsion of energy to help my attempt to regain composure. Every step I take is one more step I regret. Walking away from her isn't the answer but sticking around while he consumes every corner of her heart isn't the smartest thing either.

Knowing I can't go back there tonight without ending up in her room and begging her to love me, pleading for her to give me just a sliver of her heart, I pull out my phone and call Liam. It rings twice, then goes to voicemail. I call again. It's apparent he's screening his calls, and I don't have the patience for that shit right now.

He answers on the second ring. "Dude, don't you know how to fucking text?"

"Can I crash in your room tonight?" Sitting on the front steps of the math and science building, I watch as a few people walk along the sidewalk chattering with companions.

"She finally kicked your ass out? That's rough, man."

"She didn't…" My voice trails off on a frustrated breath. I'm not getting into this shit with him now or ever. "Can I just crash?"

"You know I don't give a shit, but I'm not sharing my bed or helping you blow up the fucking air mattress." I sigh in relief.

"Thanks, man. I'll be there in a few minutes."

My trek across campus to the dorms doesn't go as smoothly as one would hope considering my mood.

"Hey there, Daniels." The feminine purr comes from beside one of the many statues marking the campus.

I look over and see a girl I recognize, but don't know personally. She has to be a cleat chaser, or someone from one of my classes.

I nod in her direction, but turn my attention back to the sidewalk, refusing to engage any further.

"You looked stressed. I can relieve some of that for you." *Cleat chaser.*

She's absolutely gorgeous, long brown hair, piercing hazel eyes, fingernails long enough to do the type of back damage I crave, but the sight of her makes me sick. And that's when I realize, I'm in trouble. A couple months ago, I wouldn't have even bothered finding a bed. I would've dragged her into a dark corner and fucked her standing up. Now, I don't even carry a condom in my wallet. Why would I when the only girl I can imagine being inside of lives in the same apartment?

I scrub my hand over my face and shake my head. I've got it so fucking bad, I can't even be upset about it. Hundreds of women willing to sleep with me with little to no effort on my part—all of these options, including the one standing in front of me hiking her skirt up a little higher to reveal her lace garter belt and thigh-high stockings—and my dick doesn't so much as twitch in interest.

"No thanks," I mutter and walk away.

Thankfully, she doesn't chase me down and try to convince me otherwise. I've dealt with several girls these last couple weeks who have struggled with my rejection, and the things they offer as a means to convince me to fuck them are pitiful. Hell, not even that—I can't count the offers of "just let me suck your dick" I've gotten since I started school here.

Later than I expected, I make it to Liam's dorm room. He yells for me to come in when I knock. I've never been here before, but he warned me about his weirdo roommate. It's only when I step inside do I realize just how damn weird the guy is. His entire side of the room is full of screens—not even a bed, just computer equipment—which are currently filled with some space game. He's wearing Beats headphones and doesn't even bother acknowledging my presence as I step inside.

I jerk a questioning thumb over at him and Liam just shakes his head.

"What are you working on?" I ask, surprised to find him sitting at his tiny desk with his head bent over an actual textbook.

"Fucking World History," he bitches.

"I don't think I've ever actually seen you with a book before."

"Yeah, well, I shouldn't have this one out, but that sophomore chick I was banging found out about the freshman chick I fucked last week and she won't do my damn assignments anymore. She even warned all the other chicks in class about me, so I can't find anyone to do them. Fucked up, right?" He looks over at me, expecting commiseration, but he doesn't find any.

"Sorry, man." I slap him on the back, trying to seem as comforting as possible. I wonder how the guy is still in school and on the team if this is how he is.

"Air mattress is in the closet. I hope you don't mind the light." He nods his head to his oblivious roommate. "Jackass over there will be up all night playing video games and jerking off, and from the looks of this shit, I won't be getting much sleep either."

"No big deal. I appreciate it." I reach into the closet and grab the air mattress out, knowing I won't get any sleep tonight either.

I've spent weeks falling asleep with Olivia wrapped in my arms and waking up with her warm breath on my bare chest. There's no way I can rest easy knowing she's alone in the apartment, but I have the twisted hope that she is wondering where I am and missing me as much as I miss her.

***

My alarm blares in my ear what seems like only an hour after I finally passed out. Feeling like I got crushed by a bulldozer, I sit up in the dip of the air mattress and my ass hits the ground since it lost half of its air last night.

"Damn it," I grumble, looking at the time on my phone. I had to have reset the alarm when it went off the first time even though I have no recollection of it. With ten minutes to get to class, I don't have time to go home for a shower, or even to change my clothes.

I slip my shoes on and roll the air mattress up as fast as I can. Liam is passed out face down with his head on his history book, drool pooling and ruining the pages, and his creepy-ass roommate is passed out in his office chair. Stopping by the bookstore, I grab a notebook and a pen, because my books are still in my backpack at the end of the couch where I dropped them yesterday after finding Olivia watching those damn videos.

I groan as I sit down in my first class, hoping it goes by as fast as possible and praying I can concentrate on something other than Olivia Dawson.

Chapter 35

Olivia

A tear rolls down my cheek when my suspicions are confirmed. I close his bedroom door, an ache I can't describe spreading throughout my chest. I hoped he eventually came home and slept in his own bed, but I never heard him come in. I waited up until the early hours of morning, praying, but to no avail. He should be home from class by now.

Knowing he didn't sleep in this apartment makes me wonder where he did stay, and with whom. Simone comes to mind and the thought sours my stomach. He doesn't seem like the type, but he was more upset than I've ever seen him.

I walk into the kitchen and get a bottle of water from the fridge. Coffee would be too strong for my stomach this morning. I grab my laptop and pull it into my lap as I plop down on the sofa. It's midafternoon and I know he'll be home soon. I refuse to let him ignore me today. I let him walk out last night without a word, but that can't happen today. I need him as much as he seems to need me, a realization that hit not long after he was gone. We have to work through this. There's a way to compromise here, but we can't do that if he's gone—hell, it may not even be an option depending on what he did last night after he left in a rage.

I surf around on social media for a while, wondering why I even bother. I don't post, never comment or engage... I even have my status always set to offline, but I can't help it. I do care about what my former friends are doing and how their lives are going, even if they don't realize I'm creeping on their pages.

An email alert dings, so I open that window.

The only time Bryson has emailed me was when he confirmed the list of house rules I demanded he acknowledge when he first moved in, but sitting in my inbox is an email from him. The subject line is blank, which is ominous. My hand trembles as I move the mouse, hovering over the email. I'm terrified it's going to detail his plan to move out and break his lease.

I push the laptop away, staring at the seemingly innocuous name, knowing it's going to change my life forever. Rip the Band-Aid off, right?

I give in, preparing myself for the pain, only to find the email contains a smiley face and a Word document titled *Love Letter for You*. I grin at it. Even as upset as he was last night, he sends something like this. A crumb of hope that what we were building isn't destroyed settles inside me.

I click on the attachment with a wide smile on my face. It opens, then closes immediately. I click on it again, and the same thing happens. Is this some sort of joke? Finally, after the third click, the letter opens, only there are no words on the screen, just random parts of the alphabet... computer code is what it looks like.

The attachment closes and my computer screen flickers a few times. My heart begins to sprint. Trying to close out of my email program is fruitless. Nothing my mouse clicks on is working. I hold the power button with shaking fingers until the screen blinks off. Waiting an agonizing five minutes before rebooting, I'm calmer when it begins to start up like normal, but it's short-lived.

When the home screen pops up, almost every folder on my desktop is gone. My heart pounds in my chest as I frantically click different things, but nothing happens. It's as if my computer is on lockdown. I knew Bryson was upset last night, but this is beyond anything I imagined he'd be capable of.

Tears stream down my face and an ache I haven't felt since watching Duncan's live feed the day he passed crushes my chest. Nothing is working. I shut the computer down once more, but when it comes back on, even less is on my desktop.

"What's wrong?" the devil's voice asks, forcing me to snap my eyes up to him.

I shake my head, refusing to speak and turn my attention back to my ruined laptop. An eternity of clicking and futility in trying to open programs only makes the pain in my chest grow. With losing Duncan all over again and Bryson doing something so abhorrent, I feel like I'm having a heart attack.

I clutch my chest as sobs wrack my body. Bryson takes a step closer, holding his arms out, but I shuffle back, my eyes burning a hole into him.

"Don't fucking touch me!" I scream. "You did this!"

"Did what, Liv? I can't help you if you don't tell me what's wrong." His face twists in confusion, no longer the handsome calmness I've come to expect from him.

"You're so fucking bitter and vindictive," I sob. "What did you think, getting rid of the last thing I had of him would make me love you?"

He takes a stumbling step back, as if I slapped him in the face.

"I haven't... I didn't... Liv?" He reaches for me again and words I can never take back tumble for my lips, each one a fiery lash.

"I could never love you like I love him. He was my entire life. Those videos were all I had left of him. Are you so damned selfish you'd destroy me just to keep me from watching them?"

I hang my head in my hands and the weight of the useless laptop on my legs defeats me even further. With shaking hands and a battered heart, I shove it off my legs, taking no pride when it slams to the floor and skitters away in two pieces—just like my life, torn in two directions. Just when I was letting him in, just when I was opening myself up to him, his true selfish colors come out. Knowing everything I've done, all the times I took a step with him even though it ate me up inside, rips me to my core.

"He's gone," I cry. "I gave you something he should've always had," I shout, all my pain shooting out like a slap to his face. "He should be here, not you! I should be sharing a bed with him. You asked if you were a surrogate? You're less than that. You could never replace a fraction of what Duncan was capable of. You're nothing to me."

Break him. Just like he's broken you.

He stands silent only a few feet away, yet still too close for my liking.

"I opened that email with a hope that I hadn't ruined what we had." I point to the shattered computer near his feet. "What a fucking joke. You could've walked away. You didn't have to erase him."

"I could never walk away from you, Liv." He sounds as broken as I feel, and the messed-up part is I revel in his pain. It can't possibly be a fraction of what he's done to me.

"Well," I say without a tremble in my voice, rage taking over the despondency I'm feeling, "I'm not giving you a choice. You need to leave. Pack your shit and get out of my apartment. I never want to see you again."

"You don't mean that," he whispers, the pleading in his voice visible in his dark eyes.

"You have no idea just how serious I am, Bryson. Get out!" I don't even recognize my own voice as I screech at him.

"I'm not leaving you. I'm not giving up on us."

I hold both of my hands up to ward him off when he walks closer. My upturned hands close into fists and meet his chest in a violent burst of energy when he steps within reach. I pound his muscled flesh as he wraps his arms around me, holding me as close as he can even though I'm fighting for him to let me go.

"I trusted you," I whisper when my energy wanes sooner than I anticipated. "I hate you."

"Hate me today, beautiful. I can take it." His voice is calm and soothing, the opposite of what I want, but exactly what I need.

I stop fighting him when he scoops me up in his arms and carries me to my room. He settles us both on my bed, not even bothering to pull the blankets back. The broad expanse of his chest and the heat emanating from his body comforts me just as it has so many times before, but this time, I'm more broken than I've ever been.

Closing my eyes, I try to pretend Duncan is here. He's the one holding me, promising me everything will be all right. The strength in Bryson's arms, the masculine scent clinging to his clothes along with the deep timbre of his voice, are all reminders that Duncan is gone.

He left me in a crying heap while he faded away in a hotel room with only a doctor there to comfort him in his final moments. He didn't love me enough to have me there to hold his hand, to kiss his lips when his breathing grew shallow. He robbed me of our final goodbye, tore the life I imagined we could have together away from me, just as Bryson did today with one simple click of a mouse.

I'm not enough, never enough. The realization that I'll always be alone, always be hurt by the men I care for hits me as I fall into an exhausted sleep.

Chapter 36

Bryson

I whisper promises I'm not certain I can keep against the top of her head long after her breathing evened out. I have to remind myself she's angry and hurt, but her words cut me deep. From what I gather, she got an email that caused the videos of Duncan to disappear.

I could've argued with her, showed her my sent mail in my account to prove I didn't do something like that, but she was breaking right before my eyes and proving my innocence became secondary. Words were said—words I have no hope of ever getting out of my head. My chest aches at the vehemence she used. There was not a trace of the emotion I saw in her eyes two nights ago. It was replaced by hatred and repulsion. I don't know if there's a way to come back from that. I don't know if she'd even want to.

Knowing when she wakes she'll push me away again has me holding her even closer now. She whimpers against my chest, but I find a shard of hope when she clings to my shirt rather than pushing me away. In my head, I imagine she knows it's me holding her, when I know there's a very real possibility, she's in Duncan's arms in her dreams.

Regardless of what the outcome will be, I know I have to do everything in my power to fix this. Even though the last thing I want to do is leave her right now, I kiss her forehead, whisper words I've never spoken to a woman before into her soft hair and get out of the bed.

Gathering up her shattered computer in the living room, I pray Liam's roommate is as good at fixing computers as he is playing games.

***

"He's not here," Liam's manic roommates says when he finds me standing in the hallway.

I knew he wouldn't be here. He's at the baseball practice I chose to miss to go back to the apartment to try to fix things with Olivia.

"I know. I'm here to see you."

His eyebrow quirks up. "I charge two-hundred and fifty dollars for term papers, and they no longer come with the guarantee of beating the antiplagiarism system the professors are using. They updated their system and fucked up my enterprise."

"That's not... I'm not here for a term paper." I step further into the room, holding out the bag with the broken computer even though he sat down and swiveled his chair, putting his back to me.

"We're in the middle of mid-terms. If you wanted Adderall, you should've prepared by hitting me up at the beginning of the semester like the smart ones did."

I want to argue that if they were in fact smart, they wouldn't need fucking pills to study, but I need him to help me and pissing him off wouldn't benefit me right now.

"I'm not here for Adderall either. Listen, man. I need to get the files, videos, and shit off this computer." I hold the bag out to him, hating myself for actually wondering whether Olivia would recover if they really were gone forever.

It makes me an asshole, but I've fallen for a girl who will never love me back, and that stings like a bitch. I don't want him gone, or his videos destroyed. I just want to be a part of her life, a part of her, and I'm not certain that's possible since she uses him and the videos as a crutch and a tool to push me away around every corner.

"I can't put this shit back together. This old as fuck computer isn't even worth it," he mumbles as he pulls the pieces out of the grocery bag.

"I don't need you to fix the thing, I just need the videos, pictures, and shit off it."

"Dude, seriously, you can just get more porn. I mean, I'd be pissed if my collection was gone, but most of the fun is building it back up again." He grins in my direction, but his inability to hear what I'm needing is driving me mad.

"It's not porn. Fuck, it's not even my computer. My girl got an email, said it was from me. I didn't send an email, but then her files and shit vanished. I need you to get those files back for her."

"Just the videos?"

I shake my head. The videos are bad enough, but I'm sure there's more. "Pictures, videos, voice messages—anything. I need them back."

He shakes his head. "Not gonna be cheap."

"I don't give a fuck about the money. I just need that shit back." Hope sparks in my chest. I may not end up with the girl, and I may be handing her back the very thing that will keep me separate from her, but her already broken heart shattering before my eyes is not something I want seared into my brain forever.

"Give me an hour." He turns away from me. "You can leave. I don't like being supervised."

"The fuck am I gonna do for an hour?" I was just going to pass out on Liam's bed since I slept like shit last night.

"I suggest you go get your girl a new computer and a jump drive to put all this shit on once I get it back. Possibly stop by an anger management meeting on the way. Control that devil you got inside you and shit like this wouldn't get broken."

I don't even argue with him about his misconceptions. All I heard was it's only going to take an hour for him to give me Olivia back.

Taking part of his advice, I leave campus to get a computer for Olivia. The bookstore sells computers, but even the shitty ones they carry are overpriced. Once inside the electronics store, I find the smartest looking guy in the computer section and have him help me find the best computer money can buy.

"Do you need it for gaming?"

I shake my head. "No, just like getting online, watching videos, maybe Netflix and shit," I tell him as my fingers graze the keys of a ridiculously expensive laptop.

"You don't need that one then, dude. It has too much stuff you won't use." He directs my attention to a different computer.

"I need something with an awesome firewall. Something that prevents email hackers from getting in and ruining my life, destroying everything I've spent weeks building up."

He narrows his eyes at me, trying to get a read on what I'm saying. I clamp my mouth shut, feeling like a fucking idiot.

"They got your porn stash, huh? That fucking sucks, man. This one," he says, pointing to a sleek black and gray laptop, "will work best for what you need it for."

"It's not for porn," I correct, exasperated. "Just watching videos."

He winks at me as if he doesn't believe me, and I roll my eyes, giving up on the fight. "This one comes with a great firewall already in place. If you don't feel like it's enough, we sell programs that will lock your shit down like Fort Knox."

"I'll take both, please." On the way to the register, I grab a handful of jump drives, because only having one isn't going to be enough.

An hour and a half after leaving the psycho roommate, I'm back in the dorm room.

"Please tell me you were able to recover them," I say as I walk in, not bothering to knock.

His face is somber when he turns around. "I was certain you were hoping to save your porn, man. I only opened one video, dude, I swear. I know I shouldn't have, but fuck."

I cross the room, wanting to strangle him, just knowing he watched the video of Olivia masturbating with Duncan—the same video I stroked myself to when I heard it from the other side of her door.

"You motherfucker."

He holds his hands up in surrender. "I remember watching that shit live when it happened."

I stop in my tracks. The suicide video, not the one I was thinking of.

He swallows hard, his neck bobbing in effort. "That shit was all over campus, man. I don't let shit like that get to me, but Liam and I were roommates last year as well, and that guy doing that shit fucked him up. He hasn't been the same since. I take it your girl is the one the guy is talking to?"

I nod my head. "Yeah, she is. Were you able to get them all?"

"I think. I mean, I don't know how many there are, but I got everything that was on there."

I try to hand him a jump drive, but he holds his hand up and rejects it, offering over five instead. "I made copies, just in case."

"I appreciate that. How much do I owe you?"

He shakes his head. "Not a dime, man. I'm just glad I could save that stuff for her. This is the email address the virus came from."

He hands me a slip of paper. "I mean, that's my email except for the extra period."

"That's how they get people to open it up. That virus hasn't been around since the year two-thousand, but technology has changed so much since then, it's no longer as detrimental as it used to be."

"You sure I don't owe you anything?"

He shakes his head before turning back to his computer and pretending like I was never here, and for that, I'm grateful.

I slide all five jump drives into my pocket as I leave the dorm and get into my truck. I spend the drive back to the apartment wondering how my arrival is going to be taken. Even doing this for her, she may still ask me to leave and I'd have to at some point. I can't forcibly hold her against my chest forever. Eventually, she'll call the damn cops on me.

Walking back into the apartment, I realize she's still sleeping. I quietly place the new laptop and jump drives on her dresser and crawl back into bed with her. Smiling softly when she nuzzles against my chest, I hold her tight, knowing this may be the last time she'll ever be in my arms.

Chapter 37

Olivia

The heat of his body engulfs me and I stiffen in his tender embrace, unsure why he's even here. The horrible things I said to him... the lies I spewed from my mouth when I was upset and angry.

"Please don't," he begs, his warm breath gusting over my unruly hair.

"Why would you do something so terrible?" I ask, thankful my back is to him so he can't see my lip quiver.

Silent tears fall from my eyes and dampen the pillowcase. My entire body aches, not unlike the way it did the day Duncan passed away.

He releases one arm from around me and points toward a bag on top of my dresser. "I had Liam's roommate recover the files. He made five jump drives with all the things from your computer on them. The email address the virus came from wasn't mine. It had an extra period. I'd never do something like that to you, Liv. I hated finding you watching those videos, especially after sharing such an intimate moment with you, but I'd never hurt you in that way. I know you need him. I just want you to need me too."

His words come out in a rush, as though if he doesn't get them all out now, he wouldn't have another chance.

Relief washes over me as my eyes stay glued to the bag, the need to verify that I haven't lost Duncan completely burning in my chest.

"I got you a new computer, too. The guy at the store assures me the firewall protection on it will stop this type of thing from happening again, but if it does, your files are all backed up."

I feel safe in his arms, nurtured and loved, but it's difficult to let go of the rage and anger I felt earlier. In the deep recesses of my mind, I didn't believe he could do something so vile, but the proof was right there in front of me. The email wiped all of my recorded memories, leaving my computer and heart useless. The files may have been recovered, and for that I'm eternally grateful, but it doesn't negate the fact that I turned on him so easily.

Will my whole life be this way? Will I turn against everyone who cares for me, all the while holding onto a man who is gone? The very same man who urged me to move on even though I could see the heartbreak in his eyes along with his insistence.

"I didn't mean what I said," I confess, praying he believes me, even though I only seem to speak in half-truths these days.

"I know, beautiful. You were hurting." His words are soft and placating, but I can't tell if he actually believes me or is only telling me what I want to hear right now.

I turn in his arms and reach up to cup his face. "I should never have said those things, Bryson. I shouldn't have allowed myself to believe you'd do something like that."

His eyes soften just before he closes them and nuzzles his face into my touch. This man is amazing, and I seem to push him away at every turn. I swallow against the lump building in my throat when the small band of diamonds on my finger catches the light. Weeks ago, it would've felt like a betrayal, seeing Duncan's ring against the healthy skin of Bryson's face. Today, however, I'm comforted knowing he's here, holding me, forgiving me, standing by my side.

"You deserve better than me," I whisper. "You deserve someone who can love you with their whole heart."

His eyes open, the dark orbs growing wet from unshed tears. They wreck me, just as they did yesterday when he came home early and caught me on the computer.

"Possibly," he agrees, and my heart clenches, afraid he's going to pull away. I know it would be for the best, but still pray he's willing to settle for less than one hundred percent of me. "But, Liv, there's no other woman in the world besides you. I'll take what I can get."

"You shouldn't settle. I can't give you all of me when I'll never be whole again."

He wipes a tear from my cheek and leans in to place his lips on my forehead. "You will. One day, you'll be unbroken, and I'll be here every step of the way. If you'll have me, I'm not going anywhere."

For the first time since I woke up, I pull him closer to my chest. His relieved breath warms the skin of my neck and shoulder.

"I can't let him go completely," I confess.

"I'd never ask you to." He pulls his head back, gripping both sides of my jaw in his big hands. "But moving on isn't the same as letting go."

Tender lips brush against mine and his willingness to stick by my side even when I'm always trying to push him away seals up one of the tiny fissures in my injured heart, making it just a fraction more durable.

He shifts his weight so he's lying on his back and I'm splayed at his side and on his chest. I close my eyes as his hand runs up and down my spine.

"Tell me about him." His words are sensitive and pleading. His request doesn't feel like a demand for knowledge, but more an opportunity to understand what things were like between the two of us.

I falter for a brief second, unsure if opening this door to him, allowing Bryson into this part of my past is the best thing. I always considered my time with Duncan sacred; precious moments only the two of us shared.

I take a moment to imagine the shoe being on the other foot, how I would feel if Bryson had lost someone he loved so much. I don't know that I could be as considerate of his feelings as he has been with mine. I can easily admit he's a better person—stronger than anyone I've ever known.

"We met my freshman year of high school, before the first bell rang for class to begin." I close my eyes as I begin to reflect, giving a voice to the memories that have only been in my head.

He holds me closer, urging me on, giving me the strength to continue.

"He was a year older, sitting near the front steps with a group of his friends. They were older, of course. Duncan was always associating with the older kids, almost as if he was too good for kids his own age. That's the impression I got from him that first day anyway. It couldn't have been further from the truth. I soon realized he wasn't hanging out with the other kids; they were hanging around him. His personality, his charm, his ability to care for others was like a magnet no one could resist."

I laugh against Bryson's chest thinking about Duncan sitting there with messy hair, braces on his teeth, and acne.

"Even though he was catcalling, acting obnoxious, yelling out, 'Hey, sweet cheeks, don't act like you aren't impressed,' I was drawn to him. His friends laughed at his playfulness, but when I stiffened at the attention and just walked away, he stopped, which I wasn't expecting. I anticipated him calling me worse names, sure that the goading he was getting from his friends would only egg him on, but it didn't. When I looked back one last time before going into the school, I saw disappointment in his eyes. I thought I'd been lacking until he apologized later at my locker and I realized he was disappointed in himself."

I pause, waiting for his judgment, waiting for him to call Duncan an asshole and try to convince me it was an incredibly shitty way to start a relationship, but it never comes, so I continue.

"We were pretty much inseparable after that. We started out as friends—my dad was pretty strict and according to him, boys shouldn't have even been on my radar—but neither of us dated anyone else. It's like we knew we were waiting for each other, even though the agreement was unspoken. I was terrified of making a move, even after I knew I was head over heels by the beginning of my sophomore year. He was the one who kissed me after a football game. It was quick," I chuckle, remembering the shock on his face when he pulled away and I didn't slap him. "We didn't discuss it, but from then on, he found many more opportunities to kiss me.

"I started hearing chatter in the halls. He'd told anyone who would listen that I was his girl. We sort of just went from friends to being in a relationship overnight. No one was shocked, though. They could see what we were trying to deny for the longest time.

"He first got sick the second semester of his junior year, not long after we declared ourselves together. The diagnosis was almost immediate. Acute myeloid leukemia." My voice cracks at mentioning the disease that ripped him from us, but I choke down my pain and continue. "His parents, like my own, are very wealthy—only the best medical attention for their son. We were hopeful. He started treatments right away. By the end of his senior year, the doctors declared he was in remission—against all odds, they somehow beat the disease plaguing his body."

I close my eyes and grip Bryson's shirt in my hand, needing a break from the pain, yet wanting so bad to speak of him out loud. With renewed strength, I begin again.

"One year," I whisper. "One year, we had him back, healthy, almost like his old self. He was still too weak to play ball, but they put him on the team anyway. He missed fall semester but was at every practice. I was in my senior year in high school when he proposed."

I hear him swallow, his only response to the story so far.

"He insisted it wasn't too soon. 'When you know, you know,' was all he'd ever say. My dad wasn't as excited. He felt we were too young. The summer between my senior year and first semester of college, he began to grow weaker. Later on, he admitted he'd been feeling bad for a while, but refused to accept he was sick again. I'm so mad at him for that."

I shake my head against Bryson's chest. "I *was* so mad."

"You can still be angry, Liv. Every emotion you felt then, every one you feel now, is completely okay."

I swallow roughly, knowing that being unable to let go of some of the emotions I've clung to for so long has caused problems between Bryson and me. I don't tell him that, though, I simply placate him with a nod.

"When the leukemia came back, it was so much worse than it had been before. They tried everything—every drug, new treatments, and experimental medicine. Nothing worked. They moved him across the country for the last round of treatments. When the doctors declared him terminal, he finally got to come home. I couldn't function. Every thought, every action on my part, was for him. I stopped going to class. Nothing mattered but him and his recovery. I wouldn't listen to anyone when they tried to explain that it was hopeless. I never felt like it was hopeless," I choke out, barely able to say the last words as emotion overcomes me. I sob into Bryson's chest, the pain in my heart all too real again as he holds me tighter.

Chapter 38

Bryson

"Shhh," I whisper in her hair as her tears soak my shirt. "I'm here, beautiful."

After several long minutes, her grip on my shirt loosens and I'm certain she's fallen back asleep until she shifts slightly against me.

"Thank you," she says almost incoherently, her voice getting lost against my chest. "Thank you for letting me talk about him. For not judging or interrupting with your opinions. Everyone I've tried to talk to since it happened shuts me down. They got frustrated with me. You just listening means more than you can know."

I tilt her chin up, my eyes skating between hers. Tear-stained and swollen, she's still the most gorgeous woman I've ever held in my arms. "I'll always listen to you. You can tell me anything, anytime you need to. Don't ever feel like you can't tell me the truth."

I close my eyes for a moment, hating that what I say next may be a step toward our future or the last step in what we have building. My heart could shatter with my next breath, but I have to know. She loves so fiercely, so damn deep—I long for that from her.

"I need to know, Olivia. Tell me there's a chance for us. That eventually you'll find room for me too. I'm losing myself to you." *Lost, gone, you own me.*

My heart hangs in the balance as a tear rolls down her cheek. She cups my face and shakes her head slightly.

"It's too late, Bryson."

Shattered, destroyed, wrecked.

"If you asked that question weeks ago, I could have said eventually."

I shift my weight to get off the bed, but she clings to me harder.

"You misunderstand." Reaching down, she grips my hand and places it over her frantically beating heart. "You're already here. There's no eventually. I may get angry or sad and try to pull away, but never doubt, even on my most self-loathing days, I care for you."

My heart thunders in my chest as she peers up at me. "I'm going to kiss you now."

"Please," she pants against my lips.

With unhurried intention, my mouth moves over hers, our tongues working in sync. Hands roam and legs shift. It's futile to fight the erection throbbing in my jeans, so I don't even attempt to, deciding to ignore it instead. Olivia has different ideas, though.

I quell her fingers as they try to open the button on my jeans.

"That's not what I expect," I tell her. The slight shake of her head as her lips find mine again is the only acknowledgment I get from her.

Making out with a girl, knowing I could have her if I wanted her, yet not taking that extra step is a different situation for me. She was so angry earlier, that even as much as I want to make love to her right now, it doesn't feel right. I don't want her to think it's the only thing I'm after.

I slow our kissing until it's nothing more than soft pecks and gentle stroking hands.

"Go with me to the party tomorrow night."

She shakes her head, immediately refusing the invite.

"Please?"

"Parties aren't really my thing. Never have been."

It doesn't surprise me. Her whole adult life has been dedicated to Duncan, his illness, and then the grief over losing him. She's not the type of person to let go and give in to common young adult dalliances. With Duncan being so sick, I imagine they avoided all types of social gatherings, if anything to keep him from coming into contact with germs and illnesses that could've proven to be fatal.

I need to go, but I won't do it without her. Wherever she's at is where I have to be.

"It's Halloween. You can wear a mask and no one will even know who you are." I nuzzle her neck, nipping the delicate flesh below her ear, and smile when a soft whimper escapes.

Her head shakes again.

Time for the big guns.

"It's my birthday," I confess in her ear.

She gasps and pulls her head back to look in my eyes. "Really? I'm such an asshole for not knowing that."

I smile at her. "So, don't be an asshole. Be my birthday date to the party."

"I didn't get you a gift."

I laugh at the absurdity of her words. "You've already given me the greatest gift, Olivia. One I'll treasure for the rest of my life."

Her face falls, tears suddenly forming in her eyes. "What I said earlier. Please don't believe those horrible words."

I gave you something he should've always had.

Even now, after her confessing she didn't mean it, after assuring me I'm in her heart, they still sting, burning deep in my gut and contaminating the beautiful moments we've shared. I know they will for a long time to come. That's the crazy thing about words spoken in anger— they have the ability to plant doubt, ruin the sweetest of moments, and make you question every damn thing that has ever been said, every soft touch and tender emotion.

"You were hurting. You thought I purposely hurt you. I know you wish you could take them back. Hell, I wish you could too, but it doesn't matter now."

"It matters," she argues.

"Will you be in my arms when we wake in the morning?" Her face softens and a small smile forms on her lips.

"Of course."

"Will you let me hold you? Be okay when my mouth seeks yours out in the middle of the night because my skin against yours just isn't enough?"

"Yes," she pants, breathless.

I shift my weight, maneuvering between her legs, rotating my hips until her eyes flutter closed and lips part. "Will you come to me if you're upset? Let me explain if you feel like I've done something wrong?" This is such a big one for me. How easily she can question my intentions burns the most.

Slowly opening her eyes, she peers up at me with reverence and adoration.

"Always," she whispers.

"Then don't worry about the words you said, beautiful." I kiss her again. "Go to the party with me?"

When she opens her eyes this time, the pain is gone, the doubt is nowhere to be found, and peace shines in the depths of her gorgeous blue eyes.

"I'd love to be your birthday date to the party."

I smile from ear to ear and kiss her stupid.

***

Olivia's lips find mine in the fragile glow of the early morning light. She wakes me with beseeching touches and greedy hands.

"Mmmm," I hum as her lips trail over my chin and her hands explore my stomach.

My hands reach for her, and I realize she stripped out of the clothes she was wearing when we fell asleep several hours ago when I only find exquisitely bare flesh.

I raise my hips a few inches off the bed when her intentions to pull my boxers off are made known. Last night, this didn't seem like a good idea, but early this morning, with her initiating, I couldn't think of a better way to start the day. I close my eyes and let her hands roam all over my body, groaning when she intentionally avoids my cock.

"Tease," I mumble, but then gasp when hot, wet lips wrap around me. With wide eyes, I glance down at her. Even with me in her mouth, I register a devious little smirk.

I want to believe she's never done this before either. In my head, I've glorified her pureness, aiming to take every one of her firsts, but it becomes abundantly clear she either has experience or she's an oral savant. Clutching her hair as a means to ground myself in the moment, I close my eyes again and take everything she's offering.

Short nails dig into my thigh as her tongue traces every pulsing vein in my erection. The scorching heat of her mouth combined with the cool air of the room bombards my senses. Her whimpering moans when she takes me into her throat an inch too far force a tingle in my blood that incites my need for release.

"It's too good, Liv. You're going to make me come." I attempt to shift my hips back while cupping her cheek to make her slow down, wanting it to last, never wanting to leave her mouth.

Her tongue sweeps over the tip of my cock and slides down until it's fluttering against my seizing sac.

"That's the whole point," she coos before taking me in her mouth again.

"Fuck," I moan just as the first vibration of my orgasm hums through my body.

She eagerly swallows and searches for more by sucking, stroking, and licking me, until the surfeit of sensation forces me to pull her off. Licking an escaped drop of cum from her lips, she smiles at me, as satisfied with herself as I am.

She collapses beside me, and I flip on top of her the very next second.

"Happy birthday," she says as I push away a lock of hair hiding her face.

"Birthday blowjobs are the best." I cringe at my words when her face falls, realizing she thought she was the first one. Fuck, right now I wish this was the first time someone sucked me off on my birthday and regret the fact that it was something I sought out each year.

She turns her head, breaking eye contact with me.

"Jealous?" I ask playfully, hoping to turn this morning back around.

I turn her head back to me, kissing her lips, grateful she hasn't pushed me away.

"So, I admit, it's not my first, but I think starting a new tradition is in order." Tilting my head down, I take one of her nipples into my mouth, feeling it furl against my tongue.

"Yeah? What kind of tradition?" she asks, breathless, pushing more toward me when I feign pulling away.

"This one," I say, moving down her body and lashing my tongue against her clit.

"I love traditions," she says on a moan, jealousy and my stupidity forgotten.

Chapter 39

Olivia

"I've already told you why," Bryson says with a stupid smirk on his face as he puts the truck in park.

"*It's my birthday and I get to do whatever I want all day long* isn't a good enough excuse to make *me* do whatever you want for the entire day," I chide. "You better be glad I love you."

Damn it. I twist my head to look out the window, hoping he takes it in the playful way I meant it.

"You coming?" he asks, graciously ignoring my slip of the tongue.

Looking over to find him holding out his hand, I slide across the seat and clasp it, allowing him to pull me out of the truck straight against his chest.

"You haven't changed your mind about the party, have you?" His eyes implore mine, searching for contrition. "I won't force you to go."

I shake my head back and forth. "I won't ask you to stay home."

"I would," he confesses. "I don't want you to be uncomfortable."

"I will be uncomfortable, just like the first baseball practice with you, but I think it's something I need to do. And going will make you happy." I almost get lost in his dark eyes. "I want to make you happy."

He closes his eyes and presses a light kiss on my lips. "You do make me happy."

Guilt swarms in with the sudden need to apologize again for the way I treated him, but he doesn't allow for it as he takes a step back and tugs me to the entrance of the Halloween costume shop.

***

"What are you doing here?" The annoyance in Bryson's voice forces me to my feet and I walk closer to the open apartment door.

A woman in an obscene she-devil costume stands on the threshold and I tilt my head at the familiarity, begging my heart to stay calm.

"You weren't invited," he continues.

"Happy birthday to you too, brother."

Emerson. Jesus, I feel like a psycho. Weeks ago, I would've slithered away and hid in my room from the pain, but today, I was ready to claw her damn eyes out when I thought it was Simone.

I smile at Emerson as she walks past Bryson into the apartment. She pulls off her mask and sexy little devil horns, giving me a wink as Bryson closes the door a little too hard.

"Happy birthday," I whisper to her, then roll my lips between my teeth when I notice the almost sneer on Bryson's face.

"Thank you." She plops down on the couch, but jumps up quickly, pulling her barbed tail out from under her. "Since it's my birthday, I need you to do me a favor."

I raise an eyebrow at her. We went shopping and to lunch once, and while I had a great time, we're not on any level where I'd do favors for her.

"You need to change. The party we're going to… well, let's just say it's not that type of party."

I look down at my costume, smiling when Bryson walks up and wraps his arm around me.

"Don't let her change your mind, Liv. We're adorable."

"This is a college party," she argues, waving her hand up and down, indicating our costumes. "I totally get you being a cheeseburger— it's okay for the guys to dress like idiots—but really, Olivia? French fries? Not even sexy French fries."

"It's all they had left," I explain.

"At least take the tights off. Show a little leg and add more makeup," she prods.

"It's cold as hell outside," Bryson says, coming to my defense. "And she has a man. There's no need for her to look like a slut. I should be convincing you to put more clothes on, Emmy. Half of your ass is hanging out."

"Perfect," she says, standing from the couch. "Just the look I was going for. Everyone will notice me."

"You'll probably get more attention than you can handle," Bryson agrees. "Tonight was supposed to be about me and Liv, but now I have to worry about keeping guys off you."

"You'll do no such thing," she says, patting him on the front of his cheeseburger costume. "I can handle myself."

Bryson helps me put on my jacket as best he can, and murmurs, "I can't wait to eat your fries later."

I huff a laugh and follow Emerson out of the apartment.

"Whoa," Emerson sighs as we pull up to the party. "There have to be hundreds of people here."

Anxiety thrums through my body and my hands start to tremble.

"I'll be with you every second," Bryson assures me as he takes my hand and helps me out of the truck. "I'm not drinking and I'll kick the ass of anyone who even glances your way."

"I doubt anyone is going to be looking at me," I mutter, looking from side to side. Every woman here is dressed similarly to Emerson. It seems the less costume you have on, the better it's received by the men in attendance. Who knew Tinker Bell could be so slutty? Though, I can admit Peter Pan looks great without a shirt on. Bryson growls, pulling me closer to his side.

"And to think I was worried about the eyes wandering over you," he whispers in my ear. His warm breath on my chilled skin heats more than my neck. "Should I take my shirt off?"

I shake my head and grin. "I like your cheeseburger."

"I knew I should've gotten the fucking Tarzan costume. I'd freeze my nuts off all night if it meant your eyes stayed on me."

I turn in his embrace, both hands on his chest, fingers toying with the sesame seeds on his costume. "Jealous?"

"Murderously so," he confesses, kissing my lips.

Public displays of affection generally aren't my thing. Most everything Duncan and I did was accomplished in private, but I like that Bryson is so open about his claim over me. The world melts away as his lips ravage mine in full view of anyone who may look this way.

"Can I be the pickle on the side of this insanely hot meal you guys have going on?"

"Fuck off, Ashford," Bryson says against my lips.

"But seriously," Liam continues, "maybe I can be the vanilla shake."

I turn my head and smile in his direction.

"I'd give anything," he whispers, turning his attention to the devil in red beside us, "*anything* for this Sataness to wrap her lips around my straw and suck."

Bryson tenses beside me, but Emerson beats him to the punch—literally. The slap registers in my ears as I see Liam grab his cheek before Emerson wanders off.

"Jesus, that woman is hot," Liam says, his eyes following her until the crowd swallows her up.

"Calm down," I say to Bryson, who's seething beside me.

"Olivia, you're the most captivating order of fries I've ever laid eyes on," Liam says.

"You look fucking ridiculous," Bryson huffs.

There is so much truth to that statement. He's wearing a black tank top, black pants—which are nothing unusual. It's the strapped-on, bright red penis jutting from his crotch that is oddly hilarious and perfectly in character with Liam's personality.

"What exactly are you supposed to be?" I ask.

He holds up several colorful rings. "Ring toss. Wanna play?"

I shake my head but have to grab hold of Bryson's arm to keep him from punching his friend in the face.

"I'll pass, but thanks for the offer."

He takes a step closer, wrapping his arms around me for a hug, and Bryson's growl doesn't go unnoticed.

"I'm so glad you're here, Ollie," he whispers in my ear. "Is he treating you right? Making you happy?"

I nod against him, gripping the back of his shirt as emotion swells in my throat. Liam was one of Duncan's close friends—another person who was there for me that I shoved away when my grief got too bad.

"Your dick is poking me," I joke, taking a step back, trying to ward off the melancholy threatening to ruin the evening.

"I'll kill you," Bryson threatens as Liam reaches down and strokes his phallic Halloween costume.

"I'll share it with you, too," he quips.

Bryson wraps both of his arms around me, protecting me from the non-threat, claiming me as his own. I lean into his embrace, watching the slight nod of approval from Liam. It means more than he could ever imagine.

"More for your sister then," Liam says before bolting away from the ass beating Bryson so desperately wants to give him.

"Such a fucking idiot," he mumbles against my neck.

"He's really a great guy," I argue. "He and Duncan got really close. Liam championed quite a few of the fundraisers that were held on campus the year Duncan was in attendance."

"Really?" he asks, his voice marked with disbelief.

"Yep. I know it's hard to believe, since he doesn't seem to have a serious bone in his body. Duncan told them they weren't necessary since his family didn't need the money, but Liam insisted building awareness was just as important. He donated the money to St. Jude's."

"That almost makes me feel guilty for the ass kicking he'll get if he tries to mess with my sister."

I laugh and kiss his jaw. "You might as well track him down now, then. If he has his sights set on Emerson, you can bet it's going to happen."

"Don't ruin my night," he pleads, attempting to smack my ass, but being hindered by the thickness of my fries. "Let's go inside."

We make our way through the throngs of people, getting genuine compliments on our costumes from some as we pass. There are a few girls standing and talking in a small group on the porch, and one looks over at me with such longing on her face, it makes me want to grip Bryson closer—until I realize she's freezing and her envious eyes are on my warm costume, not my man.

I chuckle to myself as we cross into the house. Loud music washes over me as I scan the gyrating bodies on a makeshift dance floor taking up the entire living room.

"Dance with me," Bryson whispers in my ear, pulling me toward the crowd.

I follow his lead, though we look like complete idiots. I can barely get my arms around his stacked lettuce, tomatoes, and double meat patties, and he seems to be having the same difficulty with my fried potato sticks.

"We look ridiculous," I mutter in his ear.

"I wish we were home alone, naked, dancing like this. I can't really show you my skills with all this shit between us." He licks my neck and nips at my earlobe.

"I'm well aware of your skills," I pant as his mouth finds mine.

***

An hour later, I'm a sweaty mess. We've danced to every song that's been played, only slowing for the occasional interruption from team members stopping by to tell Bryson happy birthday.

"I'm going to find the restroom," I tell him as he speaks to JJ.

Saddened that Ainsley isn't here, I make my way down the hall to the restroom, hopeful it's empty. I turn my gaze away from the couple making out in the hallway until a flash of red catches my eye. I'll be damned if Emerson doesn't have Liam pinned against the wall as they kiss and grope one another. I may have said Liam gets what he wants, but it seems Bryson's twin has turned the tables.

I smile, realizing who the aggressor in this situation is. Liam may have finally met his match.

Chapter 40

Bryson

"This is my most favorite part of the day," Olivia whispers, trying to get closer to me. "How long have you been awake?"

Grazing a finger over my stomach, she glances up at me with a devilish look in her eyes.

"Not long." My voice cracks when her hand wanders lower. Pushing her hair off her shoulder, I run my fingers over the soft skin of her back.

My need to be inside her is almost overwhelming, but I've vowed to let her lead the way, making her responsible for how far we go. Waking up each morning with her in my arms is amazing and absolute torture all rolled into one.

"Spend the day with me?" I ask, reaching for her hand and bringing her fingertips to my lips.

"Of course," she agrees, then kisses my chest.

I look down at her, my chest filled with more warmth than I know what to do with. This girl slays me. "I want to leave the apartment. Maybe head to the dog park, have lunch at the diner—you up for that?"

"Sure," she answers, and I don't hear the annoyance in her voice that usually accompanies my requests to leave the apartment.

"We need to get out of bed," I tell her. "If I lay here much longer, I'll never want to leave."

She nips the skin above my heart. "I like the idea of staying in bed all day. We can have a movie marathon, order pizza or something."

Groaning, I shift my weight from under her and sit on the edge of the bed. "Not the kind of marathon I'd want if I stayed in this bed all day."

"Hmmm," she purrs, forcing me to look back at her.

Man, is she beautiful—laid out on her back, perky breasts exposed, dusky-rose nipples puckered and begging for attention. I pull the sheet from her body and stare down at her. White panties against her milky skin make for one hell of a sight.

Leaning forward, I take one nipple in my mouth, tugging at it with my teeth until she whimpers a soft moan.

"You think you can tempt me with this gorgeous body of yours?"

She nods arrogantly, and she's right. My cock is throbbing, begging to keep going. But staying inside all the time isn't healthy for her. She may very well be using her nakedness for just that reason, and I'm not playing into her tricks... but God, how I want to be inside her.

"Get dressed," I say with a soft peck to her lips before walking out of the room, a victorious grin on my face.

***

"You seem happy today," I say, reaching across the table and grabbing her hand.

Her eyes dart from my contact to around the busy diner.

Satisfied no one is paying attention to us, she looks back at me. "I have hope for the first time in a long time."

"Hope for what, beautiful?"

She shakes her head and looks back down at our hands. "That things are getting better. That I can miss him without swimming in grief. That I can move on without feeling guilty one hundred percent of the time."

"I hate that you feel it at all." I swallow the thickness building in my throat. "You feel guilt over us... over me—what we've done?"

"Sometimes," she answers without a second of hesitation.

I look out the window away from her, trying to focus on the people coming and going rather than the pain in my chest.

She squeezes my hand, but I don't have the ability to meet her eyes. I told her I didn't want her to give him up completely, and I meant it. But the fact that she could regret us, what we've shared... I swallow hard and take a few calming breaths before turning my eyes back to hers. "You feel guilt or regret?"

"Aren't they the same thing?"

I shake my head. "No, they're not. Guilt is when you feel like you've done something intentionally to hurt someone you care for. Regret is unintentional, but your actions hurt someone and you wish you could change what you've done."

She stares out the same window I just pulled my eyes from. I mentioned her happy mood mere minutes ago and now it's gone. I watch a lone tear roll down her cheek, and my heart constricts.

"I can't hurt him if he's gone," she says, looking back at me.

I raise an eyebrow, urging her to understand what I'm trying to imply.

"And I don't regret a second I've spent in your arms."

I give her a weak smile.

She sighs. "So, no guilt and no regret. I'm just sad then, I guess. My mother thinks I should be on antidepressants."

My face must change slightly at her admission because she narrows her eyes.

"Do you think that, too?" she asks, her tone defensive and her face guarded.

I shake my head. "I didn't say anything, Liv. What do you think?"

After taking a sip of water, her fingers trace the condensation on the outside of the glass. "Looking back, I think a few months ago my mother may have had a point. Now? I have more good days than bad."

I get up from the booth and join her on her side, pulling her against my chest and resting my chin on top of her head. "I'm glad you're having good days."

"You're like my light," she whispers, and my heart blooms.

"I'm not," I counter. "You can do this all on your own."

"I don't want to," she says, looking up at me.

"You don't have to," I say before kissing her on the lips.

She doesn't push me away or chastise me for the open display of affection. She just leans in closer and gives as good as she gets.

"You're my light too, beautiful."

***

"I'm glad we ate lunch first," I say, pulling Olivia back against my chest.

We're back at the dog park, watching the different breeds run around and play.

"Me, too," she agrees. "It would've been way too cold and damp to sit on the ground first thing this morning."

"What about that one?" I ask, pointing to the tiny beagle puppy running after a bigger dog.

"He's adorable, but I still don't want a dog. I struggle to take care of myself most days."

"You wouldn't have to raise our fur baby on your own. I'd be there to help you."

She stiffens against me and I repress a sigh, wondering what part of our conversation is troubling her now. At the rate this day is going, I regret leaving the bed this morning. I know we have to work through all this stuff, but I didn't intend to ruin our day.

Turning her in my arms, I repeat the same thing I've told her a dozen times before. "I'm here, Olivia. I'm not going anywhere."

I watch her mouth open, already knowing what she's going to say, and place a finger over her lips.

"Don't give me that tomorrow is never promised shit either." She grins against my finger. "I don't want to be worried about what tomorrow may bring, but at the same time, I don't want you to be afraid to picture me in your future."

"I can't plan a lifetime right now, Bryson. I did that once and losing that fairy tale nearly destroyed me."

"So, let's not plan a lifetime. Let's make short-term plans."

She grins at me. "What do you have in mind? I'm thinking some sexy shower time would be a great short-term goal."

"We can definitely do that." I lean in and kiss her lips. "But I was thinking something a little further out. Like Thanksgiving break."

"What about it?" she asks, settling back against my chest.

"Let's get out of town. Spend a few days together alone." I lean in closer to her ear. "Maybe plan for that bed marathon you wanted earlier."

She chuckles. "I was thinking *Orange is the New Black* or *House of Cards*."

I nip at her earlobe. "Maybe the bed marathon *I* was wanting then."

"If I didn't know you any better, I'd think you were talking about sex," she teases, a smile in her tone.

"Bingo," I say near her ear.

"That makes no sense. You push me away more often than not. Was it bad for you the one time we did have sex?"

I twirl her around so fast, her ponytail slaps me in the face. "It was amazing. Don't ever think it wasn't."

"But we haven't done it again. Something about it turned you away."

I break eye contact with her. "The day after was one of the worst days in my life. The day after that was pretty fucked up too. I feel like I pushed you too far—like we went too far and you lashed out at me. I can't handle too much more of that, so I figured we should take sex off the table."

She chuckles, straddling my lap and pushing me flat on the grass. "It was just a bad couple of days. That won't happen again."

"You don't know that," I argue. "I'd rather have you like this, happy and a little horny, than satisfied sexually and hating me."

"That's where you're wrong." She leans in closer, her mouth brushing against my ear. "I'm way more than a little horny."

"We should head back to the apartment before we get arrested," I groan as she rotates her hips, whimpering as she rubs herself against my straining erection. For a moment, I fight my own words, reveling in the heat of her body against mine. "Never mind."

Rolling over, I flip her onto her back. She bats at my chest with her hand and pushes me away. "Fine, back to the apartment."

Chapter 41

Olivia

"Mmmm. You're very attentive," I purr as Bryson runs soapy hands all over my body.

"You're fucking irresistible," he growls. "Every second I'm around you, I have to fight to keep my hands to myself." He nips at my neck, keeping his hand busy on my stomach.

I angle my head further to the side, giving him full access. His hands, his mouth, and the heated water pouring over our bodies is a spectacular way to wake up and get ready for the day. My body hums for him, but he's the one who keeps pulling back. It's been several days since we nearly ripped each other's clothes off at the dog park, and that's as far as it has gone. We've only made love one time, but my body craves him every second of the day.

"I never mind your hands on me. Touch me as much as you want, but only if I get the same allowances."

I reach behind my back and stroke the erection he's been taunting me with since we got up.

"Deal," he pants in my ear when I give him a hard squeeze.

Skilled fingers wander lower, teasing my body in the most delicious way. His free hand skates around my hip and applies pressure to the center of my back. I bend at the waist, releasing him and placing my hands on the wall.

"You're perfect," he says, running both hands down my back before gripping my hips. His hot and insanely hard shaft lies in the crease of my ass cheeks, so close, yet so far away from where I want him—where I need him.

I shift my weight, praying he can take a hint.

"This what you want?" he taunts, taking a half step back and striking my clit with the head.

"Please." I moan like a harlot when he slides inside.

Banding an arm around my middle, he pulls me to standing, toying with my nipple as I arch my back toward him.

I turn my head to meet his lips over my shoulder and whimper, my needy body less than patient for him to move. He's static inside me, as if waiting for something, and I'm willing to give him anything he wants in this moment.

"I'm bare," he confides in my ear. "Tell me this is okay, Liv."

My body begins to tremble at the sensations flooding through me, but I squeeze my eyes shut, torn between what I want and the responsible thing to do.

"I'm not on birth control," I confess.

A slight backward shift of his hips forces my internal muscles to clamp down, begging him to stay, refusing to release him.

"I'll pull out," he promises with another shift of his hips.

I push back, taking him fully inside, an unspoken permission I hope won't come with dire consequences.

With one hand toying with my peaked nipple and the other hand between my legs, striking at my clit, he sets a punishing rhythm. I grasp at his arms, holding on for dear life as fire runs through my veins, settling low in my stomach. This is the antithesis of the first time we made love. This is hard, fast, glorious fucking. As much as I cherished the first time and the emotional connection I needed in the moment, I love him this way, too.

"You need to come, beautiful," he pleads in my ear, pinching my clit between two fingers. He thrusts harder as my orgasm continues to build, and I detonate, trembling and convulsing around his rhythmic thrusts.

He fucks me through it, prolonging my release until his grip has to tighten to support me.

"Your mouth," he breathes in my ear.

I hiss when he pulls free, not wanting his cock to ever leave me. He urges me to turn around and lower with a slight pressure on my shoulders. The second my lips wrap around his engorged head, he comes, and I grip his thighs as he mindlessly drives into my mouth, coaxing his release.

"Fuck," he groans, taking a step back, having to reach for the wall to keep from falling.

There's nothing to clean. She swallowed every last drop.

My back straightens at the memory and I rise to standing as Bryson reaches for me, leaning in to kiss me, but I turn my head at the last second, gloom settling over me.

"Hey," he says, applying gentle pressure on my chin so I have to look at him. "What's wrong? Was I too rough? I can dial it back next time... but I thought you enjoyed it."

"It's nothing," I lie.

"Don't do that. This is exactly what I was worried about." He wraps his arms around my slick body, pulling me to his chest. "Don't pull away from me. I'll forgo sex if this is what's going to happen every time."

"What we just did... it was the very same thing you did with Simone in this shower," I say, feeling overwhelmed and defeated at the same time. "At least I swallowed every drop, too," I continue, my voice as hollow as my stomach feels. "Less to clean up I suppose." I shrug and rough hands on my upper arms pull me from his chest.

"No," he insists, his eyes meeting mine, his voice hard, determined. "I've never had sex without a condom before. And Simone may have sucked my dick in the shower, but it was your face I saw. It was your hands touching me. It was the only way I could come."

I nod my head, but I can't meet his eyes. Isn't that the line guys always feed women to make them feel better? I reach for the shampoo, wanting nothing more than to finish up and put distance between us, but his hand clasps mine, bringing my knuckles to his lips.

"If I could take back everything I've ever done with other women, just to give you my firsts, I would." His imploring eyes search mine for understanding. "Only you."

The tension in my shoulders eases as the thoughts paralyzing me only moments before drift away. This sweet, amazing man has given me no reason to doubt his words, his sincerity, yet I did. I'm broken in a lot of ways, but he just wants to fill all the gaps I'm unable to piece back together. I smile up at him, offering my lips for a kiss. His lips seal over mine and my heart flutters at the warmth, taste, and sensations flooding my body. It's all him. Breaking the kiss, he leans his forehead onto mine and smiles before nudging me to turn around. Moments later, his hands are in my hair, massaging my scalp, as he takes over the duty of washing and conditioning. Something he doesn't have to do, but it makes me feel cherished, all the same.

Clean and dried off, I leave the bathroom with a small smile on my face, only for it to fall when I find my mother walking down the hall to my room. Closing the door quickly, I clutch the towel tighter around me.

"Mom, what are you doing here?" I do my best to not sound flustered, but I have no idea how long she's been here or what she's heard.

"I haven't heard from you in a few days. I was on my way to the store and thought I'd stop by and see if you wanted to tag along, maybe grab some breakfast." Her face is hopeful, no hint of the wariness I'd expect had she'd been here longer than a minute.

"Ummm," I begin, only to cringe when the bathroom door opens behind me.

"I was thinking I'd have you for breakfast," Bryson says, wrapping an arm around my waist and kissing my shoulder.

My mother gasps, and I feel his head snap up as his body tenses behind me. Slowly opening my eyes, I expect to find disappointment and ire on her face. Instead, I see an amused grin and a sparkle in her eyes.

"Mrs. Dawson," Bryson says, wiping the water from his hand on my towel before offering it to her.

A dash of relief fills me as I thank my lucky stars that I didn't step away from the bathroom door. Bryson is stark naked behind me and the last thing I need is my mother seeing the goods to add to this embarrassing moment.

"Bryson," she says, shaking his proffered hand. A blush forms on her cheeks. "Well, it seems you have breakfast plans already."

I stand absolutely still, mortified by the mirth in my mother's voice, only to be further embarrassed when Bryson chuckles behind me.

"I can wait," he tells her with a serious tone. Bending down, he whispers in my ear, "I still need a towel."

I jump, startled as the bathroom door clicks behind me. His words register and I remember the task I was on before my mother made an appearance.

"I'm going to go," Mom says, turning toward the front room.

I stare after her, unsure of how to act or what to say. My parents have always been open about sex—I'm certain they assumed Duncan and I had taken that leap years ago—but I've never been in this kind of situation.

"Mom," I call after her.

She looks over her shoulder, a grin on her face. "Enjoy your day, Olivia. Be safe."

I chuff a flustered laugh as the door closes behind her.

"I'm going to change the damn locks," I mutter to myself as I open the bathroom door to find Bryson leaning against the vanity, naked as the day he was born, arms crossed over his chest and a crooked smile on his face.

"*I can wait?* Are you kidding me right now?" His smile grows before a chuckle escapes his lips. I slap his chest before walking back out. "Get your own damn towel."

Minutes later, we meet, both fully dressed in the kitchen.

"Your mom didn't seem to mind," he says, kissing the tip of my nose. "Why are you so flustered?"

"I'm embarrassed. What if she came in while we were naked on the couch or even in my room making all sorts of noise?"

"She didn't. Just tell her we shower together to save water. Better for the environment." His hands snake up the front of my tank top and I slap them away.

"We were in there for over an hour and there was no misreading your declaration of meal plans."

His laugh causes my own lips to turn up.

"Sorry about that." He tilts his head to the side. "My offer still stands."

"You're ridiculous," I chide, stepping around him to open the fridge. "I think we'll have omelets for breakfast, since I don't think I'll be able to let you do that without picturing the look on my mother's face."

"Omelets sound perfect." He kisses the top of my head and backs away. Looking over my shoulder, I see him heading into the living room. "But, Liv?"

I raise an eyebrow at him.

"The only thing you'll be thinking about when I eat your pussy is how hard you're going to detonate when I finally let you come."

A shiver of anticipation runs over my body and settles low in my belly. One thing I know about Bryson Daniels is he is more than capable of delivering every dirty promise his mouth makes. I honestly can't wait for the week and a half until Thanksgiving break gets here and we can have more than a couple days to spend together.

Chapter 42

Bryson

"Where exactly are we going?" I pull my eyes from the road to look over at Olivia before snapping them back to the task at hand. Eyes sparkling and a gorgeous glow to her cheeks, she's practically transformed over the last month.

"It's a surprise," I tease.

She glances at me warily. "I don't really like surprises."

"You'll like this one," I assure her.

"We're staying all week?"

I wanted to have my arms around her before springing my full plans on her, making the chances of her refusing or insisting I take her back to the apartment less likely.

"Most of the week," I answer.

I feel her eyes on me, but I don't take my gaze off the road. It's Thanksgiving break and along with the much cooler temperatures we've already had this fall, the broadcasters warned of sleet and ice this morning.

"My mother has asked us to join them for lunch on Thursday."

"Thursday?" Mild annoyance marks her tone, but I keep my eyes forward, letting her work through it alone. "As in Thanksgiving dinner?"

I shrug my shoulders. "Just lunch on Thursday."

I try to hide the amusement in my voice.

"My parents want to meet you. We've been together for over two months now." I risk a look in her direction, only to find her eyes focused out her window. "My mom has been hounding me about it."

"Why do they want to meet me?" she asks the window, her breath steaming up the glass. She turns to look at me. "What if they don't like me?"

"They'll love you because I love you." She stiffens at the words, but mere moments later, her face softens and a small smile forms at the corners of her mouth.

I force myself to look away, back to the road. I've said those words to her hundreds of times while she's been sleeping, but this is the first time I've told her while she's aware.

Silence fills the cab and I wonder if I've said them too soon—if uttering those words now not only dampers our trip, but also the relationship we've been building.

She shifts in her seat, turning her body toward mine before she speaks. "Do you think we're moving too fast?"

I shake my head. "I just want you to meet my family. I want them to get to know the girl who's captured my heart."

She nods in my periphery, but she doesn't say anything else.

"We're not moving too fast, Liv. It's not like I've bought a ring yet or anything." I sigh, focusing on the highway ahead as the silence between us stretches.

I thought the lack of speaking before was bad, but by the time we pull up to the cabin a few hours later, I'm nearly deaf from the lingering absence of noise.

"This is beautiful," she says, leaning closer to the windshield, as if we hadn't just spent two uncomfortable hours together.

Normally I'd force her to talk, but due mainly to my fear of rejection, I allow it this time.

***

"Thank you," Olivia whispers.

"For what?" I ask, my voice soft. Tugging her closer to my chest, I grind against her ass, and tease, "I haven't even been inside you today."

It's Wednesday and we've been in secluded bliss for four days, finding alternative amusements when we discovered we not only ended up with no service, but the cabin doesn't even have a television. We've both woken up with blissful smiles on our faces and fallen into bed with content yet exhausted sighs each night. It's almost as if she's a brand-new person. I only see sporadic glimpses of the woman she was several months ago. Her transformation has been nothing short of dramatic, and I'm honored to walk this journey with her.

"For bringing me here. For helping me make new memories." I still my hips at the seriousness in her tone.

"I want to make a lifetime of memories with you," I confess against her naked back.

Her contented sigh and the shimmy of her hips as she snuggles further into my embrace soothes an aching part in my soul that has been wondering if she's happy with me, if she can see us together a year from now, twenty years from now.

I roll her onto her back and sweep hair from her face before cupping her chin.

"I love you," I whisper.

A soft smile takes up residence on her lips and in her eyes as she reaches her mouth up to mine. That she hasn't said the words back yet doesn't go unnoticed, but I know she will in time. She's still coming to terms with the idea that moving on and being happy is something she can do.

My hand roams down her stomach, exploring her bare flesh as she clings to my biceps.

"These are new," I observe, tracing the small abdominal muscles now peeking out from under her skin. "You've gained weight, too."

She giggles when my fingers find and tease her most ticklish spot.

She tries to back away, smacking at my hand. "You can't say that to a woman. It's rude."

"You're stronger, more durable," I say close to her lips. "Just means you can handle me a little rougher."

She quirks an eyebrow up. "You implying I haven't handled you well yet?"

I shake my head before lowering my mouth to nip at her bottom lip. "You handle me perfectly."

"I've been doing yoga," she says, distracting me before my seeking mouth lands on her nipples.

I peer up at her, a devious smirk on my face. "Really?"

She nods her head. "While you're in class, I do workout videos on my computer, ordered a few DVDs. In fact, it's the only disc I brought. Never took it out after my last workout."

I slide off the bed and pull her up with me.

"What are you doing?" she asks but follows along as I tug her toward the living room.

"We're going to do yoga."

"Right now? I thought we'd work up a sweat in a different way."

"Oh, we're going to work up a sweat, beautiful." I pull her to my chest, my hard cock standing proud between our naked bodies. Gripping her hips, I lower my palms, taking her ass in my hands. "I want you to suck my cock while you're in downward dog. Then I want to see how far you can arch your back when I fuck you in puppy pose."

She moans into my mouth when my tongue breaches her lips.

"That sounds awesome for you. But what do I get?"

I lay down on the soft rug in front of the fireplace and stroke my cock, precum pooling at the tip as she licks her lips. "Don't worry, beautiful. When I'm done with you, corpse pose is the only thing you'll be able to manage."

I watch, riveted as she widens her stance near my feet and bends over, her glorious breasts just out of reach.

Holding my cock at the base, I tilt it toward her slightly so she can wrap her lips around it. Aside from being inside her bare, nothing has ever felt better than her unbelievable lips wrapped around me.

I hiss at the scorching heat of her mouth and every muscle in my body clenches when she leans forward and takes me down her throat. I wrap her hair in my fist and watch as she continues her assault, her lips and tongue moving up and down my shaft. When I notice how hard it is for her to maintain the up and down motions, I hold her head and shift my hips into her eager mouth like a gentleman.

She turns her eyes up at me, smiling around my cock, letting me know I haven't fooled her. I grin until she increases the suction and my eyes roll into the back of my head. Clearly, she has the upper hand. A handful of minutes later, the tingle starts at the base of my spine.

I shift my hips to the side, falling from her mouth with a satisfying pop. "Knees and elbows, baby."

She bites her lip as she crawls back on the rug and leans forward. Olivia's lithe, flexible body amazes me when she stays on her knees, her ass high in the air and breasts lower to the rug. She's all but bent in half and the luxurious lines of her naked body enthrall me.

"So perfect," I praise, swiping a finger up her center only to find her wet for me.

"Mmmm," she moans when I ease inside her, my movements slow and controlled. "I love yoga."

I scrape my short nails down her back, loving the hiss of breath that leaves her lips before I grip her hips, draw my cock out, and pound into her.

We've been latex free for a week now, and I spend every waking moment either inside her, or dreaming of when I can have her again. Just like right now, sinking into her is just like the first time. Sweat forms on my brow as my fingers flex against the soft flesh of her hips. I grind my teeth to stave off the tingle from the orgasm trying to creep up my spine, but her moans, pants, and urges of "harder, harder" bring me to the edge almost immediately.

"Oh God!" Her voice echoes off the walls, spurring me on. "I'm going to have carpet burn on my face."

She's definitely gotten more vocal since our first few times together, and her words are almost as desirable as the tight heat of her body. Together they are a deadly combination that can easily turn me into a two-pump chump.

Not wanting to mar her beautiful skin, I pull her up and sit back on my heels. Taking over, she commands the movements, ensuring we'll both come quickly.

All I can think when I blow is we may both be in corpse pose when this is over.

Chapter 43

Olivia

"This is so weird," I mutter to Bryson, who's sitting beside me on the sofa. "How did this even happen?"

He holds his beer bottle in front of his mouth before speaking. "Emerson convinced me having all your information, including your parents' number, was important in case something happened."

"Emerson doesn't seem like such a fatalist," I argue.

He shakes his head and chuckles. "She's not, but my mom mentioned it to her, and Emmy pretty much does whatever my mom says."

"That still doesn't explain this," I hiss, waving my hand out in front of me toward the roomful of people.

"My mom broke into Emerson's phone last week when she went home. My mom called your mom, they plotted and planned, and... well," he pauses to look across the room at his older brother, Josh, and his wife, "here we are. One big, happy family."

I squeeze his thigh until he winces and pulls his attention back to me. "You're a little too happy about all of this for me to believe you didn't have a hand in it."

He feigns innocence, but the sparkle in his eyes tells me I'm closer to the truth than he'll admit.

I glare across the room, watching both of our mothers with their heads together, formulating some type of devious plan. Bryson just met my father for the first time this morning when we drove over. He'd been out of the country working on his latest business venture but is home for the holidays. Bryson was received by my father with open arms, just as I'd hoped.

The last month has been beyond amazing. I leave the apartment freely now, on my own, as well as shopping with Ainsley and Emerson when she comes to visit. The week over Thanksgiving break was exactly what we needed to solidify our relationship. It seems my parents love Bryson, and that's a relief I didn't realize I was stressed over until I heard my dad offer him a beer, something he'd never do with a man he didn't like.

It wasn't until a couple hours later when the doorbell rang and the entire Daniels family traipsed into my childhood home that I felt the walls begin to close in.

My heart pounds in my chest as I watch Emerson help her nine-year-old niece tie bows on Christmas presents while my dad and Mr. Daniels argue over whether the Broncos are going to win the game this evening. This whole scene is very surreal. I know my mother has good intentions, but how could she think for a moment I would be okay with this?

This exact situation is what Christmas looked like for us, with exception to last year when Duncan was away for treatments—only it was the Kellys in our living room and Duncan beside me, drinking eggnog and laughing with my dad.

I swipe at the tears that manage to break past my anger and pain, rolling down my cheeks.

"Excuse us," Bryson says, grabbing my hand and pulling me to my feet.

Conversations continue behind us when we walk out of the room but dissipate before Bryson places me against the wall and leans his forehead against mine.

"New memories," he whispers against my lips. "We're making new ones, Liv."

He can read me like a book; he's always been able to. He knows when my mood shifts and what's going on in my head before I can even verbalize the thoughts and feelings myself.

"It's hard to make new memories when they look exactly like the old ones," I say, my voice hoarse as more tears form on my bottom lashes.

He nods in understanding. "I don't know how to change things for you, to make it easier."

"Just hold me for a minute," I beg, wrapping my arms around him.

"I'll hold you forever, Liv. You don't even have to ask."

I pull him closer, hating that I can tell the difference between young love and mature love. It feels like a betrayal when I give a voice to the knowledge that Duncan and Bryson love so differently, but my heart soars knowing each man gave me exactly what I needed during the moments they were in my life.

"Josh is very handsome," I say, trying to pull us out of this dark moment.

He lifts his head from the top of mine. "Do I have to worry about you and my brother?"

I grin. "Your father is incredibly good-looking too."

He narrows his eyes at me, but I see the slight twitch at the corners of his mouth. "Where is this going?"

I shrug. "I just don't have to worry about you getting ugly is all."

"Good to know." He chuckles, pulling me back against his chest. "Ready to go back out and face the mob?"

"Might as well get it over with," I complain, taking a step back. "Or we can go up to my old room and make out?"

A light sparks in his eyes as he contemplates the idea. He grabs my hand and heads toward the stairs.

"Lunch is ready!" my mom calls out from the living room.

"Damn it," I mutter. "Think they'll miss us?"

Bryson changes direction from the bottom of the stairs and pulls me toward the dining room.

"Making memories, remember?" he whispers in my ear as he pulls out a chair for me to sit on.

"Memories," I repeat, looking around the table, hoping my mother doesn't ask too many questions about our relationship in mixed company.

* * *

"That was brutal," I complain as Bryson opens the door to our apartment. The last four hours with our combined parents had been more stressful than the last couple of months while Bryson and I built our relationship. Needless to say, I'm extremely grateful to be home.

"It wasn't so bad," he argues.

I scoff and raise my brow. "You weren't the one being grilled about school and plans for the future."

"Sure I was," he says, leaning down to pull my shoes off. He stands up and winks at me. "Your future is my future."

I watch his back as he walks away, his button-down shirt pulling free from his body as he makes his way to his bedroom for more comfortable clothes.

"You sure are sugary sweet today," I call after him.

He emerges from the hall less than a minute later, shirtless and tugging sweats over his naked butt. Commando is my favorite. I turn my eyes from him, doing my best to tamp down the arousal that seems to flare whenever he's around. He must think I'm a sex fiend, even though he hasn't complained yet.

"I'm sugary sweet every day, beautiful." He leans in and kisses my forehead before turning toward the kitchen. "Why? Are you getting tired of it? It's my nature. I can't help it."

"I don't want you to get tired of it. Your mom mentioned she's never seen you this way before." I stand with my hip propped against the counter as he searches for something to eat.

"Like what?" he asks, his voice echoing in the near-empty refrigerator.

"'Head over heels' I think is the term she used."

His head pops up over the door. "Maybe because I've never been head over heels before."

I frown at him. This man is amazing and charming, surely, he's been interested in other women for more than sex.

"What? Don't believe me?" His eyes narrow as he evaluates the situation. "Are you trying to pick a fight on Christmas? Trying to force my eternal love for you? Fishing for compliments?"

He closes the refrigerator door and stalks toward me.

"Women must throw themselves at you, if you act like this around everyone."

He shakes his head and clasps my hips when he's within arm's reach. "They fight over me, claw each other's eyes out when I walk by." I shiver when he runs his nose up the length of my neck. "Every woman in the world wants a piece of me."

Sighing at his playful words, I can't help but wonder how much of it is truth. Simone, the girls at the ball field—they all wanted a piece of him.

"Every woman? A little arrogant, don't you think?"

"Yet, here I am with you," he whispers against my mouth.

"With me," I pant as his hips finally make contact with mine.

"Only you." His lips take mine in a fevered kiss, one hand around my hip and the other cradling my head.

His mouth leaves mine, trailing delicious kisses down my throat.

"I love you," I whisper as his ear nears mine.

"I know," he says on a breath, trying to play off his body's reaction to my confession, but he becomes more rigid before a small tremor rocks through him.

When he pulls his head back, a wide grin splits his face.

I bite my lip to keep from mirroring him.

"One more time," he pleads.

"Just one?" I tease, my lips quirking at one corner.

He shrugs. "Maybe a million then."

"How about one time each day for forever?"

"Make it ten times a day and you've got a deal," he bargains.

"I love you," I repeat, leaning my head down to his.

His kiss is tender, worshipping, reverent, and I'm weightless as he lifts me up and carries me to my room.

When he deposits me on the bed and walks out of the room, I frown at his retreating back, but he reappears with a small box in his hands.

"We already did gifts at my parents' house," I chastise, even though my blood is pumping harder at the sight of the tiny jewelry box.

I got him a new phone since he cracked the screen on his a couple weeks ago and insisted on continuing to use it. He gifted me with more bath and body stuff—in his favorite scent, of course—than I'll ever be able to use in a lifetime, and a personalized playlist he says is our love story. I'm equally excited and nervous to listen to it.

"I didn't want to give this to you in front of family in case you hate it. I don't want you to feel obligated to respond a certain way."

My heart thunders and my hands shake to the point where I almost drop the box when he hands it to me. He climbs on the bed behind me, pulls me back against his chest, and continues to shred any restraint I had on my anxiety.

"I didn't want to ask you the question with an audience. I wanted you all to myself when you said yes." I blame the breath escaping his mouth and washing over my shoulder for the chills wracking my body as I prepare my rejection to the question he's asking too soon. I love him, there's no denying that, but four months is not long enough for this big of a leap.

My eyes catch the diamond band on my left hand, hating and loving it at the same time. I've found two perfect men—one I'll hold in my heart and one I'll spend eternity with.

"Bryson, it's too..." my voice trails off as I flip the lid of the box up. It's not a diamond or an engagement ring facing me, but a gorgeous heart bolo necklace with a baseball through it.

I look over my shoulder, my brows furrowed together in confusion.

There's a glint in his eye, as if he wanted me to believe he was proposing. Thankfully, I don't see hurt, just understanding, as if he also knows it's too early to speak of such things.

"And the question?" I prod.

"Go to opening day with me?"

"I already told you I would."

He shrugs, a wide smile on his face. "I just wanted to make it official."

He reaches behind him and pulls a shirt from the back waistband of his sweats. "I got you this, too," he says, spreading it out on my lap. The front has the Oregon State Beavers logo and the back has a big number two with his name above it.

"I want everyone to know you're mine." His arms wrap around me as he kisses my neck.

"I want that too," I tell him, pushing him until he's flat on his back and I'm straddling his waist. "Looks like I owe you another gift."

He waggles his eyebrows. "What do you have in mind, beautiful?"

I shrug. "A little of this, a little of that."

"You know how much I love a buffet."

His arms move north under his head while my mouth moves south.

Chapter 44

Olivia

"You, my smoking hot short stop, are going to be late for the game," I tell Bryson as he runs around the apartment looking for the last few things for his gym bag that I suggested he get together last night.

"You're still coming, right?" His eyes land on the necklace he gave me at Christmas. I only take it off to shower and that's because it tangles in my wet hair.

"I wouldn't miss it for the world." I kiss his lips and chuckle with a soft push against his shoulders when he tries to take it further. "Emerson will be here in a bit to pick me up. We're going to swing by and grab Ainsley, then we'll be at the ballpark."

He stands, reaching down to cup my cheek. "Cheer for me."

"You know I will." I smile up at him and tilt my head into his touch. "I'll embarrass you and you'll never want me to attend another game."

"Impossible. You look great in my jersey," he says before scooping up his gym bag and walking toward the door. "I love you, Liv."

"I love you, too."

For the first time in a while, I sit quietly on the couch and take stock of my life. The bad days are gone for the most part. The worst since before Thanksgiving being just a week ago, but I imagine the anniversary of Duncan's death will always cause me grief and sadness.

Bryson held me while I cried, and I did something I thought I'd never do. I offered him the chance to watch a few of our videos together. He held me close and laughed at some of Duncan's humor and his tears wet my shirt at some of our pain. The whole thing was amazingly cathartic.

Spending each day doing common domestic things over the last couple of months has been good, but it's falling asleep with his lips against my skin and waking up with his arms wrapped around me that means the most. I never knew my heart would heal as much as it has, and I owe most of that restoration to him.

A sharp knock on the door pulls me from my reflection. I grab my purse and jacket, knowing it's Emerson on the other side.

I give her a quick smile and lock the door behind me.

"Well, aren't you just the perfect girlfriend," she says while my back is to her. "He's got you wearing his number and everything."

I grin at her when I turn back around, but don't say anything.

She wraps her arm around my shoulder as we make it to her car. "Thank you."

Her voice is low and filled with an unnamed emotion.

"For what? Wearing a shirt?"

She shakes her head and my eyes scan her face, seeing how serious she is. This isn't joking about being whipped or having Bryson wrapped around my finger. We've had those conversations before, and this doesn't feel like that.

"Thank you for loving him so fiercely. Thank you for being the sister I've never had."

I stop us in our tracks and wrap her up in a hug. She holds on, squeezing as if she can't let go, so I break our connection first.

"I love you, too, you know?" I bump her shoulder with mine as we make it to the parking lot.

"Who doesn't?" she says with a quick smirk.

I shake my head and snort. Sometimes, I wonder if the twins didn't have their emotions reversed in utero. Bryson is the loving, doting, occasionally emotional one, and Emerson, although built with an amazing body every woman would love to have, is cocky, arrogant, and full of herself.

Opening day for Oregon State is incredibly crowded. Parking was a time-consuming feat, and the rush of people toward the entrance gate was incredibly similar to how I imagine the Pamplona Running of the Bulls would be. It took me nearly forty minutes to make it to my seat. Emerson opted to grab a glass of beer on the deck while I went straight to our section in the covered area behind home plate.

Ainsley texted that she wasn't feeling well when we were on the way to her dorm. I have a feeling it has something to do with JJ, but her texts were short and clipped, assuring me she just felt under the weather with promises of attending the next home game.

The teams are just now beginning to hit the dugouts and Emerson still isn't back. I smile at Bryson and give him a quick wave when he looks over. He blows a kiss in my direction, and a small rush of heat hits my cheeks, part embarrassment, part love for that man.

"So good to see you, Ollie." I freeze, clenching my eyes shut.

The familiar voice makes me want to cry, run, and jump up and hug him all at the same time. The voice is so familiar to *his*, my eyes burn when I even consider the unearthly possibility that Duncan is standing behind me.

After Bryson was so kind, caring, and understanding during my grief on the anniversary of Duncan's death, I realized I'd never change where I am today. Bryson's arms are where I feel like I was always meant to be.

It still doesn't keep the slight feeling of shame from hitting me as I sit here at an Oregon State baseball game wearing a big number two and Bryson's last name on my back.

Knowing I can't ignore them, I turn my eyes and give a tiny smile. "Mr. and Mrs. Kelly. It's good to see you, too."

A tender smile is on Mrs. Kelly's lips. "Your mom says you're doing well. We spoke last week."

I nod, swallowing hard to try to remove the lump that has formed.

"Number two," Mr. Kelly says, pointing to my jersey. "It was always a good number on you."

I give them both a weak smile. What do I say right now? I never told Bryson I've worn this number on my back for years. That it was Duncan's number when he played ball in high school. Or that I realized they wore the same numbers during fall training and the first practice I went to when the girls in the stands were fawning all over him. When I woke up this morning and put this number back on my body, I had never felt more proud to wear it again, but now, with Duncan's parents here, his dad pointing it out, all the kismet energy I felt is washing away.

Mrs. Kelly reaches for my hand, and I offer her mine with quivering lips and trembling fingers. "Don't be upset, Ollie."

Her voice is comforting, just as it has always been, even in dire moments. She's always been strong, even when her son was withering away. She's always held herself together and her faith never faltered even while she was losing her only child, proclaiming Duncan was no longer suffering.

"Your mom told us how happy you are, how wonderful Bryson is to you." Her genuine smile helps to ease my nerves just a little.

"It's too soon," I whimper as tears build behind my eyes. She shakes her head, refusing my words. "I've abandoned him."

"No, sweet girl," Mr. Kelly says, taking my other hand. "You're happy, and that's what he always wanted."

The tears fall freely, rolling down my cheeks and releasing onto my shirt from my chin.

"Do you love him?" I nod, unable to deny my feelings for Bryson, refusing to taint the fact that I've given him my whole heart with a lie, even though I know it may cause them pain. "That's all that matters. Love doesn't work on a schedule, Ollie. More often, it finds us when we need it the most."

"I'll always love Duncan, too." I don't know why I feel the need to tell them, but it feels good when the words release.

"We know," Mr. Kelly assures me. "He would be happy for you. He *is* happy for you, of that I'm certain."

They each release my hands after a gentle squeeze.

"I didn't expect to see you today," I confess, changing the subject as I try to get my emotions under control, even as my tears refuse to stop falling.

Mrs. Kelly hands me a tissue as her husband begins to speak.

"Oregon State is my alma mater, as you know. We're also here because we've started a baseball scholarship in Duncan's name. They're going to introduce the recipient during the stretch."

We sit and talk through the game as Bryson's team fights hard to maintain a one run lead, only to lose it in the ninth. Not once does the shame for being here and loving Bryson return as we talk about everything under the sun, including the fact that I still haven't returned to school—a conversation I've had more than once with Bryson.

We say our goodbyes as the teams leave the dugouts and head back to the locker room with their heads hanging low, disappointment on each of their faces. I hate that they lost. It's not that big of a deal considering how many games they'll play, but I know how bad it can be for moral at the start of a season.

"They seem like nice people," Emerson says as we walk out of the complex. She joined us about twenty minutes into our reunion, even chatted along and interjected a few times, but never questioned who they were.

"Duncan's parents," I explain.

"Oh," she says, her voice soft. "Wow. Are you okay?"

"I am now." I smile in return, feeling a huge weight lift off my shoulders. Until they gave me their heartfelt approval of being with Bryson, I didn't realize how much I needed it. It's almost as if the final piece I knew was missing has fallen into place.

She rubs her hand over my back as we head to the truck. We've had a couple conversations about my history with Duncan, and I know Bryson has filled in the rest. She's always been respectful of the heaviness the subject brings.

Her hand tenses on my back, causing me to follow her eyes across the parking lot. Bryson, JJ, and Liam make their way toward us, smiles on each of their faces. Well, Liam looks like he's on the prowl once he spots Emerson, and JJ's mouth turns down in a frown when he notices Ainsley isn't with us.

"I thought SLS was coming?" JJ questions once he's within earshot.

I smile when Bryson positions himself around my back, arms around my waist. "She texted and said she didn't feel well."

"She was fine last night," he says, letting that little morsel of information slip.

I cock an eyebrow up at him and Bryson chuckles in my ear, but it's Liam who comments. "Shit or get off the damn pot, JJ."

"Pot, kettle," Emerson mutters.

The sudden tension in Bryson's arms doesn't go unnoticed. I pat his forearms in reassurance. I know he doesn't like the idea of Liam and Emerson, but he can't deny the chemistry they have, and I know he can see how much he's changed over the last couple months as Emerson keeps him dangling in the wind. I never thought it would be Liam who insisted on a wholesome relationship, but stranger things have happened. Emerson wants no part of commitment, and Liam is the one insisting on it before he takes things further with her.

Of course, Bryson hates every second of it.

I turn my attention away from JJ's defeated face and the stare-off going on between Liam and Emerson. I cup Bryson's newly bearded face in my hands, relishing the feel of the soft hairs on my fingers. "I'm sorry for the loss."

He kisses my lips in full view of everyone around me. "Just one game, beautiful. We'll beat 'em next time."

"I know you will," I agree.

"I want to get you home," he whispers in my ear. "Celebrate opening day with you opening your legs."

He's grown increasingly dirty as time has gone by. I don't know whether he's just now getting to how he behaved with other girls, or there's something about me changing how he responds physically. I hate to think he may have felt like he couldn't be himself completely from day one, so I convince myself we're evolving together.

"Not much of a celebration. We do that almost every day." I kiss his lips, nipping the bottom one before pulling away.

"I celebrate every second I spend with you." He leans in, taking my lips in a passionate kiss that should probably be reserved for the privacy of our own home, but I'm past caring. The only thing I have on my mind is this amazing man who helped me through some of my weakest days and loved me during my darkest nights.

"That's a lot of seconds," I tell him when he eventually pulls away.

"Billions," he agrees. "And I'll love you madly with each and every one."

Epilogue

Olivia

Three Years Later

I smile at my family, including Bryson, his family, and the Kellys as I'm showered with mortar boards along with the rest of my graduating class. Graduation, a day I never thought would happen four years ago. Having a future filled with love and understanding wasn't something I could even fathom on my best days after Duncan passed away. Now, the possibilities are endless, no goal unreachable.

I started back to school in the fall, one year after meeting Bryson—one year after my life started over. Today is the first graduation of several I have coming, my end goal being a psychologist who counsels those struggling with their grief of losing a loved one. I want to pay it forward by helping others who struggle daily just to get out of bed; those who are so weighed down by their grief, they can't seem to function. I know exactly how they're feeling and hope to prove to them that there is a light at the end of the tunnel.

"I'm so proud of you," my mother says, wrapping her arms around me. Tears glisten in her and my father's eyes as I brush windblown hair behind my ears.

I hug all the people who came to share in this special day, saving my favorite for last. It feels like an eternity before Bryson wraps his arms around me, turning us both in a circle as he kisses my lips.

"Congratulations, beautiful. I'm so fucking proud of you," he proclaims, pecking my mouth with kisses between his words.

"I couldn't have done it without you," I admit.

His face turns serious as he lowers me to the ground and cups my cheeks in his big hands. "Yes, you could have. I'm just glad you didn't have to. I'm glad you still have a few more years of school, though. Strip studying is one of my favorite things." He waggles his brows.

"Mine, too," I confess against his lips, adding, "I'm not wearing any panties."

He growls into my mouth. "Don't tell me shit like that when we have to spend the next several hours with our families."

I give him a devious smirk. "We can skip it."

Light shines in his eyes, featuring a glint I've never seen before. "Not this time, beautiful. Today is special in more ways than one."

The ride to my parents' house in the back of the limo my father insisted on is torture. Bryson whispers dirty things in my ear the entire way, causing me to squirm as both our parents sit mere feet away. The Kellys opted to drive themselves to lunch but will be joining us shortly.

There is nothing unusual about today's lunch. We all seem to get together as often as we can. Only, today is in celebration of my accomplishments, which leave me a little uneasy. Being the center of attention has never made me comfortable.

I've grown closer with the Kellys over the last couple years, hating the distance I created after we all lost Duncan. They've welcomed Bryson with open arms, never once making me feel like they were ashamed of me for being with him.

I smile at Mrs. Kelly across the table as she chats animatedly with my mom and Emerson. It's the aura around Emerson that causes me concern. Liam isn't here. They are normally inseparable, but he's been oddly absent the last couple weeks. I've asked Bryson what's going on, and he assured me things are fine and I just needed to focus on finals. Trusting him always, I did just that, but looking at the fake smile on my friend's face as she tries to hide the fact that she's breaking apart inside makes me wish I asked more questions.

Bryson squeezes my hand under the table. "She'll be fine."

I turn to him. "I know that distant look. Has she lost him forever?"

He shakes his head no, but I see the doubt clouding his eyes. "They have to work through some things. It's not our place to interfere."

Her mood lightens a bit as lunch goes on. I'm bombarded with questions about summer plans and when we're moving out of the tiny apartment we've lived in since our beginning.

"So many questions," I tease, even though I'm growing frustrated. This lunch should've been over an hour ago. Naked in our bed at home is the only place I want to be right now.

"Does that feel good?" is the only question I want to hear when Bryson's mouth skates down my body, satisfying my neediness.

Bryson releases my hand and stands from his chair. I push mine back, thankful he's finally going to make our excuses so we can leave.

"One more," he says loud enough for everyone to hear.

"One more what?" I turn my head to him, watching in shock as he drops down beside me in clear view of everyone I love.

"Just one more question." He grips my hand, looking up at me as he kneels on the floor.

A tear rolls down my cheek and his fingers twitch in mine, itching to wipe it way like he's done countless times in the years we've been together.

"Unless you're tired of questions?" he asks as a playful smirk turns the corners of his mouth up.

My breathing comes in fast, panting breaths loud enough for everyone in the room to hear. My brain fills with so many chaotic thoughts, I can't single any one bit of logic out.

"I love you," he begins. "I'm absolutely certain I was put on this earth to love you and only you. You're the part of my heart I didn't know I was missing. Make me whole, beautiful. Marry me?"

Tears of turmoil roll down my face. I know I'm his only love, but I can't regret what I had, even if for a short while, with Duncan.

I turn my eyes from him, seeing the exact moment the anxiety hits him because I didn't answer immediately. My eyes fall on Mr. and Mrs. Kelly across the table. A wide smile marks his face, but she has her hands clasped to her mouth, tears also rolling down her cheeks, escaping from her closed eyes. When they open, love and a keen peacefulness stare back at me. A slight nod of her head assures me they are not only okay with this, but just as happy as I am.

I turn back to Bryson, ready to jump in his arms and accept his proposal when my eyes land on the familiar band of diamonds, now part of a gorgeous ring topped with a magnificent round cut diamond.

My eyes dart up to his and back down to the ring.

"He'll always be a part of you," he whispers, only loud enough for me to hear. "That means he's a part of us."

I nod my head, meeting his eyes and holding them with mine.

"I'm dying here, beautiful."

"I love you." Not exactly what he wants to hear, but I feel the need to express it.

"I love you, too. Do I need to repeat the question?" The same glint of mischievous seduction he had every time he asked me that when we were studying for finals sparkles in his eyes. Stalling while studying meant I knew the answer. Toying with him gave me time to wonder about the reward I was going to get when I answered right. The gleam in his eyes betrays his understanding of the situation.

He licks his lips, and the rest of the room just fades away. I no longer hear the joyful sobs of my mother, or Emerson gasping. Their loving energy and approval still floats all around us, but Bryson and I are alone in this moment.

"What's my prize?" My mouth turns up in a coy smile. The expression on Bryson's face tells me he's having the same visceral reaction he'd have alone in our apartment.

"Me," he answers. "For eternity. I'm here, beautiful."

"You're here," I agree. Breathlessly, I ask him, "Can you repeat the question?"

"Marry me," he says, only it's a demand, easier to say the second time around now that he's sure of my answer.

"Yes," I whisper.

His hands tremble in mine, and I wait for him to drop the small box he's been holding out this whole time.

"Final answer?"

"Only answer," I assure him.

A loud whoop echoes around the room. I know it came from my dad, but I don't turn my eyes away from Bryson as he works the ring from the box. He slips it on my finger as the room fills with cheers and congratulations.

Wrapping me in a hug, he nearly squeezes the breath out of me.

Warm air skates over my ear as he says, "I'm going to spank your ass when we get home for making me wait."

"Mmmm," I hum. "My favorite kind of prize."

THE END

Need more loving, compassionate men in your life?
Check out Love Me Like That!
Synopsis:

After living a life of betrayal and abuse, London Sykes in on her own.
She's ready to start over, leaving the past behind.
But when her car skids off the road, London is rescued by a sad, mysterious, and sexy man--a man who changes everything for her.
Kadin Cole is done.
At a cabin in the woods for his very first--and last time--Kadin refuses to return to a life he cannot endure.
With grief that suffocates him, he makes the hardest decision of his life.
But when a beautiful woman crashes into his life, Kadin is torn between his grief and his hope for a new beginning.
Now, it's up to Kadin and London to find warmth in the coldest time of their lives.
Can their passion thaw their hearts and give them a chance at something more?

Social Media Links

FB Author Page
FB Author Group
Twitter
Instagram
BookBub
Newsletter

OTHER BOOKS FROM MARIE JAMES

Newest Series
Blackbridge Security
Hostile Territory
Shot in the Dark
Contingency Plan

Standalones
Crowd Pleaser
Macon
We Said Forever
More Than a Memory

Cole Brothers SERIES
Love Me Like That
Teach Me Like That

Cerberus MC
Kincaid: Cerberus MC Book 1
Kid: Cerberus MC Book 2
Shadow: Cerberus MC Book 3
Dominic: Cerberus MC Book 4
Snatch: Cerberus MC Book 5
Lawson: Cerberus MC Book 6
Hound: Cerberus MC Book 7
Griffin: Cerberus MC Book 8
Samson: Cerberus MC Book 9
Tug: Cerberus MC Book 10
Scooter: Cerberus MC Book 11
Cannon: Cerberus MC Book 12
Rocker: Cerberus MC Book 13
Colton: Cerberus MC Book 14
Cerberus MC Box Set 1
Cerberus MC Box Set 2
Cerberus MC Box Set 3

Ravens Ruin MC
Desperate Beginnings: **Prequel**
Book 1: Sins of the Father
Book 2: Luck of the Devil
Book 3: Dancing with the Devil

MM Romance
Grinder
Taunting Tony

Westover Prep Series
(bully/enemies to lovers romance)
One-Eighty
Catch Twenty-Two

Made in the USA
Middletown, DE
15 September 2021